# Hope Larson • Jackie Ball • Elle Power • Sarah Stern

# GOLDIE VANCE ™

## *Volume Four*

BOOM! BOX ™

# GOLDIE

ROSS RICHIE CEO & Founder
MATT GAGNON Editor-in-Chief
FILIP SABLIK President of Publishing & Marketing
STEPHEN CHRISTY President of Development
LANCE KREITER VP of Licensing & Merchandising
PHIL BARBARO VP of Finance
ARUNE SINGH VP of Marketing
BRYCE CARLSON Managing Editor
MEL CAYLO Marketing Manager
SCOTT NEWMAN Production Design Manager
KATE HENNING Operations Manager
SIERRA HAHN Senior Editor
DAFNA PLEBAN Editor, Talent Development
SHANNON WATTERS Editor
ERIC HARBURN Editor
WHITNEY LEOPARD Editor
CAMERON CHITTOCK Editor
CHRIS ROSA Associate Editor
MATTHEW LEVINE Associate Editor

SOPHIE PHILIPS-ROBERTS Assistant Editor
AMANDA LaFRANCO Executive Assistant
KATALINA HOLLAND Editorial Administrative Assistant
JILLIAN CRAB Production Designer
MICHELLE ANKLEY Production Designer
KARA LEOPARD Production Designer
MARIE KRUPINA Production Designer
GRACE PARK Production Design Assistant
CHELSEA ROBERTS Production Design Assistant
ELIZABETH LOUGHRIDGE Accounting Coordinator
STEPHANIE HOCUTT Social Media Coordinator
JOSÉ MEZA Event Coordinator
HOLLY AITCHISON Operations Coordinator
MEGAN CHRISTOPHER Operations Assistant
RODRIGO HERNANDEZ Mailroom Assistant
MORGAN PERRY Direct Market Representative
CAT O' GRADY Marketing Assistant
LIZ ALMENDAREZ Accounting Administrative Assistant
CORNELIA TZANA Administrative Assistant

## BOOM! BOX™

# VANCE ™

created by **Hope Larson & Brittney Williams**

story by
**Hope Larson & Jackie Ball**
written by
**Jackie Ball**
illustrated by
**Elle Power**
colors by
**Sarah Stern**
letters by
**Jim Campbell**

cover by
**Brittney Williams**

designer
**Chelsea Roberts**
assistant editor
**Sophie Philips-Roberts**
editors
**Dafna Pleban &
Shannon Watters**

special thanks to
**Marie Krupina**

# chapter THIRTEEN

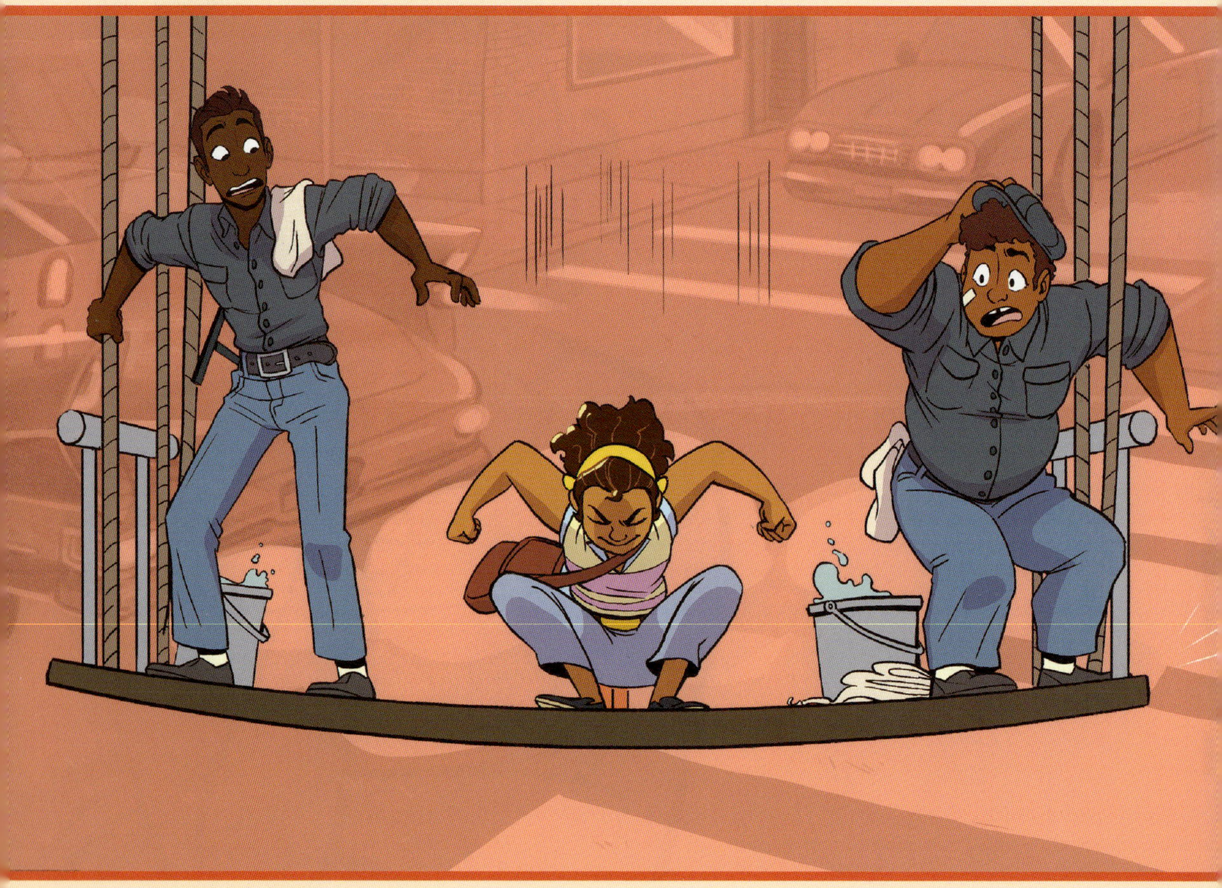

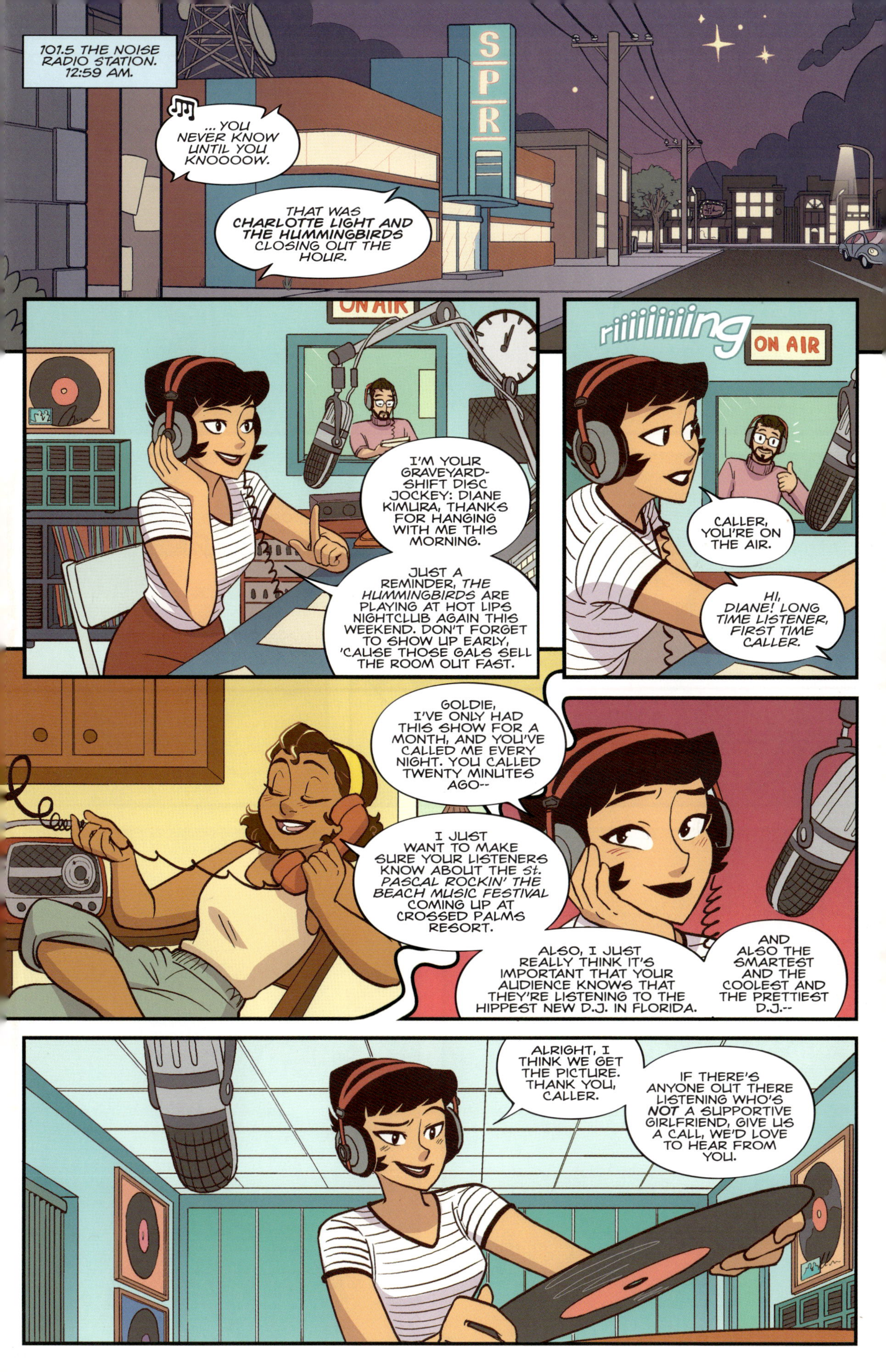
101.5 THE NOISE RADIO STATION. 12:59 AM.
...YOU NEVER KNOW UNTIL YOU KNOOOOW.
THAT WAS CHARLOTTE LIGHT AND THE HUMMINGBIRDS CLOSING OUT THE HOUR.
SPR
ON AIR
I'M YOUR GRAVEYARD-SHIFT DISC JOCKEY: DIANE KIMURA, THANKS FOR HANGING WITH ME THIS MORNING.
JUST A REMINDER, THE HUMMINGBIRDS ARE PLAYING AT HOT LIPS NIGHTCLUB AGAIN THIS WEEKEND. DON'T FORGET TO SHOW UP EARLY, 'CAUSE THOSE GALS SELL THE ROOM OUT FAST.
riiiiiiiiing
ON AIR
CALLER, YOU'RE ON THE AIR.
HI, DIANE! LONG TIME LISTENER, FIRST TIME CALLER.
GOLDIE, I'VE ONLY HAD THIS SHOW FOR A MONTH, AND YOU'VE CALLED ME EVERY NIGHT. YOU CALLED TWENTY MINUTES AGO--
I JUST WANT TO MAKE SURE YOUR LISTENERS KNOW ABOUT THE St. PASCAL ROCKIN' THE BEACH MUSIC FESTIVAL COMING UP AT CROSSED PALMS RESORT.
ALSO, I JUST REALLY THINK IT'S IMPORTANT THAT YOUR AUDIENCE KNOWS THAT THEY'RE LISTENING TO THE HIPPEST NEW D.J. IN FLORIDA.
AND ALSO THE SMARTEST AND THE COOLEST AND THE PRETTIEST D.J.--
ALRIGHT, I THINK WE GET THE PICTURE. THANK YOU, CALLER.
IF THERE'S ANYONE OUT THERE LISTENING WHO'S NOT A SUPPORTIVE GIRLFRIEND, GIVE US A CALL, WE'D LOVE TO HEAR FROM YOU.

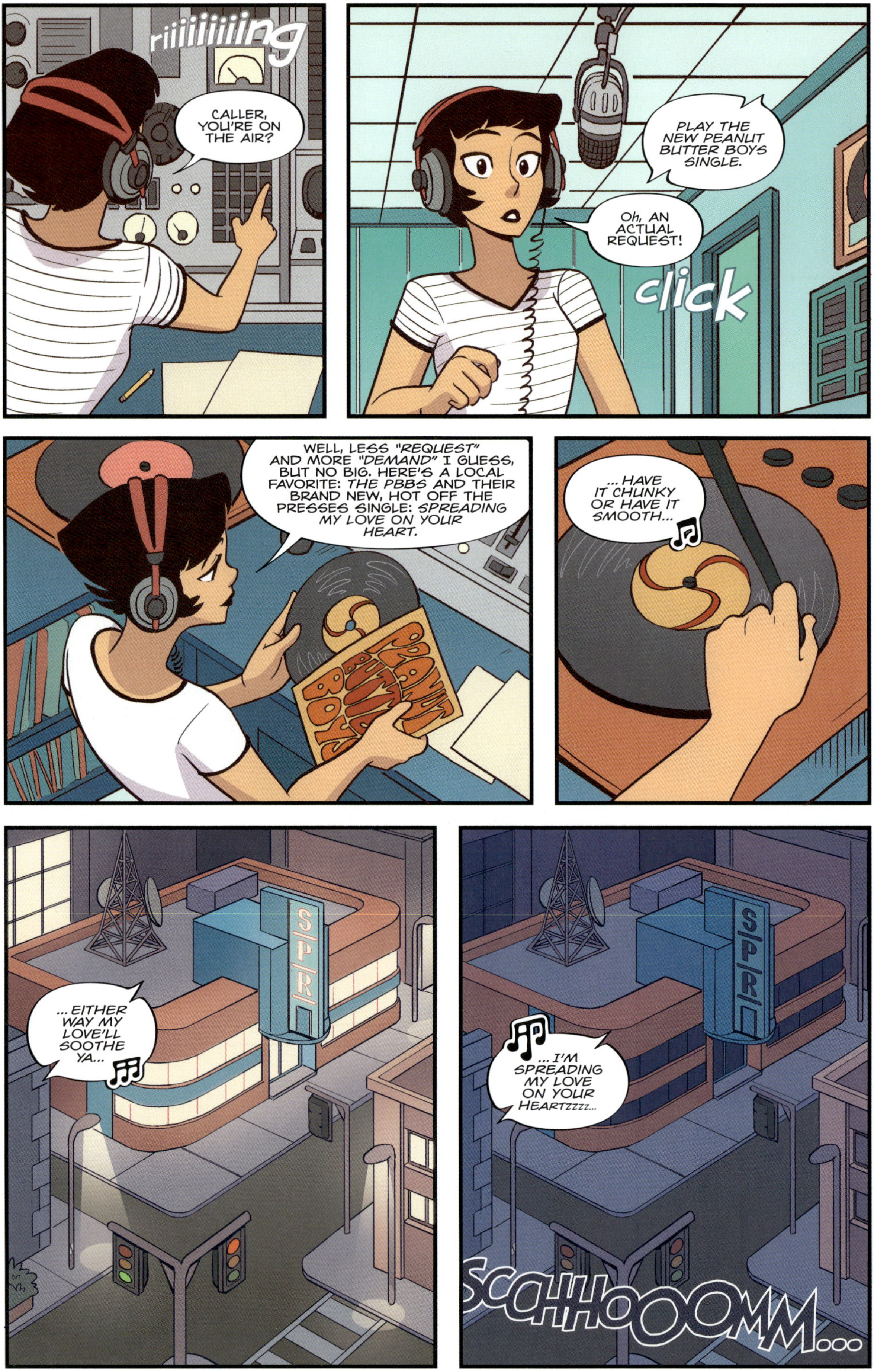
riiiiiiiiing
CALLER, YOU'RE ON THE AIR?
PLAY THE NEW PEANUT BUTTER BOYS SINGLE.
Oh, AN ACTUAL REQUEST!
click
WELL, LESS "REQUEST" AND MORE "DEMAND" I GUESS, BUT NO BIG. HERE'S A LOCAL FAVORITE: THE PBBS AND THEIR BRAND NEW, HOT OFF THE PRESSES SINGLE: SPREADING MY LOVE ON YOUR HEART.
PEANUT BUTTER BOYS
...HAVE IT CHUNKY OR HAVE IT SMOOTH...
SPR
...EITHER WAY MY LOVE'LL SOOTHE YA...
SPR
...I'M SPREADING MY LOVE ON YOUR HEARTzzzz...
SCCHHOOOMM...

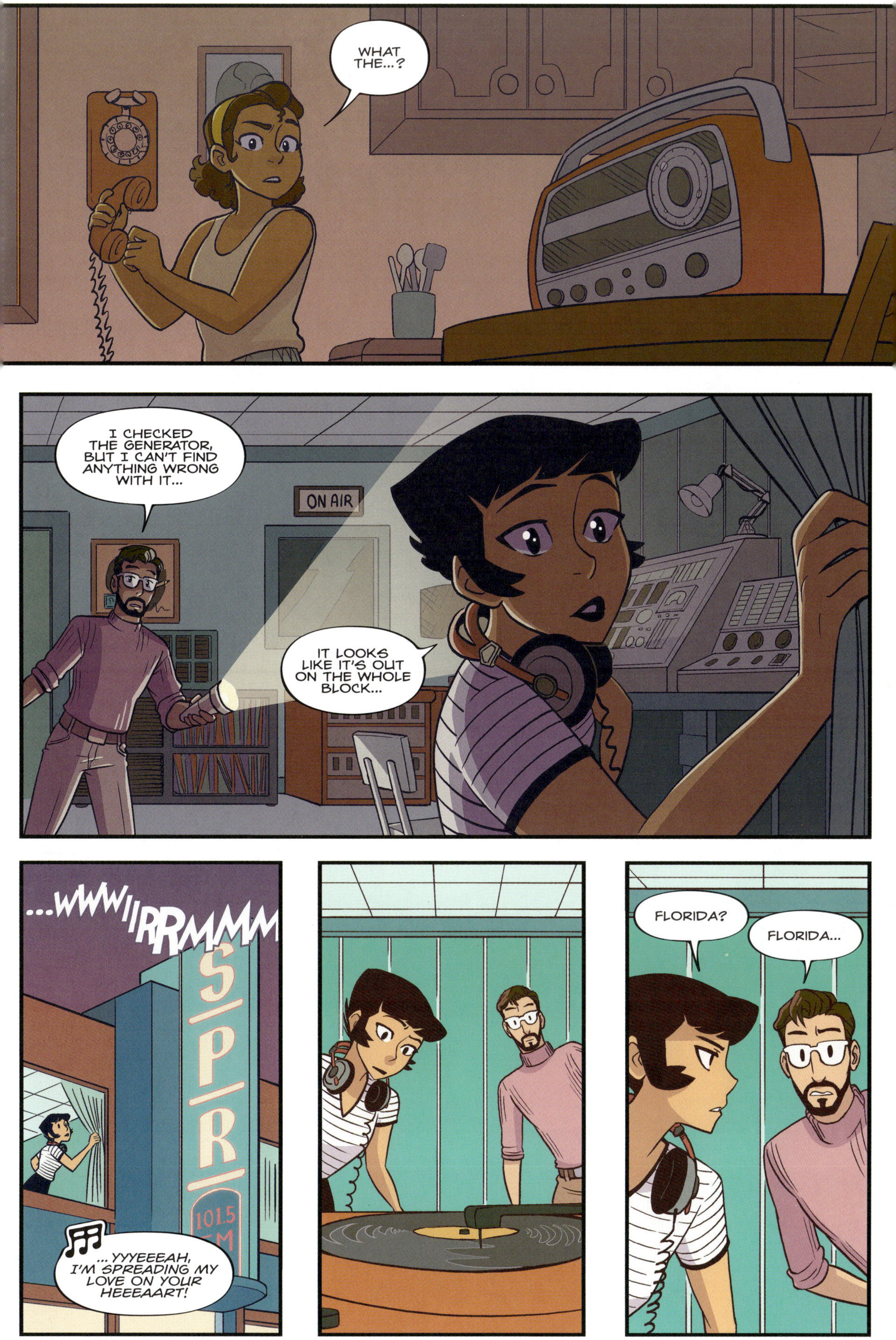
WHAT THE...?
I CHECKED THE GENERATOR, BUT I CAN'T FIND ANYTHING WRONG WITH IT...
ON AIR
IT LOOKS LIKE IT'S OUT ON THE WHOLE BLOCK...
...WWWIIRRMMM
SPR
101.5
...YYYEEEAH, I'M SPREADING MY LOVE ON YOUR HEEEAART!
FLORIDA?
FLORIDA...

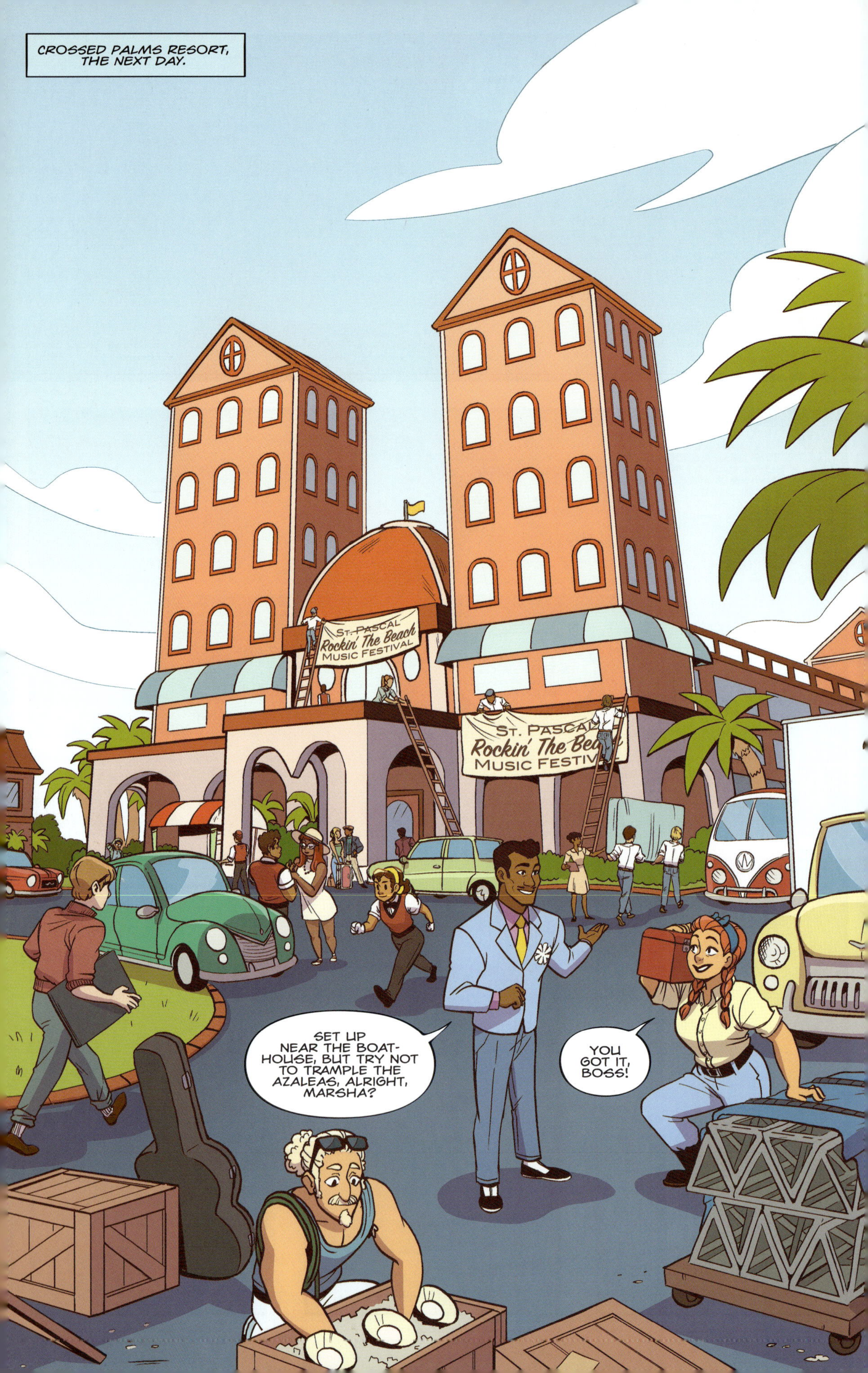
CROSSED PALMS RESORT, THE NEXT DAY.
ST. PASCAL Rockin' The Beach MUSIC FESTIVAL
SET UP NEAR THE BOAT-HOUSE, BUT TRY NOT TO TRAMPLE THE AZALEAS, ALRIGHT, MARSHA?
YOU GOT IT, BOSS!

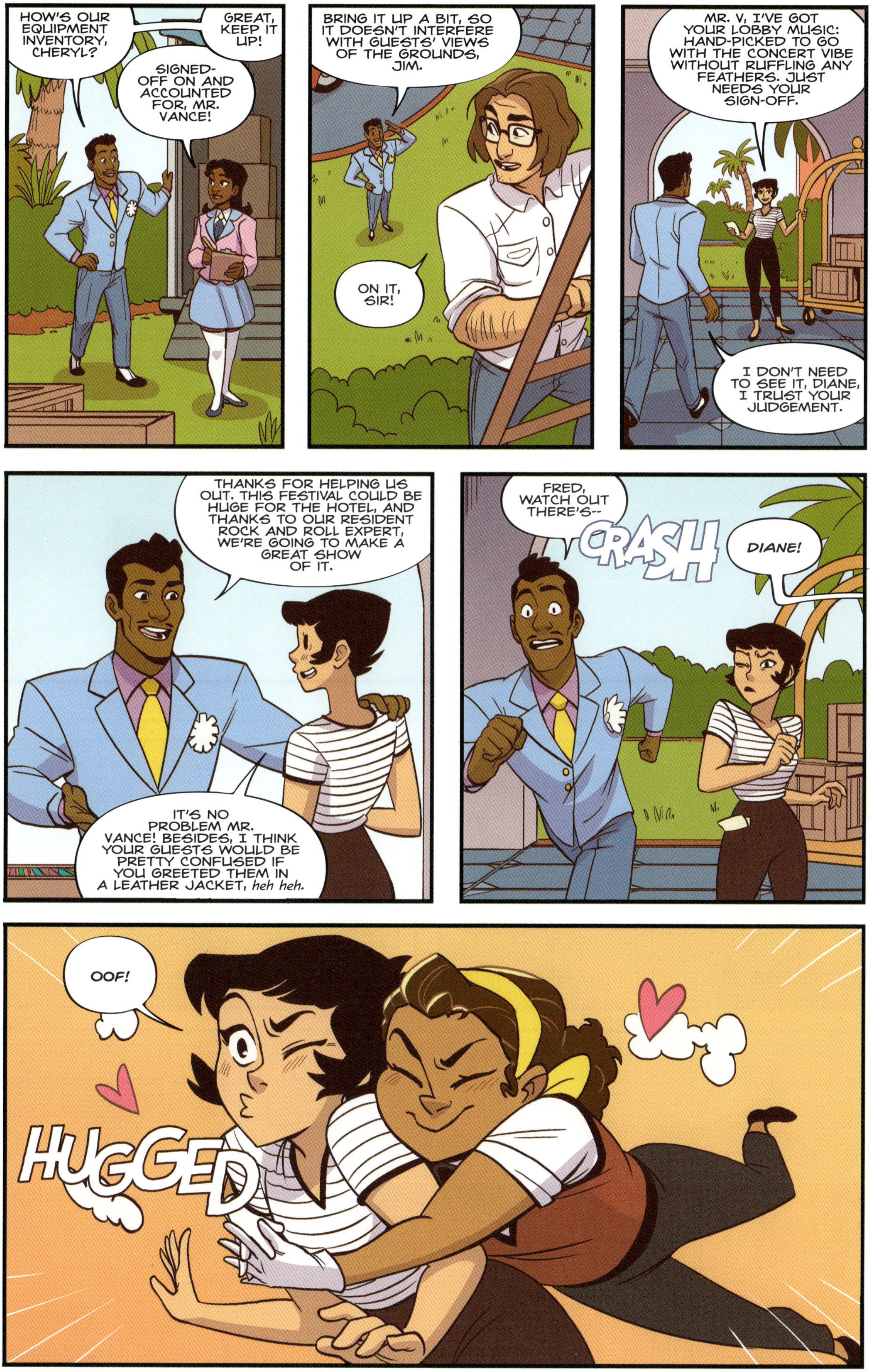

HOW'S OUR EQUIPMENT INVENTORY, CHERYL?
SIGNED-OFF ON AND ACCOUNTED FOR, MR. VANCE!
GREAT, KEEP IT UP!
BRING IT UP A BIT, SO IT DOESN'T INTERFERE WITH GUESTS' VIEWS OF THE GROUNDS, JIM.
ON IT, SIR!
MR. V, I'VE GOT YOUR LOBBY MUSIC: HAND-PICKED TO GO WITH THE CONCERT VIBE WITHOUT RUFFLING ANY FEATHERS. JUST NEEDS YOUR SIGN-OFF.
I DON'T NEED TO SEE IT, DIANE, I TRUST YOUR JUDGEMENT.
THANKS FOR HELPING US OUT. THIS FESTIVAL COULD BE HUGE FOR THE HOTEL, AND THANKS TO OUR RESIDENT ROCK AND ROLL EXPERT, WE'RE GOING TO MAKE A GREAT SHOW OF IT.
IT'S NO PROBLEM MR. VANCE! BESIDES, I THINK YOUR GUESTS WOULD BE PRETTY CONFUSED IF YOU GREETED THEM IN A LEATHER JACKET, *heh heh.*
FRED, WATCH OUT THERE'S--
CRASH
DIANE!
OOF!
HUGGED

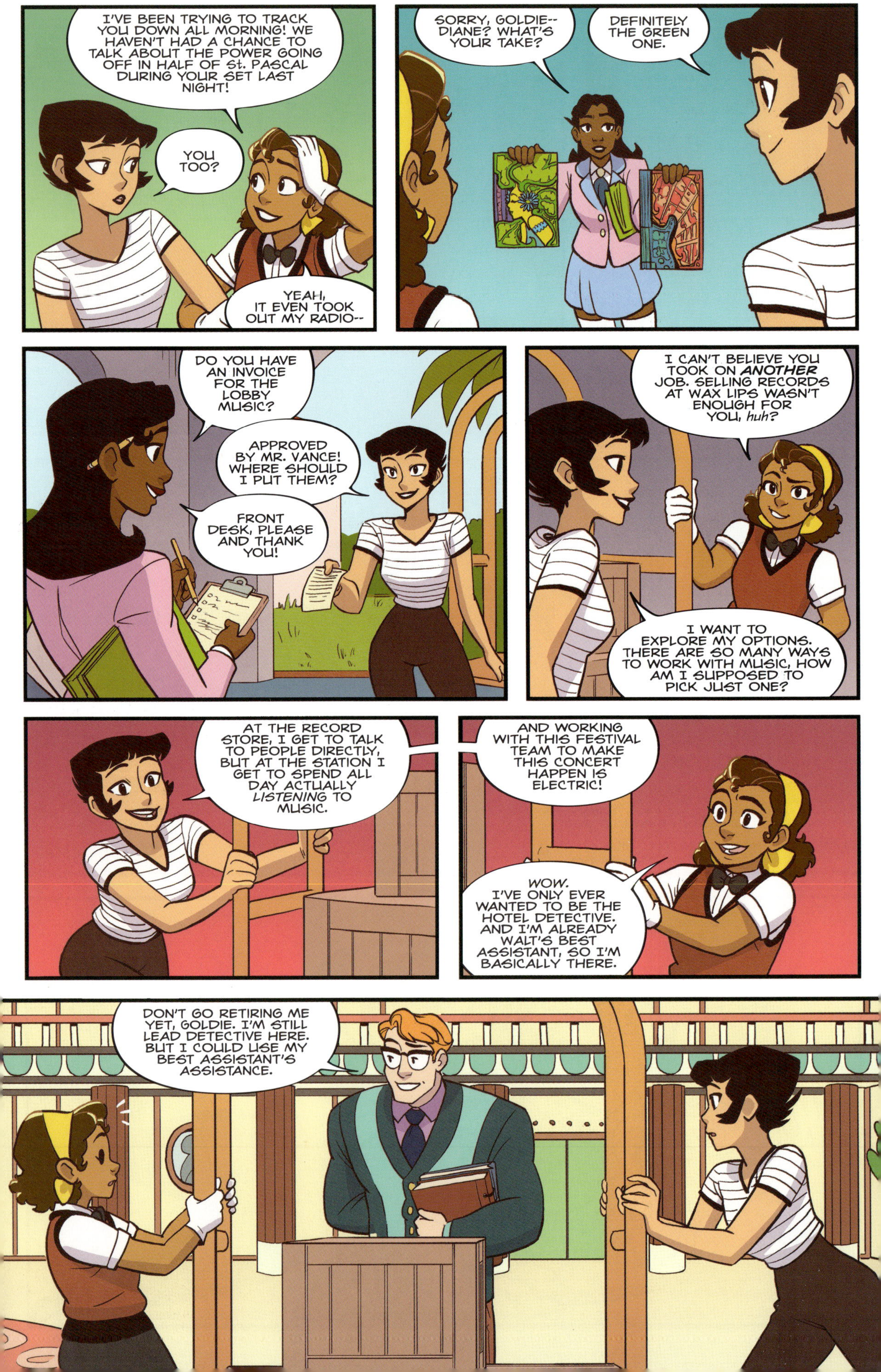
I'VE BEEN TRYING TO TRACK YOU DOWN ALL MORNING! WE HAVEN'T HAD A CHANCE TO TALK ABOUT THE POWER GOING OFF IN HALF OF St. PASCAL DURING YOUR SET LAST NIGHT!
YOU TOO?
YEAH, IT EVEN TOOK OUT MY RADIO--
SORRY, GOLDIE-- DIANE? WHAT'S YOUR TAKE?
DEFINITELY THE GREEN ONE.
DO YOU HAVE AN INVOICE FOR THE LOBBY MUSIC?
APPROVED BY MR. VANCE! WHERE SHOULD I PUT THEM?
FRONT DESK, PLEASE AND THANK YOU!
I CAN'T BELIEVE YOU TOOK ON ***ANOTHER*** JOB. SELLING RECORDS AT WAX LIPS WASN'T ENOUGH FOR YOU, *huh*?
I WANT TO EXPLORE MY OPTIONS. THERE ARE SO MANY WAYS TO WORK WITH MUSIC, HOW AM I SUPPOSED TO PICK JUST ONE?
AT THE RECORD STORE, I GET TO TALK TO PEOPLE DIRECTLY, BUT AT THE STATION I GET TO SPEND ALL DAY ACTUALLY *LISTENING* TO MUSIC.
AND WORKING WITH THIS FESTIVAL TEAM TO MAKE THIS CONCERT HAPPEN IS ELECTRIC!
WOW. I'VE ONLY EVER WANTED TO BE THE HOTEL DETECTIVE. AND I'M ALREADY WALT'S BEST ASSISTANT, SO I'M BASICALLY THERE.
DON'T GO RETIRING ME YET, GOLDIE. I'M STILL LEAD DETECTIVE HERE. BUT I COULD USE MY BEST ASSISTANT'S ASSISTANCE.

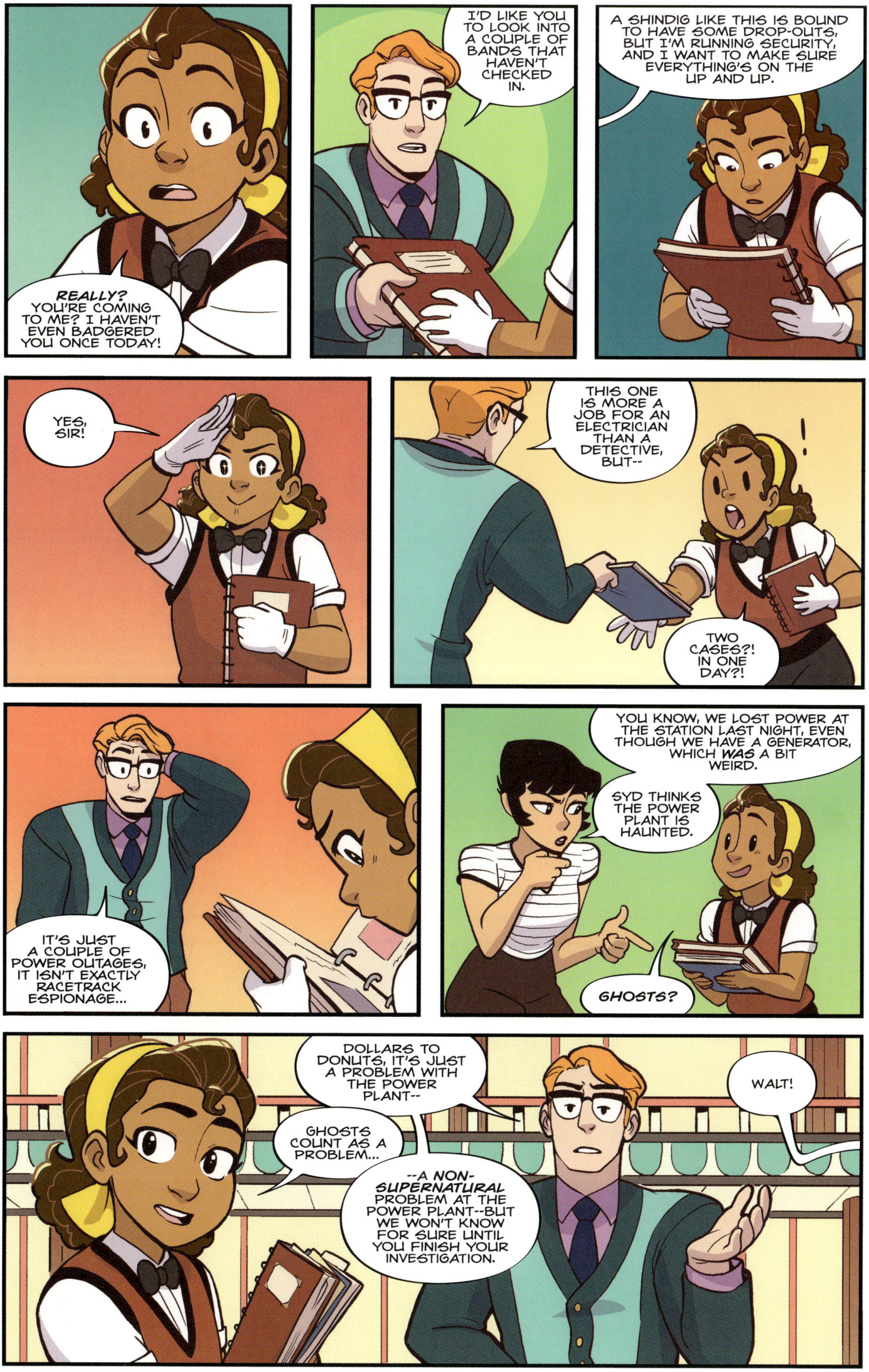
*REALLY?* YOU'RE COMING TO ME? I HAVEN'T EVEN BADGERED YOU ONCE TODAY!
I'D LIKE YOU TO LOOK INTO A COUPLE OF BANDS THAT HAVEN'T CHECKED IN.
A SHINDIG LIKE THIS IS BOUND TO HAVE SOME DROP-OUTS, BUT I'M RUNNING SECURITY, AND I WANT TO MAKE SURE EVERYTHING'S ON THE UP AND UP.
YES, SIR!
THIS ONE IS MORE A JOB FOR AN ELECTRICIAN THAN A DETECTIVE, BUT--
!
TWO CASES?! IN ONE DAY?!
IT'S JUST A COUPLE OF POWER OUTAGES, IT ISN'T EXACTLY RACETRACK ESPIONAGE...
YOU KNOW, WE LOST POWER AT THE STATION LAST NIGHT, EVEN THOUGH WE HAVE A GENERATOR, WHICH *WAS* A BIT WEIRD.
SYD THINKS THE POWER PLANT IS HAUNTED.
*GHOSTS?*
DOLLARS TO DONUTS, IT'S JUST A PROBLEM WITH THE POWER PLANT--
GHOSTS COUNT AS A PROBLEM...
--A *NON-SUPERNATURAL* PROBLEM AT THE POWER PLANT--BUT WE WON'T KNOW FOR SURE UNTIL YOU FINISH YOUR INVESTIGATION.
WALT!

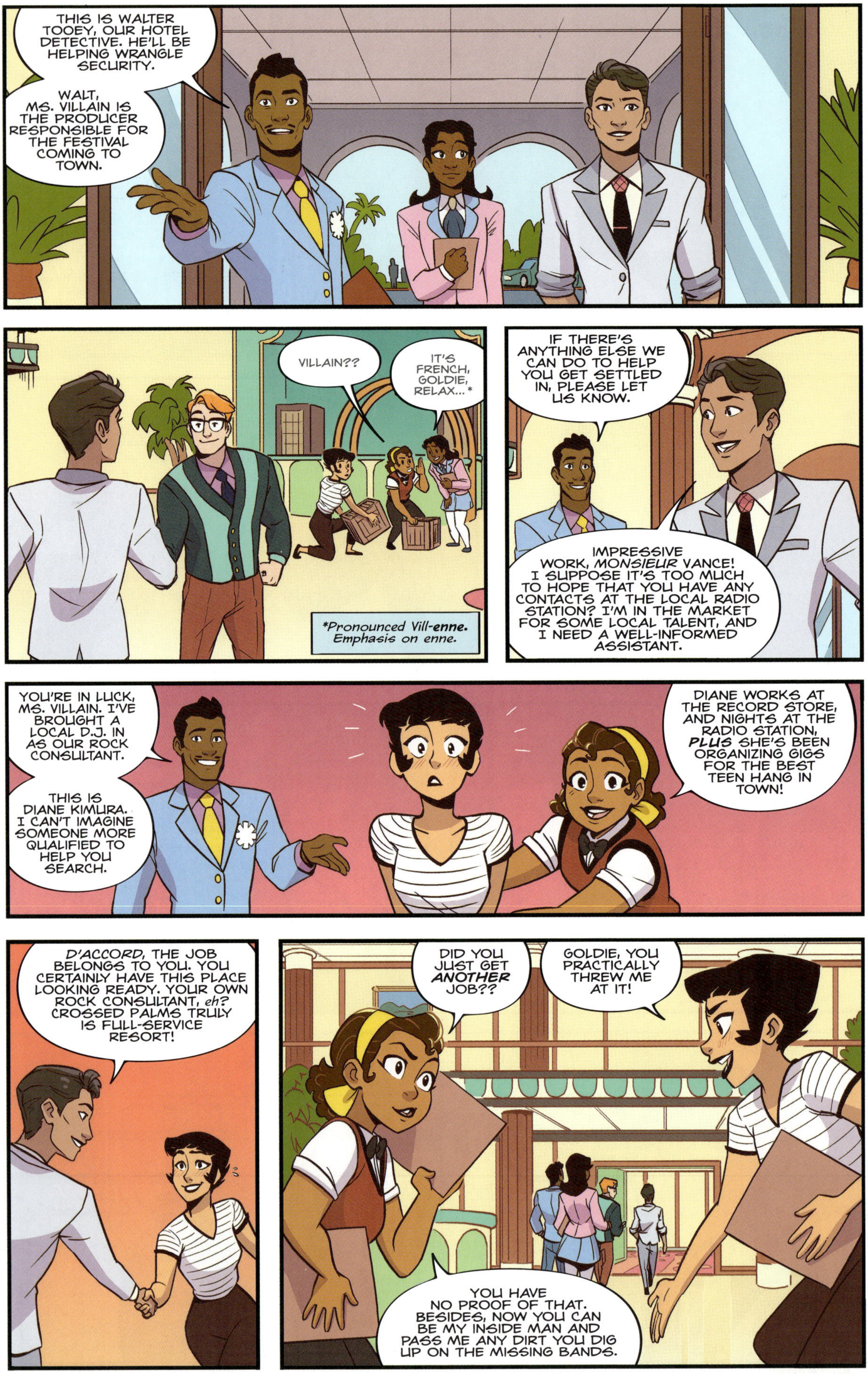
THIS IS WALTER TOOEY, OUR HOTEL DETECTIVE. HE'LL BE HELPING WRANGLE SECURITY.
WALT, MS. VILLAIN IS THE PRODUCER RESPONSIBLE FOR THE FESTIVAL COMING TO TOWN.
VILLAIN??
IT'S FRENCH, GOLDIE, RELAX...*
*Pronounced Vill-**enne.** Emphasis on enne.
IF THERE'S ANYTHING ELSE WE CAN DO TO HELP YOU GET SETTLED IN, PLEASE LET US KNOW.
IMPRESSIVE WORK, *MONSIEUR* VANCE! I SUPPOSE IT'S TOO MUCH TO HOPE THAT YOU HAVE ANY CONTACTS AT THE LOCAL RADIO STATION? I'M IN THE MARKET FOR SOME LOCAL TALENT, AND I NEED A WELL-INFORMED ASSISTANT.
YOU'RE IN LUCK, MS. VILLAIN. I'VE BROUGHT A LOCAL D.J. IN AS OUR ROCK CONSULTANT.
THIS IS DIANE KIMURA. I CAN'T IMAGINE SOMEONE MORE QUALIFIED TO HELP YOU SEARCH.
DIANE WORKS AT THE RECORD STORE, AND NIGHTS AT THE RADIO STATION, ***PLUS*** SHE'S BEEN ORGANIZING GIGS FOR THE BEST TEEN HANG IN TOWN!
*D'ACCORD,* THE JOB BELONGS TO YOU. YOU CERTAINLY HAVE THIS PLACE LOOKING READY. YOUR OWN ROCK CONSULTANT, *eh?* CROSSED PALMS TRULY IS FULL-SERVICE RESORT!
DID YOU JUST GET ***ANOTHER*** JOB??
GOLDIE, YOU PRACTICALLY THREW ME AT IT!
YOU HAVE NO PROOF OF THAT. BESIDES, NOW YOU CAN BE MY INSIDE MAN AND PASS ME ANY DIRT YOU DIG UP ON THE MISSING BANDS.

HOT LIPS NIGHTCLUB, LATER THAT NIGHT.

"WELCOME TO HOT LIPS."

THE RECORD STORE DOES WELL, SO THE OWNER FIGURED LOCAL TEENS COULD USE A PLACE TO SCOPE LIVE MUSIC.

WHEN CHUCK AND THE GIRLS STARTED THE BAND, I CONVINCED THEM TO PLAY HERE, AND THEY'VE BEEN DOING GANGBUSTERS EVER SINCE!

OUI, I SEE THAT! THIS LINE IS SERIOUS.

THESE LADIES ARE CERTAINLY ON TO SOMETHING.

*I WISH I WAS ON TO SOMETHING! THIS THIRD WHEEL BIT IS AWKWARD...*

SCHHOOOMM

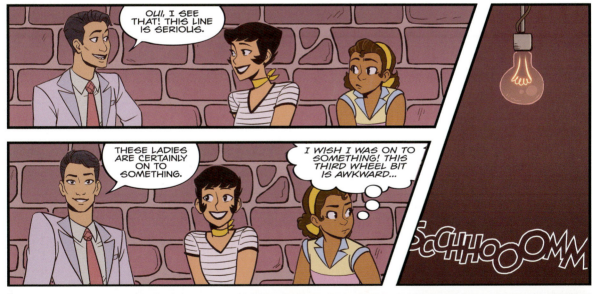

*Awwwwww!*

BRING BACK THE MUSIC!

BOO! STUPID POWER!

*NOOOOOO!*

BOOOOO!

*Ah! A GHOST!*

NO, THAT WAS JUST ME, I WAS SAYING "BOO!"

*THAT WAS QUICK. WOW, I AM GREAT AT WISHING!*

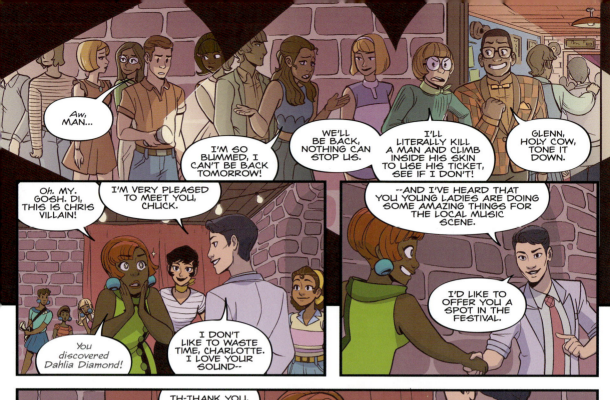

AW, MAN...

I'M SO BUMMED, I CAN'T BE BACK TOMORROW!

WE'LL BE BACK, NOTHING CAN STOP US.

I'LL LITERALLY KILL A MAN AND CLIMB INSIDE HIS SKIN TO USE HIS TICKET, SEE IF I DON'T!

GLENN, HOLY COW, TONE IT DOWN.

OH. MY. GOSH. DI, THIS IS CHRIS VILLAIN!

I'M VERY PLEASED TO MEET YOU, CHUCK.

You discovered Dahlia Diamond!

I DON'T LIKE TO WASTE TIME, CHARLOTTE. I LOVE YOUR SOUND--

--AND I'VE HEARD THAT YOU YOUNG LADIES ARE DOING SOME AMAZING THINGS FOR THE LOCAL MUSIC SCENE.

I'D LIKE TO OFFER YOU A SPOT IN THE FESTIVAL.

TH-THANK YOU. WE WOULD BE HONORED.

EEEEEEEEEE!

CAN YOU BELIEVE THAT JUST HAPPENED??

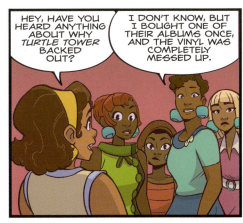

**Panel 1:**
THIS IS UNBELIEVABLE! DO YOU THINK WE'RE TAKING *TURTLE TOWER'S* SPOT? I HEARD THEY BACKED OUT...

I THINK YOU NEED TO CALM DOWN BEFORE YOU BLOW ANOTHER FUSE IN THIS JOINT...

**Panel 2:**
HEY, HAVE YOU HEARD ANYTHING ABOUT WHY *TURTLE TOWER* BACKED OUT?

I DON'T KNOW, BUT I BOUGHT ONE OF THEIR ALBUMS ONCE, AND THE VINYL WAS COMPLETELY MESSED UP.

THERE WASN'T ANY MUSIC ON IT, JUST SOME WEIRD, NASTY SCREAMING... I HAD TO GET MY MONEY BACK.

YOU LOOKING INTO THOSE DISAPPEARING BANDS?

I HEARD A RUMOR THE FESTIVAL IS CURSED...

NO, YOU *STARTED* A RUMOR THAT THE FESTIVAL IS CURSED...

WHY DO YOU--?

GOLDIE! IT'S YOU, YOU'RE GOLDIE!

DIANE NEVER STOPS GUSHING ABOUT YOU, IT'S ADORABLE! I'M CHUCK! AND THESE ARE *THE HUMMINGBIRDS:* ROSE, JEAN, AND MARG!

EVERYONE, THIS IS GOLDIE!

HRK!

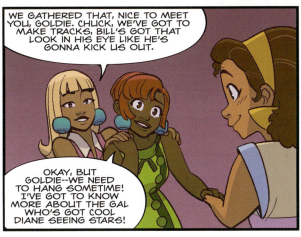

WE GATHERED THAT, NICE TO MEET YOU, GOLDIE. CHUCK, WE'VE GOT TO MAKE TRACKS, BILL'S GOT THAT LOOK IN HIS EYE LIKE HE'S GONNA KICK US OUT.

OKAY, BUT GOLDIE--WE NEED TO HANG SOMETIME! I'VE GOT TO KNOW MORE ABOUT THE GAL WHO'S GOT COOL DIANE SEEING STARS!

YEAH...

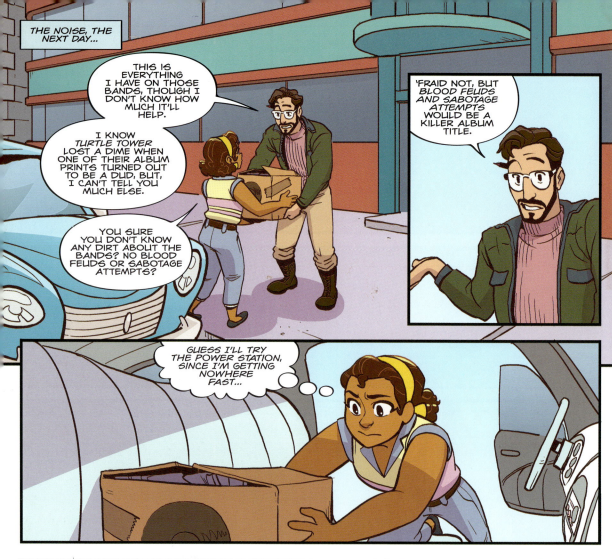

THIS IS EVERYTHING I HAVE ON THOSE BANDS, THOUGH I DON'T KNOW HOW MUCH IT'LL HELP.

I KNOW *TURTLE TOWER* LOST A DIME WHEN ONE OF THEIR ALBUM PRINTS TURNED OUT TO BE A DUD, BUT, I CAN'T TELL YOU MUCH ELSE.

YOU SURE YOU DON'T KNOW ANY DIRT ABOUT THE BANDS? NO BLOOD FEUDS OR SABOTAGE ATTEMPTS?

'FRAID NOT, BUT BLOOD FEUDS AND SABOTAGE ATTEMPTS WOULD BE A KILLER ALBUM TITLE.

GUESS I'LL TRY THE POWER STATION, SINCE I'M GETTING NOWHERE FAST...

St. PASCAL POWER PLANT...

WE HAVE NO IDEA WHAT'S CAUSING THE OUTAGES. WE'VE RUN ABOUT A HUNDRED DIAGNOSTICS, BUT WE HAVEN'T TURNED UP A SINGLE CAUSE FOR THE SURGES.

FLASH! AND YOU'RE SURE YOU HAVEN'T HAD ANY REPORTS OF CREEPY, SHADOWY FIGURES?

OR NEW HIRES THAT ARE UNUSUALLY HELPFUL AND FRIENDLY, BUT HIDING SINISTER ULTERIOR MOTIVES?

N...NO?

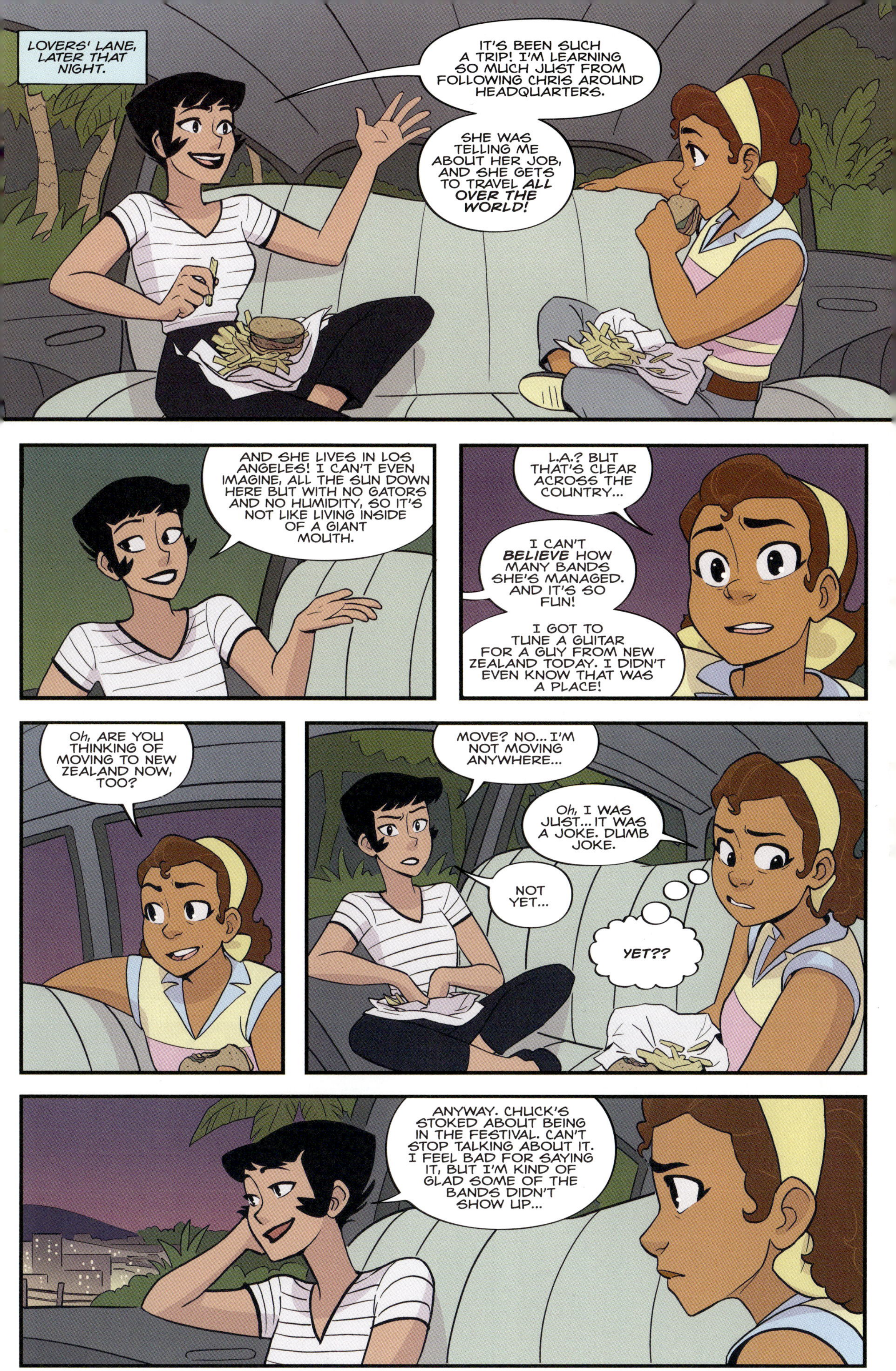
LOVERS' LANE, LATER THAT NIGHT.
IT'S BEEN SUCH A TRIP! I'M LEARNING SO MUCH JUST FROM FOLLOWING CHRIS AROUND HEADQUARTERS.
SHE WAS TELLING ME ABOUT HER JOB, AND SHE GETS TO TRAVEL ALL OVER THE WORLD!
AND SHE LIVES IN LOS ANGELES! I CAN'T EVEN IMAGINE, ALL THE SUN DOWN HERE BUT WITH NO GATORS AND NO HUMIDITY, SO IT'S NOT LIKE LIVING INSIDE OF A GIANT MOUTH.
L.A.? BUT THAT'S CLEAR ACROSS THE COUNTRY...
I CAN'T BELIEVE HOW MANY BANDS SHE'S MANAGED. AND IT'S SO FUN!
I GOT TO TUNE A GUITAR FOR A GUY FROM NEW ZEALAND TODAY. I DIDN'T EVEN KNOW THAT WAS A PLACE!
Oh, ARE YOU THINKING OF MOVING TO NEW ZEALAND NOW, TOO?
MOVE? NO... I'M NOT MOVING ANYWHERE...
Oh, I WAS JUST... IT WAS A JOKE. DUMB JOKE.
NOT YET...
YET??
ANYWAY. CHUCK'S STOKED ABOUT BEING IN THE FESTIVAL. CAN'T STOP TALKING ABOUT IT. I FEEL BAD FOR SAYING IT, BUT I'M KIND OF GLAD SOME OF THE BANDS DIDN'T SHOW UP...

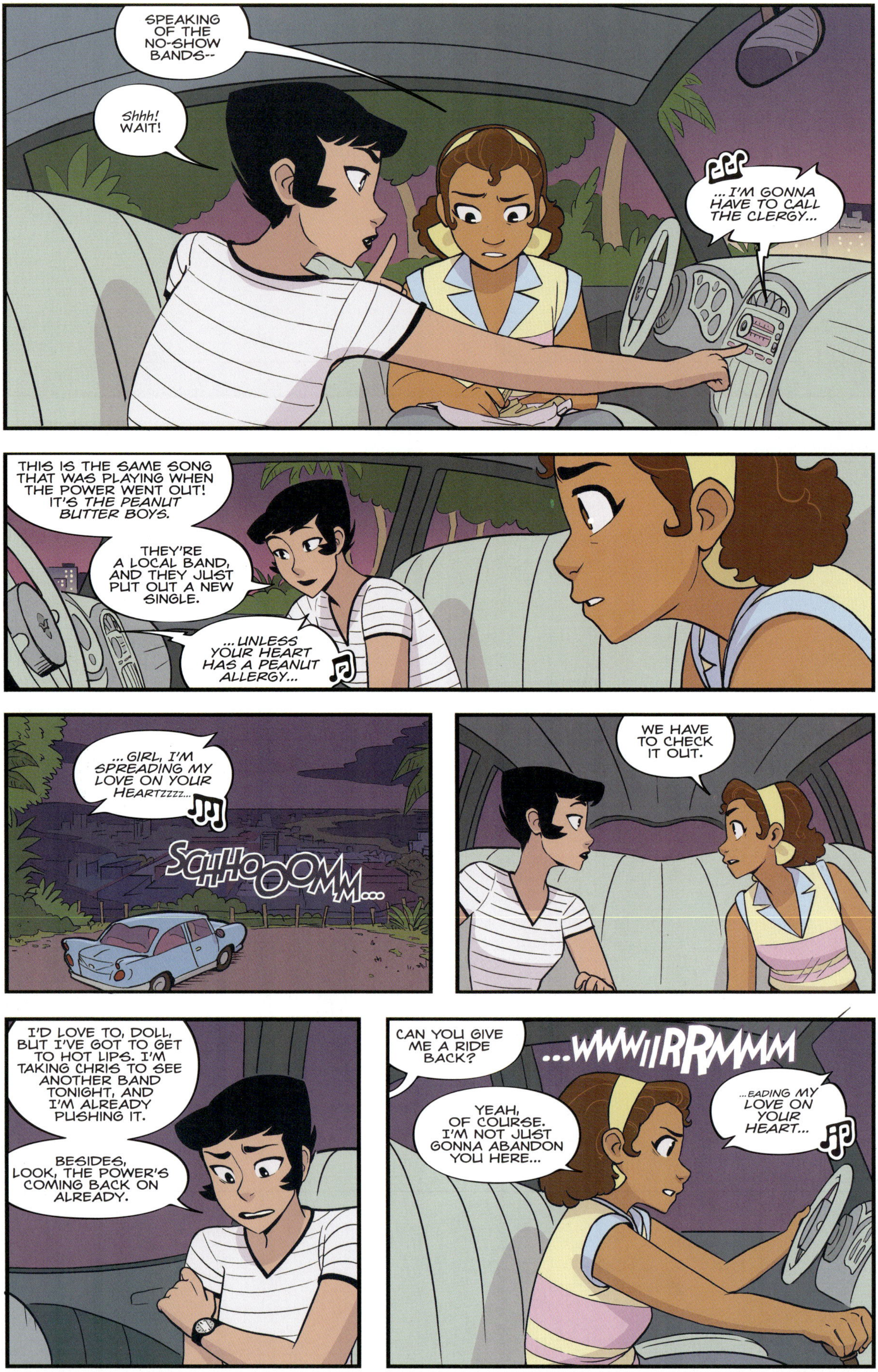
SPEAKING OF THE NO-SHOW BANDS--
Shhh! WAIT!
...I'M GONNA HAVE TO CALL THE CLERGY...
THIS IS THE SAME SONG THAT WAS PLAYING WHEN THE POWER WENT OUT! IT'S THE PEANUT BUTTER BOYS.
THEY'RE A LOCAL BAND, AND THEY JUST PUT OUT A NEW SINGLE.
...UNLESS YOUR HEART HAS A PEANUT ALLERGY...
...GIRL, I'M SPREADING MY LOVE ON YOUR HEARTzzzz...
SCHHOOOMM...
WE HAVE TO CHECK IT OUT.
I'D LOVE TO, DOLL, BUT I'VE GOT TO GET TO HOT LIPS. I'M TAKING CHRIS TO SEE ANOTHER BAND TONIGHT, AND I'M ALREADY PUSHING IT.
BESIDES, LOOK, THE POWER'S COMING BACK ON ALREADY.
CAN YOU GIVE ME A RIDE BACK?
...WWWIIRRMMM
YEAH, OF COURSE. I'M NOT JUST GONNA ABANDON YOU HERE...
...EADING MY LOVE ON YOUR HEART...

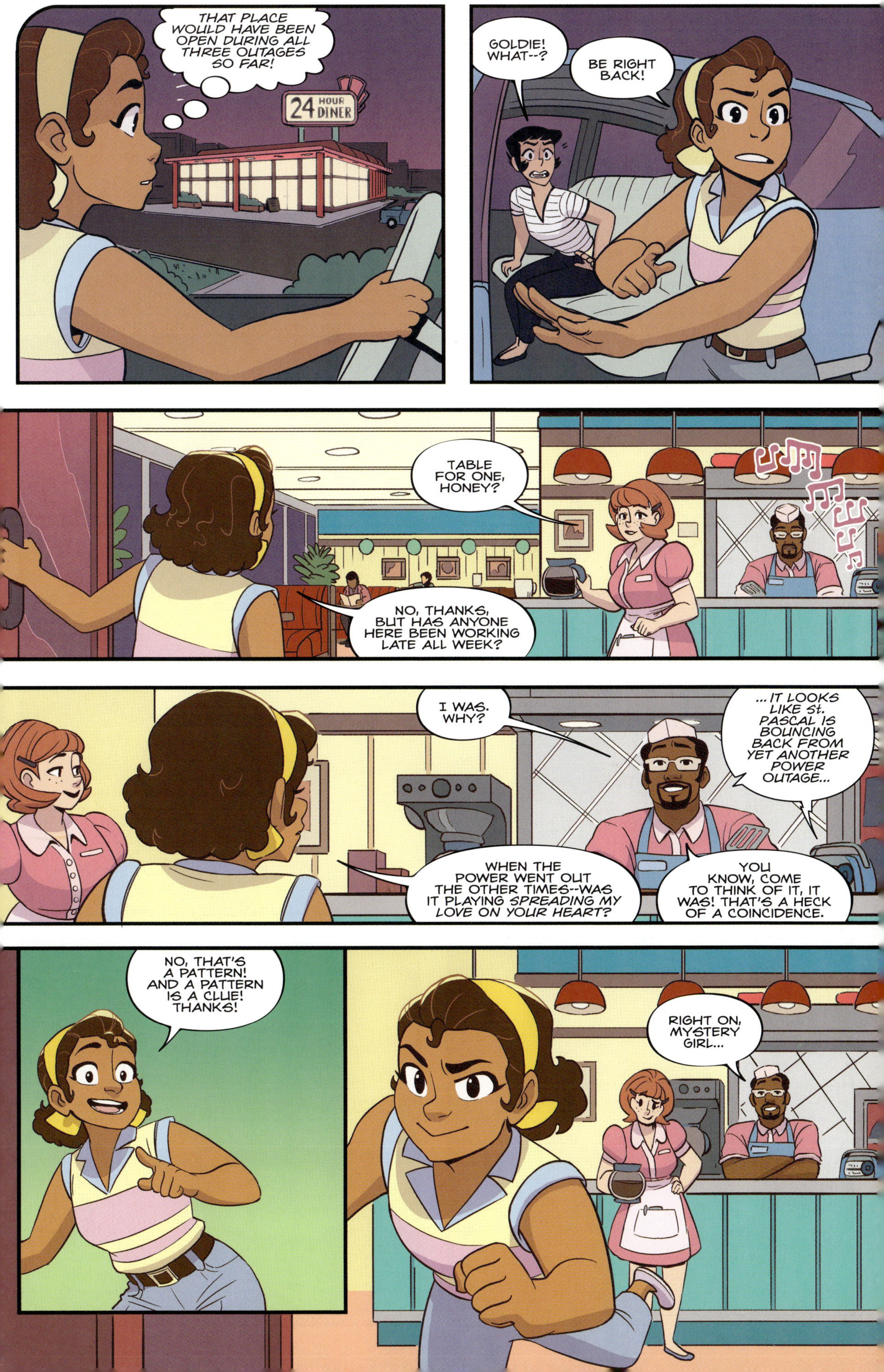
THAT PLACE WOULD HAVE BEEN OPEN DURING ALL THREE OUTAGES SO FAR!
24 HOUR DINER
GOLDIE! WHAT--?
BE RIGHT BACK!
TABLE FOR ONE, HONEY?
NO, THANKS, BUT HAS ANYONE HERE BEEN WORKING LATE ALL WEEK?
I WAS. WHY?
...IT LOOKS LIKE St. PASCAL IS BOUNCING BACK FROM YET ANOTHER POWER OUTAGE...
WHEN THE POWER WENT OUT THE OTHER TIMES--WAS IT PLAYING *SPREADING MY LOVE ON YOUR HEART*?
YOU KNOW, COME TO THINK OF IT, IT WAS! THAT'S A HECK OF A COINCIDENCE.
NO, THAT'S A PATTERN! AND A PATTERN IS A CLUE! THANKS!
RIGHT ON, MYSTERY GIRL...

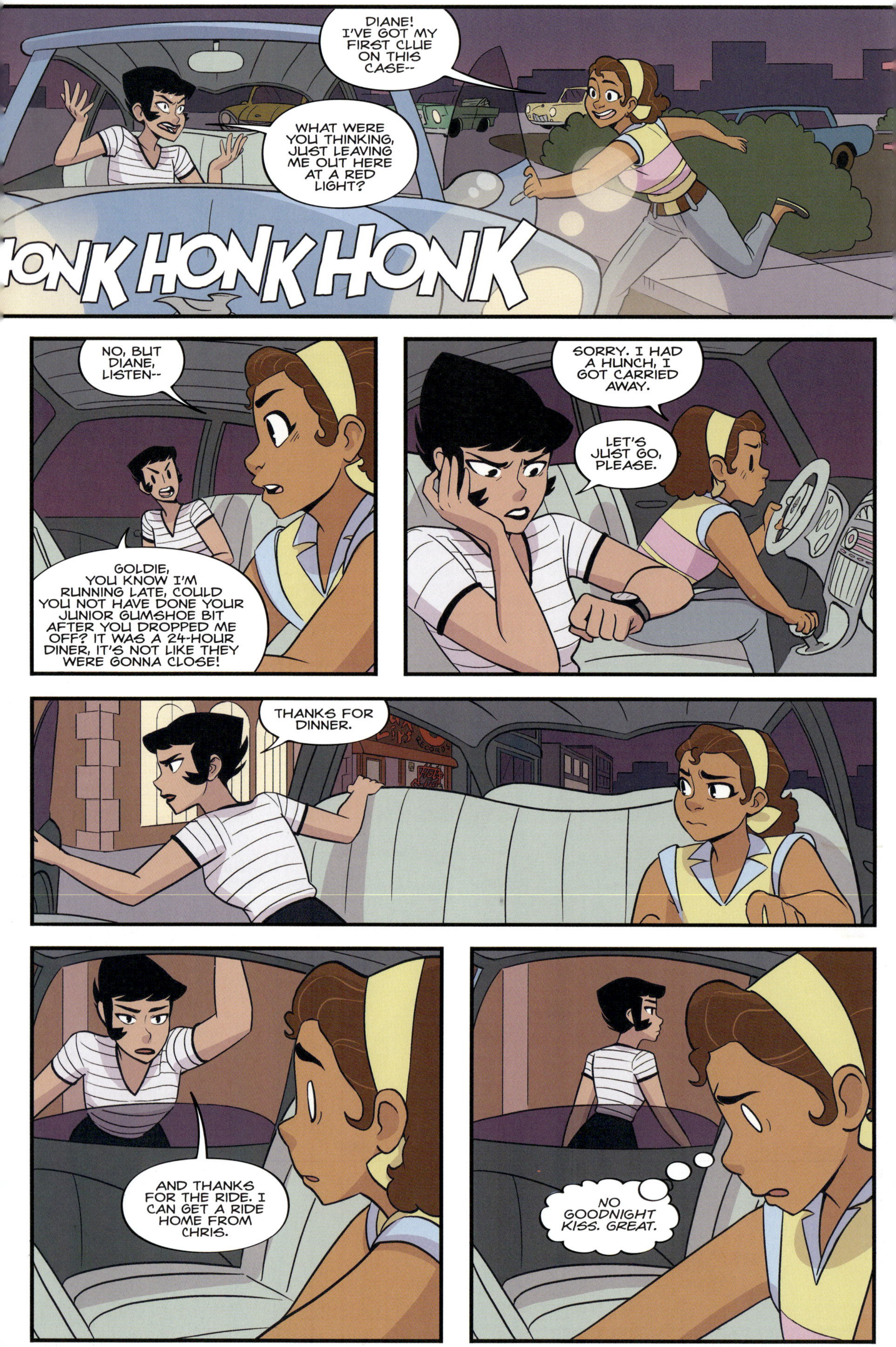
DIANE! I'VE GOT MY FIRST CLUE ON THIS CASE--
WHAT WERE YOU THINKING, JUST LEAVING ME OUT HERE AT A RED LIGHT?
HONK HONK HONK
NO, BUT DIANE, LISTEN--
GOLDIE, YOU KNOW I'M RUNNING LATE, COULD YOU NOT HAVE DONE YOUR JUNIOR GUMSHOE BIT AFTER YOU DROPPED ME OFF? IT WAS A 24-HOUR DINER, IT'S NOT LIKE THEY WERE GONNA CLOSE!
SORRY. I HAD A HUNCH, I GOT CARRIED AWAY.
LET'S JUST GO, PLEASE.
THANKS FOR DINNER.
AND THANKS FOR THE RIDE. I CAN GET A RIDE HOME FROM CHRIS.
NO GOODNIGHT KISS. GREAT.

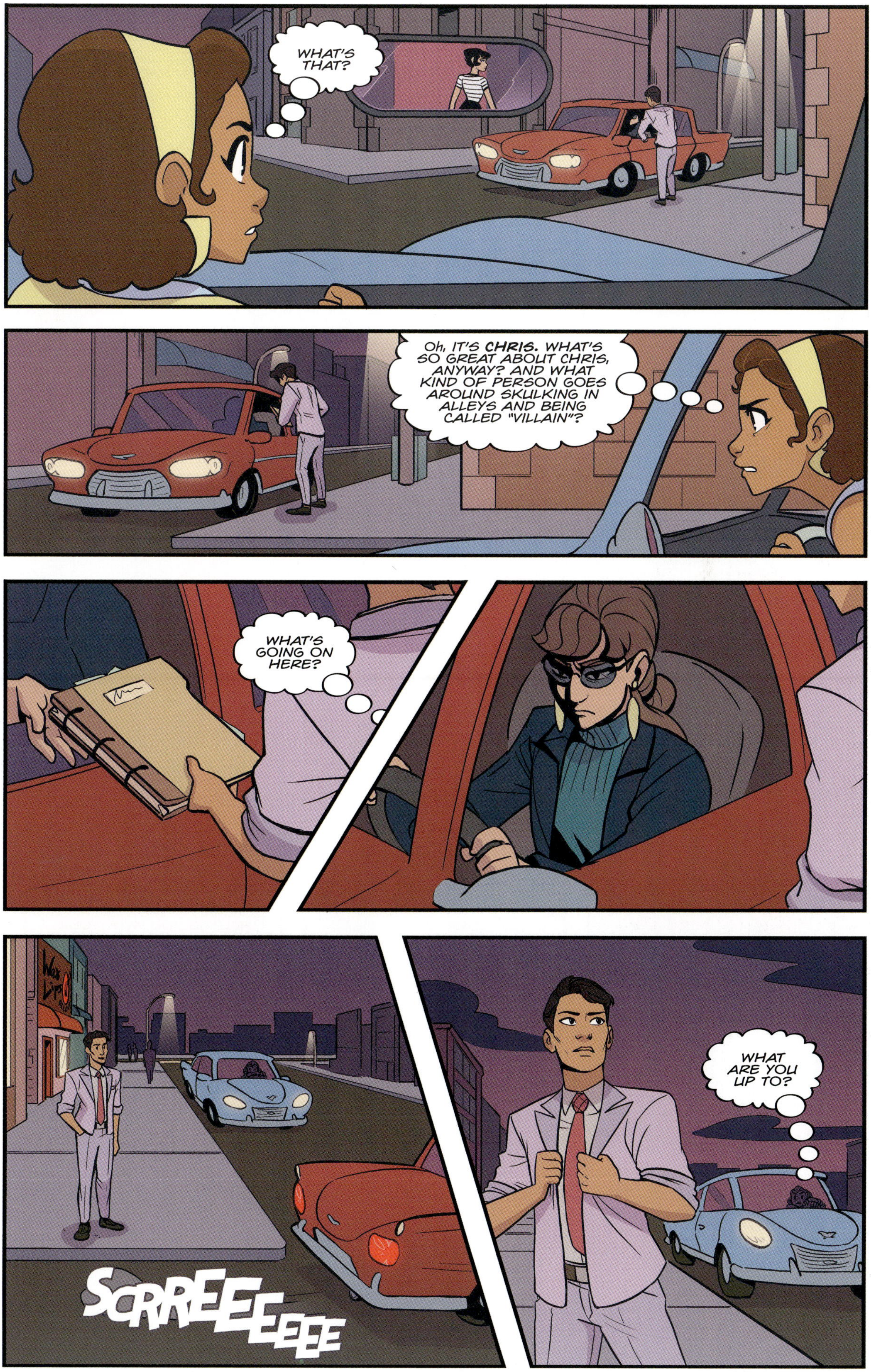
WHAT'S THAT?
Oh, IT'S CHRIS. WHAT'S SO GREAT ABOUT CHRIS, ANYWAY? AND WHAT KIND OF PERSON GOES AROUND SKULKING IN ALLEYS AND BEING CALLED "VILLAIN"?
WHAT'S GOING ON HERE?
SCRREEEEEEE
WHAT ARE YOU UP TO?

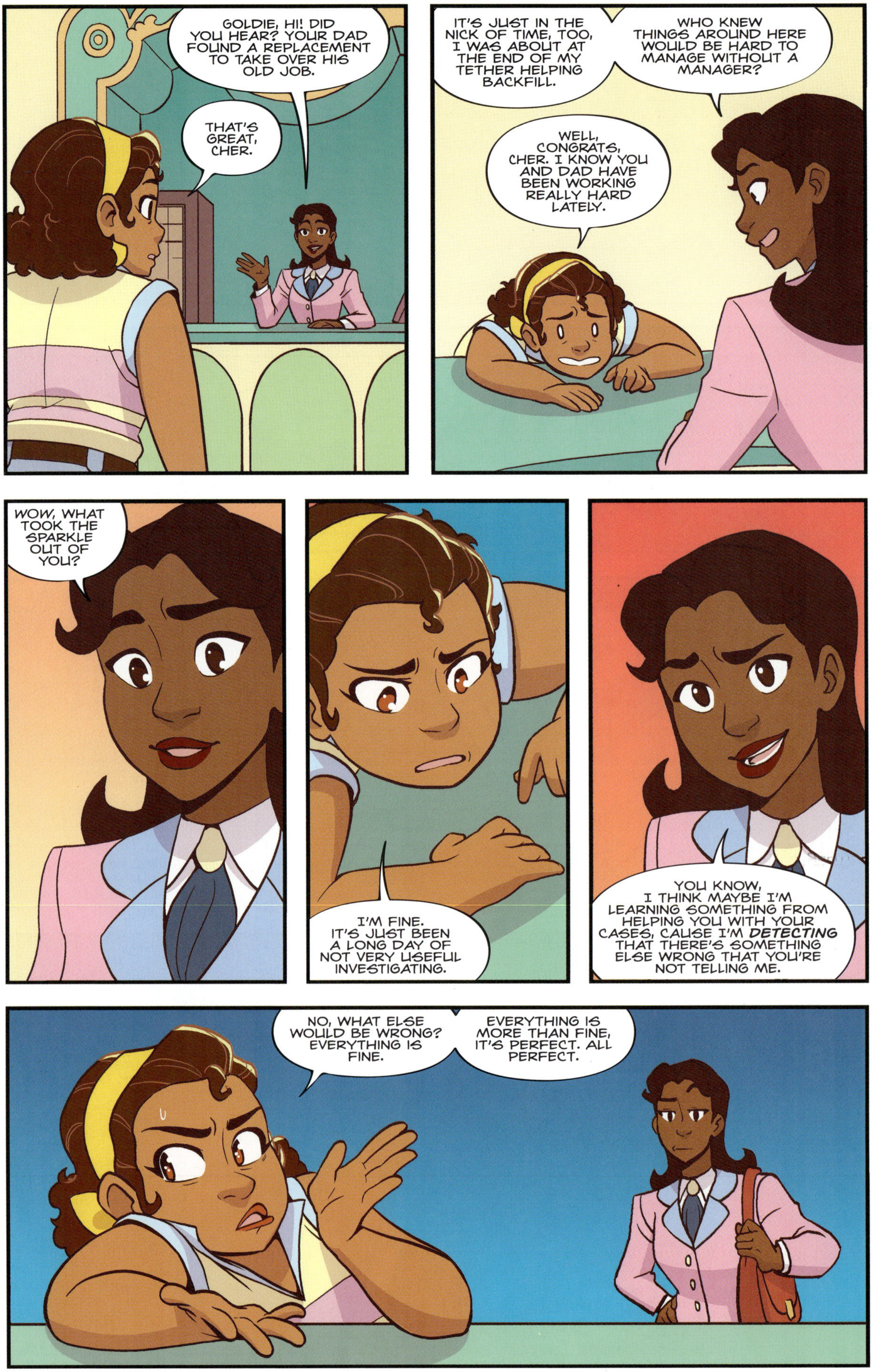
GOLDIE, HI! DID YOU HEAR? YOUR DAD FOUND A REPLACEMENT TO TAKE OVER HIS OLD JOB.
THAT'S GREAT, CHER.
IT'S JUST IN THE NICK OF TIME, TOO, I WAS ABOUT AT THE END OF MY TETHER HELPING BACKFILL.
WHO KNEW THINGS AROUND HERE WOULD BE HARD TO MANAGE WITHOUT A MANAGER?
WELL, CONGRATS, CHER. I KNOW YOU AND DAD HAVE BEEN WORKING REALLY HARD LATELY.
WOW, WHAT TOOK THE SPARKLE OUT OF YOU?
I'M FINE. IT'S JUST BEEN A LONG DAY OF NOT VERY USEFUL INVESTIGATING.
YOU KNOW, I THINK MAYBE I'M LEARNING SOMETHING FROM HELPING YOU WITH YOUR CASES, CAUSE I'M ***DETECTING*** THAT THERE'S SOMETHING ELSE WRONG THAT YOU'RE NOT TELLING ME.
NO, WHAT ELSE WOULD BE WRONG? EVERYTHING IS FINE.
EVERYTHING IS MORE THAN FINE, IT'S PERFECT. ALL PERFECT.

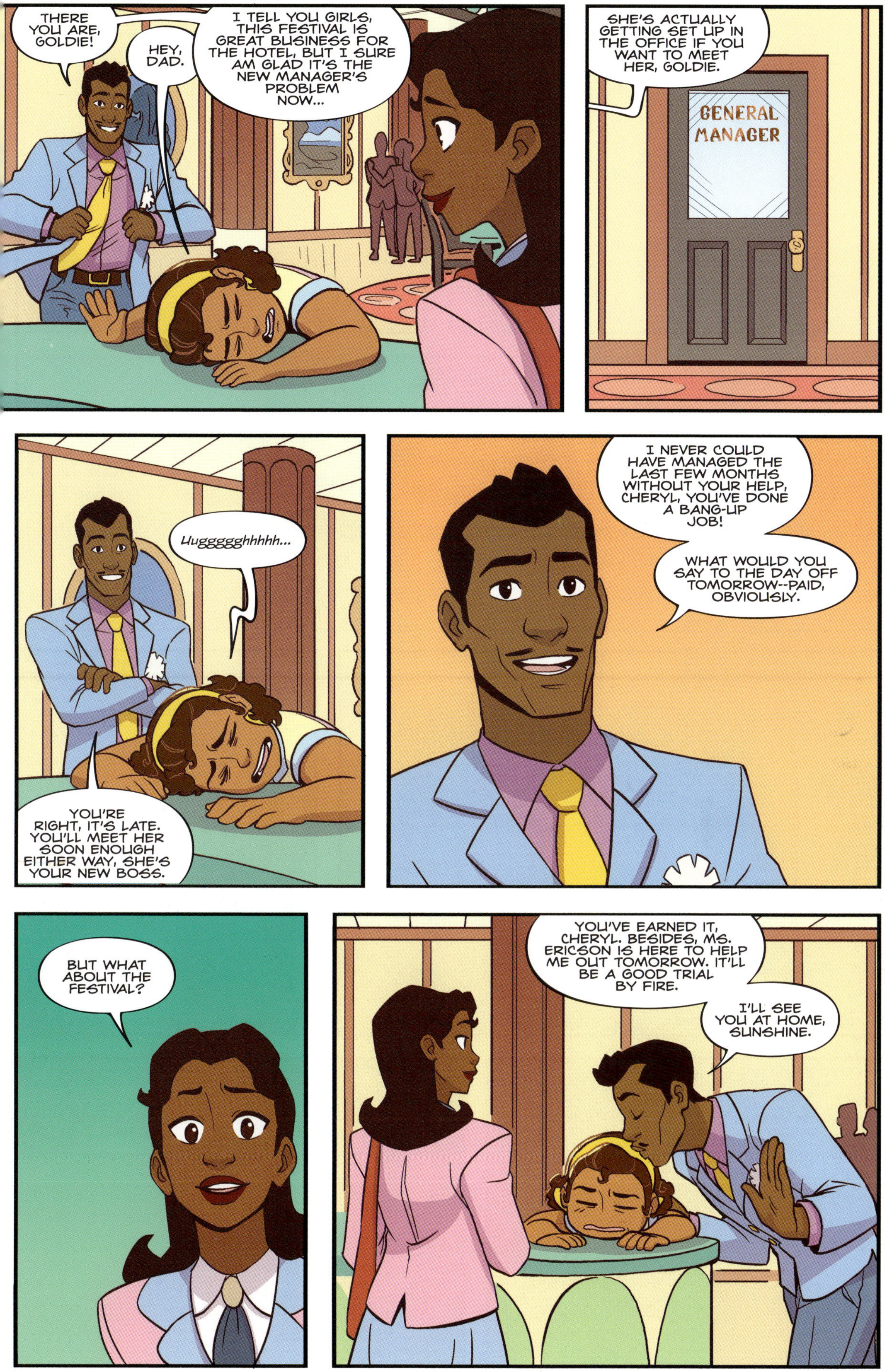
THERE YOU ARE, GOLDIE!
HEY, DAD.
I TELL YOU GIRLS, THIS FESTIVAL IS GREAT BUSINESS FOR THE HOTEL, BUT I SURE AM GLAD IT'S THE NEW MANAGER'S PROBLEM NOW...
SHE'S ACTUALLY GETTING SET UP IN THE OFFICE IF YOU WANT TO MEET HER, GOLDIE.
GENERAL MANAGER
Uuggggghhhhh...
YOU'RE RIGHT, IT'S LATE. YOU'LL MEET HER SOON ENOUGH EITHER WAY, SHE'S YOUR NEW BOSS.
I NEVER COULD HAVE MANAGED THE LAST FEW MONTHS WITHOUT YOUR HELP, CHERYL, YOU'VE DONE A BANG-UP JOB!
WHAT WOULD YOU SAY TO THE DAY OFF TOMORROW--PAID, OBVIOUSLY.
BUT WHAT ABOUT THE FESTIVAL?
YOU'VE EARNED IT, CHERYL. BESIDES, MS. ERICSON IS HERE TO HELP ME OUT TOMORROW. IT'LL BE A GOOD TRIAL BY FIRE.
I'LL SEE YOU AT HOME, SUNSHINE.

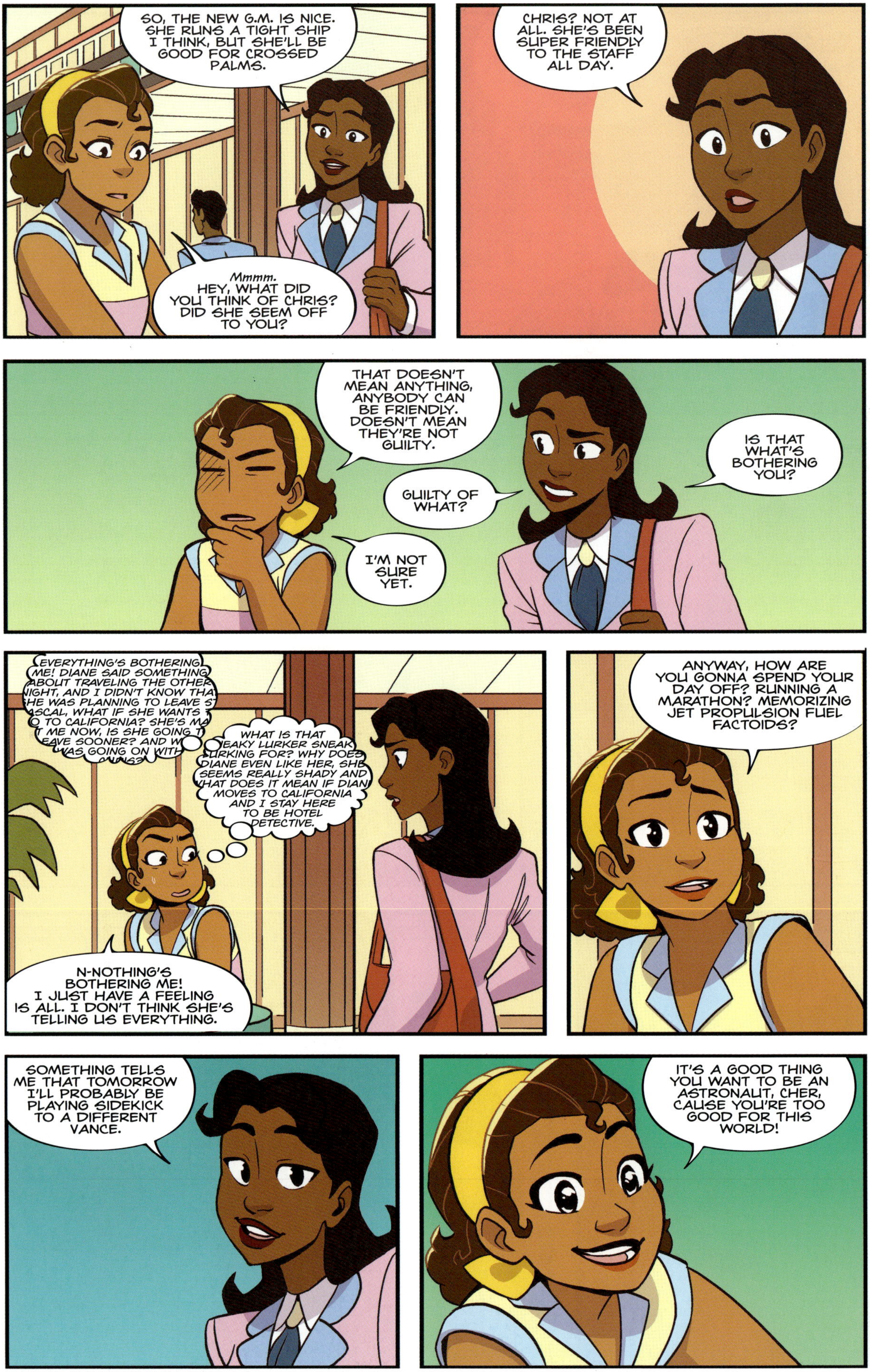
SO, THE NEW G.M. IS NICE. SHE RUNS A TIGHT SHIP I THINK, BUT SHE'LL BE GOOD FOR CROSSED PALMS.
Mmmm. HEY, WHAT DID YOU THINK OF CHRIS? DID SHE SEEM OFF TO YOU?
CHRIS? NOT AT ALL. SHE'S BEEN SUPER FRIENDLY TO THE STAFF ALL DAY.
THAT DOESN'T MEAN ANYTHING, ANYBODY CAN BE FRIENDLY. DOESN'T MEAN THEY'RE NOT GUILTY.
GUILTY OF WHAT?
I'M NOT SURE YET.
IS THAT WHAT'S BOTHERING YOU?
EVERYTHING'S BOTHERING ME! DIANE SAID SOMETHING ABOUT TRAVELING THE OTHER NIGHT, AND I DIDN'T KNOW THA HE WAS PLANNING TO LEAVE S ASCAL, WHAT IF SHE WANTS O TO CALIFORNIA? SHE'S MA T ME NOW, IS SHE GOING T EAVE SOONER? AND W WAS GOING ON WITH
WHAT IS THAT EAKY LURKER SNEAK URKING FOR? WHY DOES DIANE EVEN LIKE HER, SHE SEEMS REALLY SHADY AND HAT DOES IT MEAN IF DIAN MOVES TO CALIFORNIA AND I STAY HERE TO BE HOTEL DETECTIVE.
N-NOTHING'S BOTHERING ME! I JUST HAVE A FEELING IS ALL. I DON'T THINK SHE'S TELLING US EVERYTHING.
ANYWAY, HOW ARE YOU GONNA SPEND YOUR DAY OFF? RUNNING A MARATHON? MEMORIZING JET PROPULSION FUEL FACTOIDS?
SOMETHING TELLS ME THAT TOMORROW I'LL PROBABLY BE PLAYING SIDEKICK TO A DIFFERENT VANCE.
IT'S A GOOD THING YOU WANT TO BE AN ASTRONAUT, CHER, CAUSE YOU'RE TOO GOOD FOR THIS WORLD!

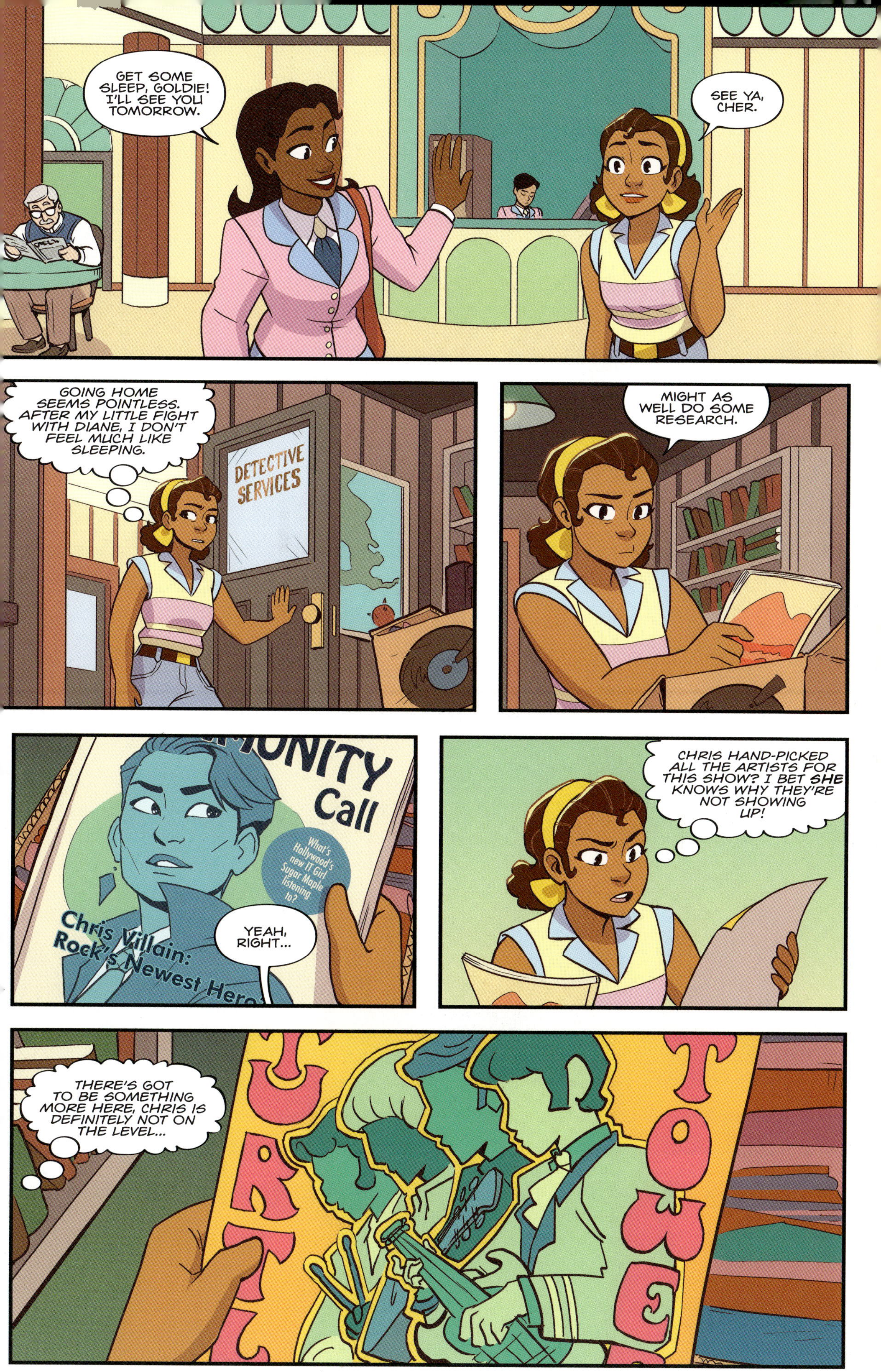
GET SOME SLEEP, GOLDIE! I'LL SEE YOU TOMORROW.
SEE YA, CHER.
GOING HOME SEEMS POINTLESS. AFTER MY LITTLE FIGHT WITH DIANE, I DON'T FEEL MUCH LIKE SLEEPING.
DETECTIVE SERVICES
MIGHT AS WELL DO SOME RESEARCH.
Call
What's Hollywood's new IT Girl Sugar Maple listening to?
Chris Villain: Rock's Newest Hero
YEAH, RIGHT...
CHRIS HAND-PICKED ALL THE ARTISTS FOR THIS SHOW? I BET **SHE** KNOWS WHY THEY'RE NOT SHOWING UP!
THERE'S GOT TO BE SOMETHING MORE HERE, CHRIS IS DEFINITELY NOT ON THE LEVEL...

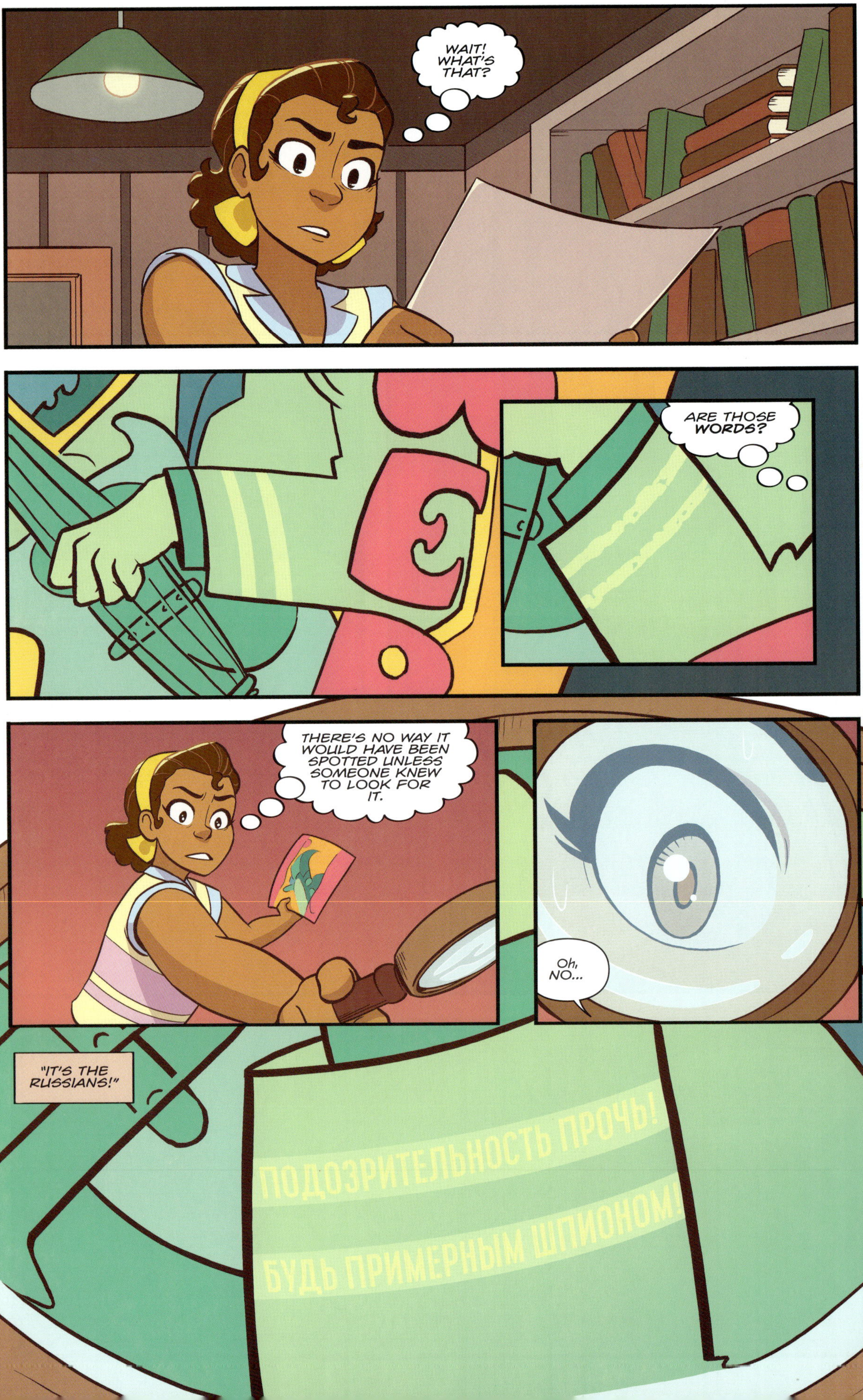
WAIT! WHAT'S THAT?
ARE THOSE WORDS?
THERE'S NO WAY IT WOULD HAVE BEEN SPOTTED UNLESS SOMEONE KNEW TO LOOK FOR IT.
Oh, NO...
"IT'S THE RUSSIANS!"
ПОДОЗРИТЕЛЬНОСТЬ ПРОЧЬ!
БУДЬ ПРИМЕРНЫМ ШПИОНОМ!

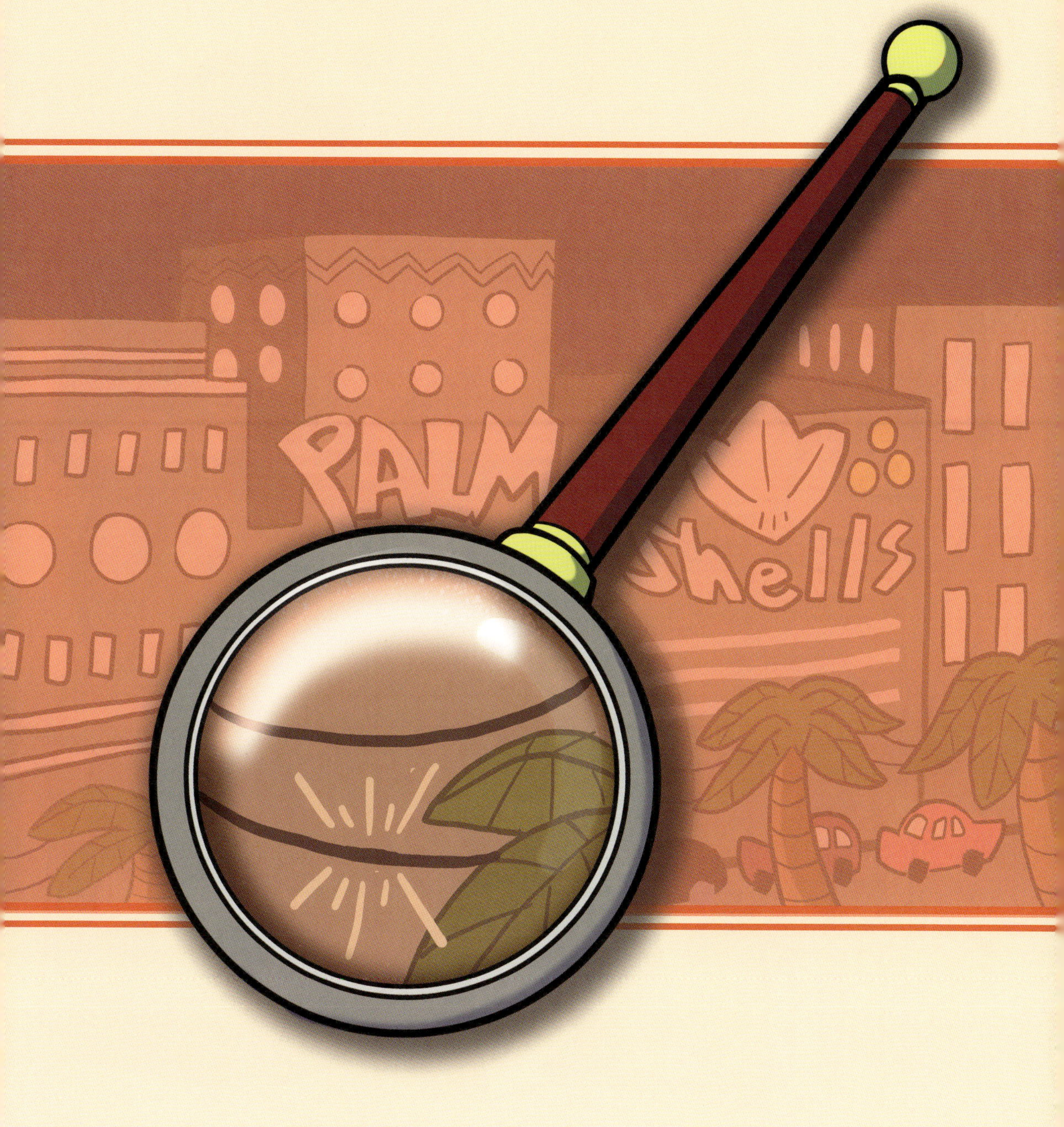
PALM
Shells

issue fourteen cover by **Brittney Williams**

chapter
# FOURTEEN

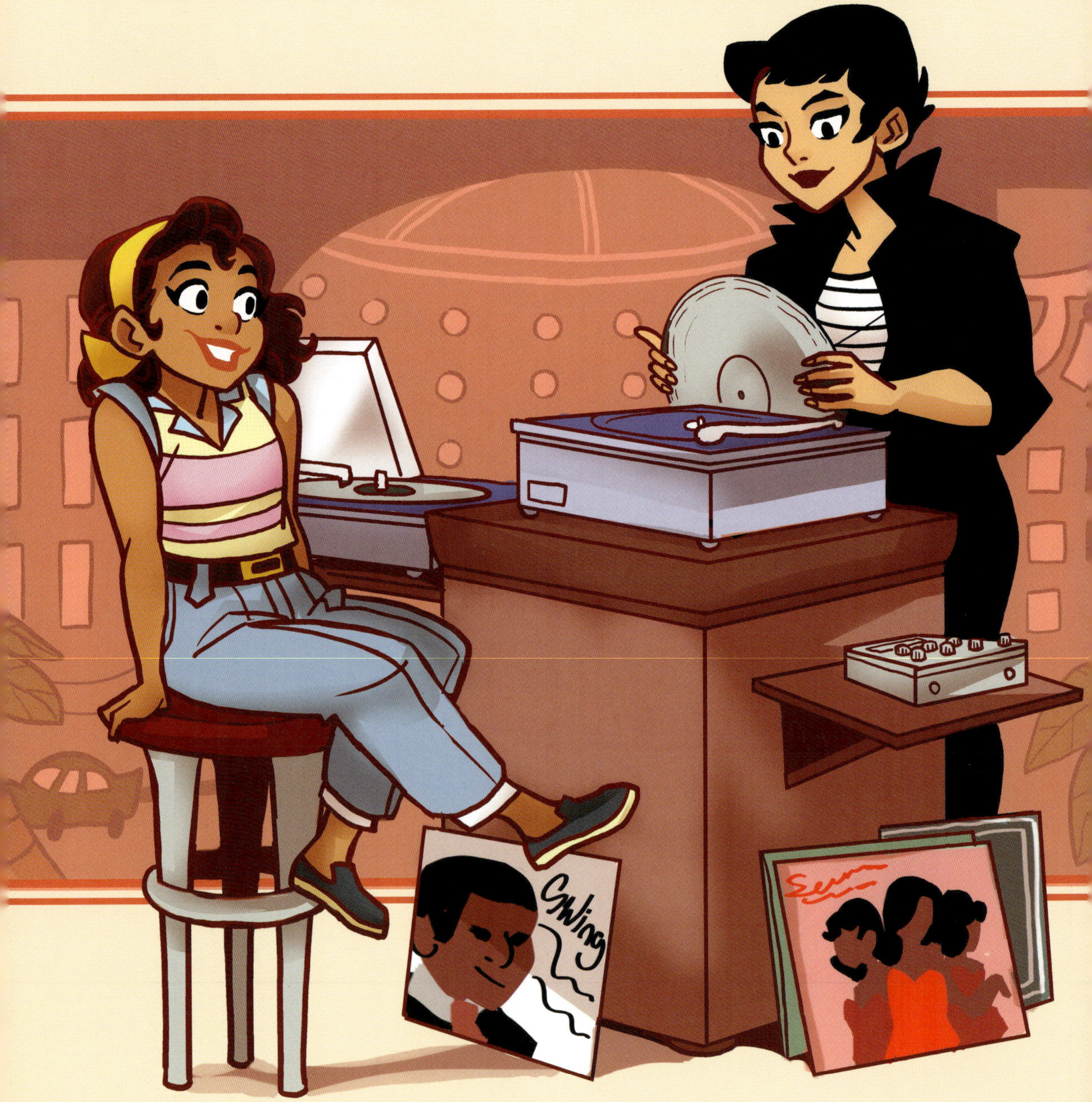
Swing

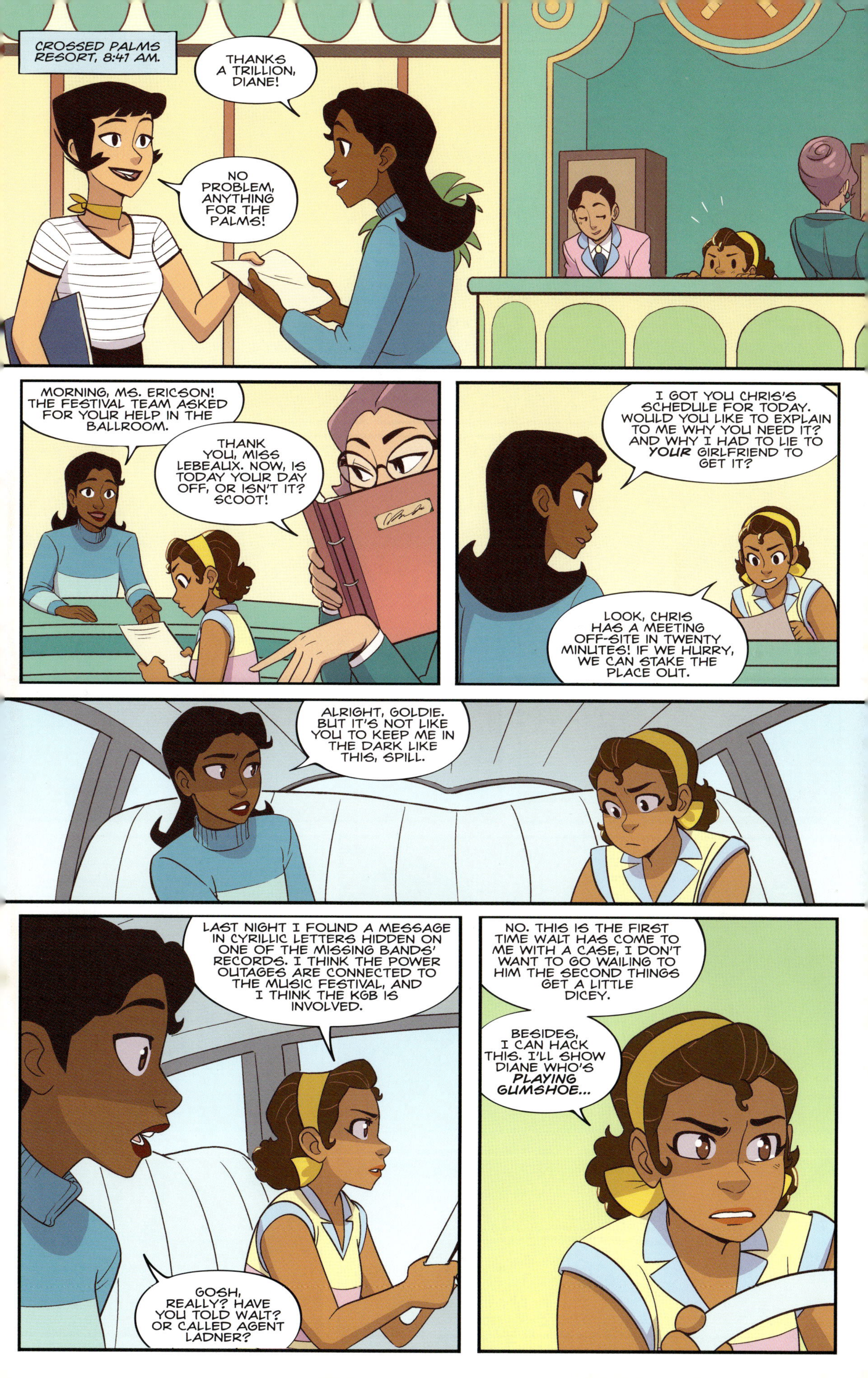
CROSSED PALMS RESORT, 8:41 AM.
THANKS A TRILLION, DIANE!
NO PROBLEM, ANYTHING FOR THE PALMS!
MORNING, MS. ERICSON! THE FESTIVAL TEAM ASKED FOR YOUR HELP IN THE BALLROOM.
THANK YOU, MISS LEBEAUX. NOW, IS TODAY YOUR DAY OFF, OR ISN'T IT? SCOOT!
I GOT YOU CHRIS'S SCHEDULE FOR TODAY. WOULD YOU LIKE TO EXPLAIN TO ME WHY YOU NEED IT? AND WHY I HAD TO LIE TO *YOUR* GIRLFRIEND TO GET IT?
LOOK, CHRIS HAS A MEETING OFF-SITE IN TWENTY MINUTES! IF WE HURRY, WE CAN STAKE THE PLACE OUT.
ALRIGHT, GOLDIE. BUT IT'S NOT LIKE YOU TO KEEP ME IN THE DARK LIKE THIS, SPILL.
LAST NIGHT I FOUND A MESSAGE IN CYRILLIC LETTERS HIDDEN ON ONE OF THE MISSING BANDS' RECORDS. I THINK THE POWER OUTAGES ARE CONNECTED TO THE MUSIC FESTIVAL, AND I THINK THE KGB IS INVOLVED.
GOSH, REALLY? HAVE YOU TOLD WALT? OR CALLED AGENT LADNER?
NO. THIS IS THE FIRST TIME WALT HAS COME TO ME WITH A CASE, I DON'T WANT TO GO WAILING TO HIM THE SECOND THINGS GET A LITTLE DICEY.
BESIDES, I CAN HACK THIS. I'LL SHOW DIANE WHO'S ***PLAYING GUMSHOE...***

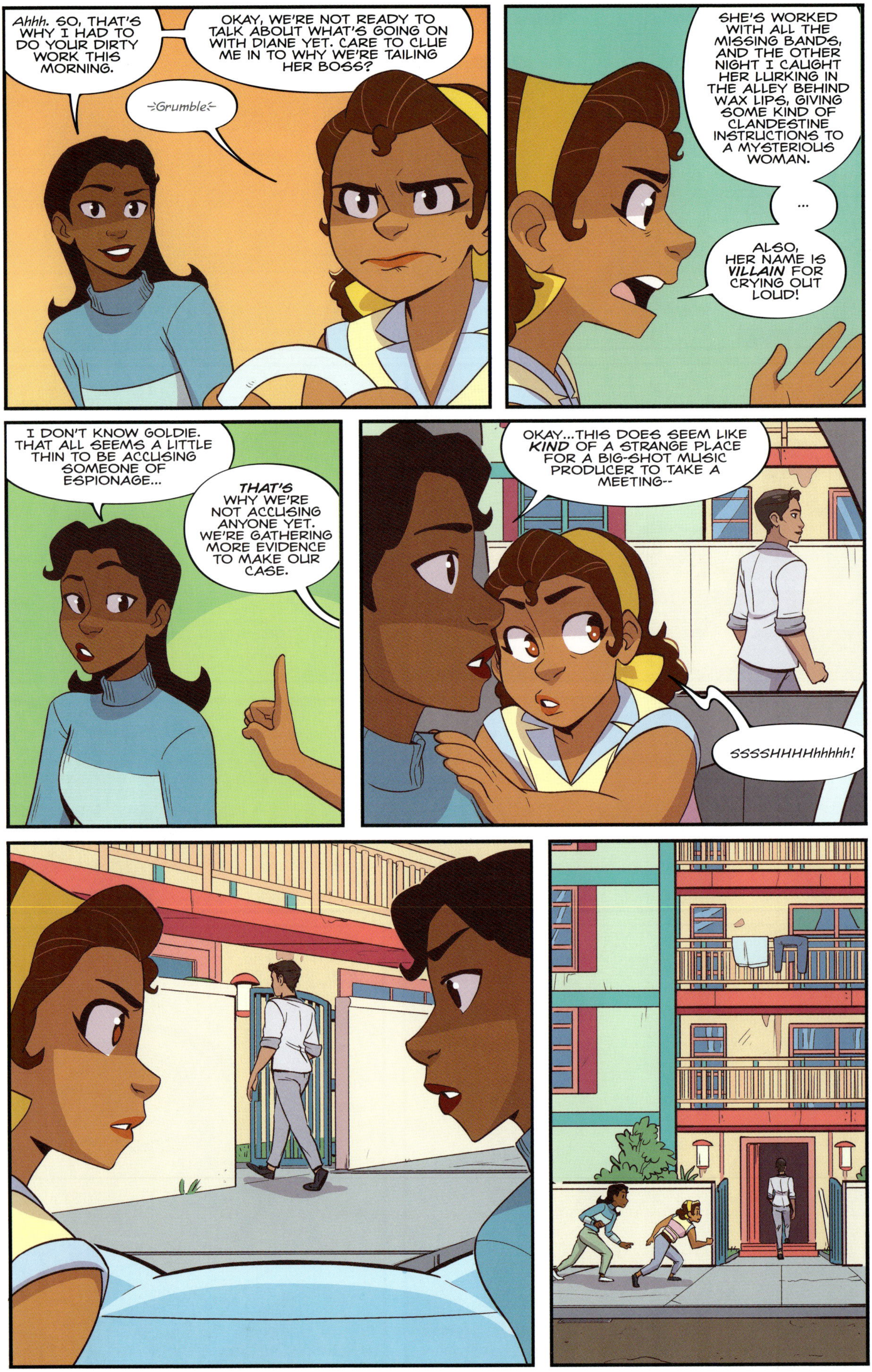

Ahhh. SO, THAT'S WHY I HAD TO DO YOUR DIRTY WORK THIS MORNING.
OKAY, WE'RE NOT READY TO TALK ABOUT WHAT'S GOING ON WITH DIANE YET. CARE TO CLUE ME IN TO WHY WE'RE TAILING HER BOSS?
Grumble
SHE'S WORKED WITH ALL THE MISSING BANDS, AND THE OTHER NIGHT I CAUGHT HER LURKING IN THE ALLEY BEHIND WAX LIPS, GIVING SOME KIND OF CLANDESTINE INSTRUCTIONS TO A MYSTERIOUS WOMAN.
...
ALSO, HER NAME IS VILLAIN FOR CRYING OUT LOUD!
I DON'T KNOW GOLDIE. THAT ALL SEEMS A LITTLE THIN TO BE ACCUSING SOMEONE OF ESPIONAGE...
THAT'S WHY WE'RE NOT ACCUSING ANYONE YET. WE'RE GATHERING MORE EVIDENCE TO MAKE OUR CASE.
OKAY...THIS DOES SEEM LIKE KIND OF A STRANGE PLACE FOR A BIG-SHOT MUSIC PRODUCER TO TAKE A MEETING--
SSSSHHHHhhhhh!

BZZZZZ

click

FLASH!

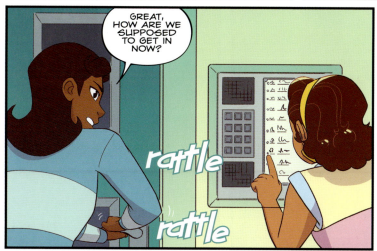

GREAT, HOW ARE WE SUPPOSED TO GET IN NOW?

rattle

rattle

BEEP BOOP BEEP

HELLO?

GOOD MORNIN' MRS. WINSLOW, MAY I CALL YOU LINDA?

WELL, I--

LINDA, MY NAME IS **ETHEL SWAN**, AND I AM A REPRESENTATIVE FOR KARY MAY COSMETICS. AND LINDA, I HAVE WITH ME AN ENTIRE JAR OF OUR *CARELESS CARESS COLD CREAM* FOR YOU TO TRY TODAY, FREE OF CHARGE!

LET ME TELL YOU, LINDA, I USE IT MYSELF AND IT IS SO DIVINE IT COULD MELT THE WINGS OFF AN ANGEL!

BZZZZZ

OH, GOODNESS, THAT SOUNDS LOVELY! COME RIGHT UP, ETHEL!

ALRIGHT, "ETHEL," YOU HAVE ANY TRICKY TRICKS FOR FINDING OUT WHICH WAY SHE WENT?

*ding*

COME ON, THE STAIRS'LL BE FASTER!

÷HUFF÷

÷HUFF÷

÷HUFF÷

I SEE HER!

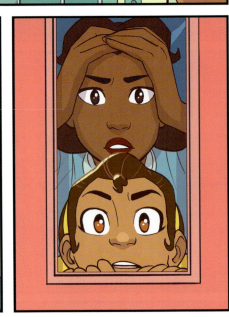

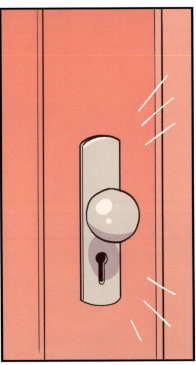

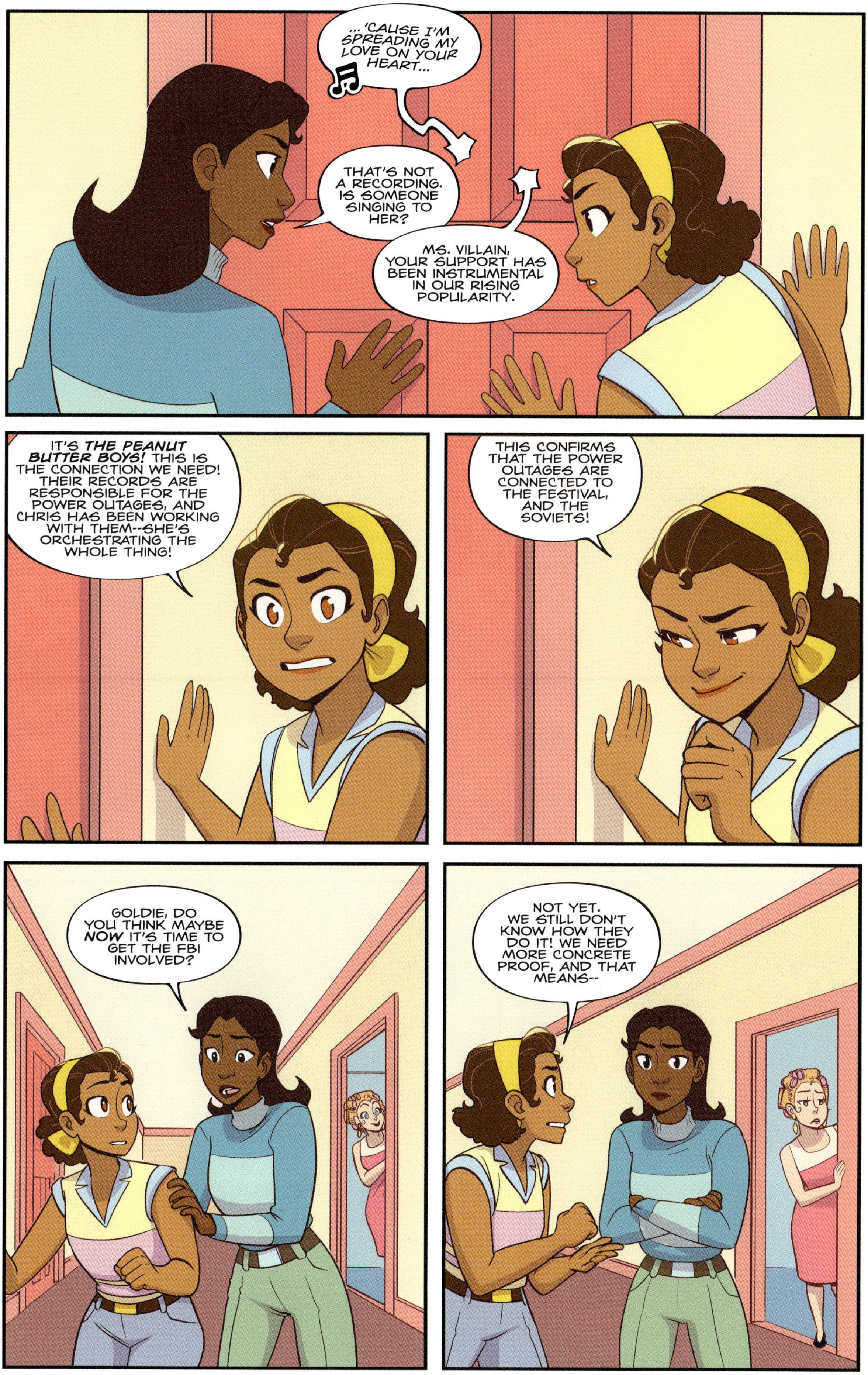
...'CAUSE I'M SPREADING MY LOVE ON YOUR HEART...
THAT'S NOT A RECORDING. IS SOMEONE SINGING TO HER?
MS. VILLAIN, YOUR SUPPORT HAS BEEN INSTRUMENTAL IN OUR RISING POPULARITY.
IT'S ***THE PEANUT BUTTER BOYS!*** THIS IS THE CONNECTION WE NEED! THEIR RECORDS ARE RESPONSIBLE FOR THE POWER OUTAGES, AND CHRIS HAS BEEN WORKING WITH THEM--SHE'S ORCHESTRATING THE WHOLE THING!
THIS CONFIRMS THAT THE POWER OUTAGES ARE CONNECTED TO THE FESTIVAL, AND THE SOVIETS!
GOLDIE, DO YOU THINK MAYBE ***NOW*** IT'S TIME TO GET THE FBI INVOLVED?
NOT YET. WE STILL DON'T KNOW HOW THEY DO IT! WE NEED MORE CONCRETE PROOF, AND THAT MEANS--

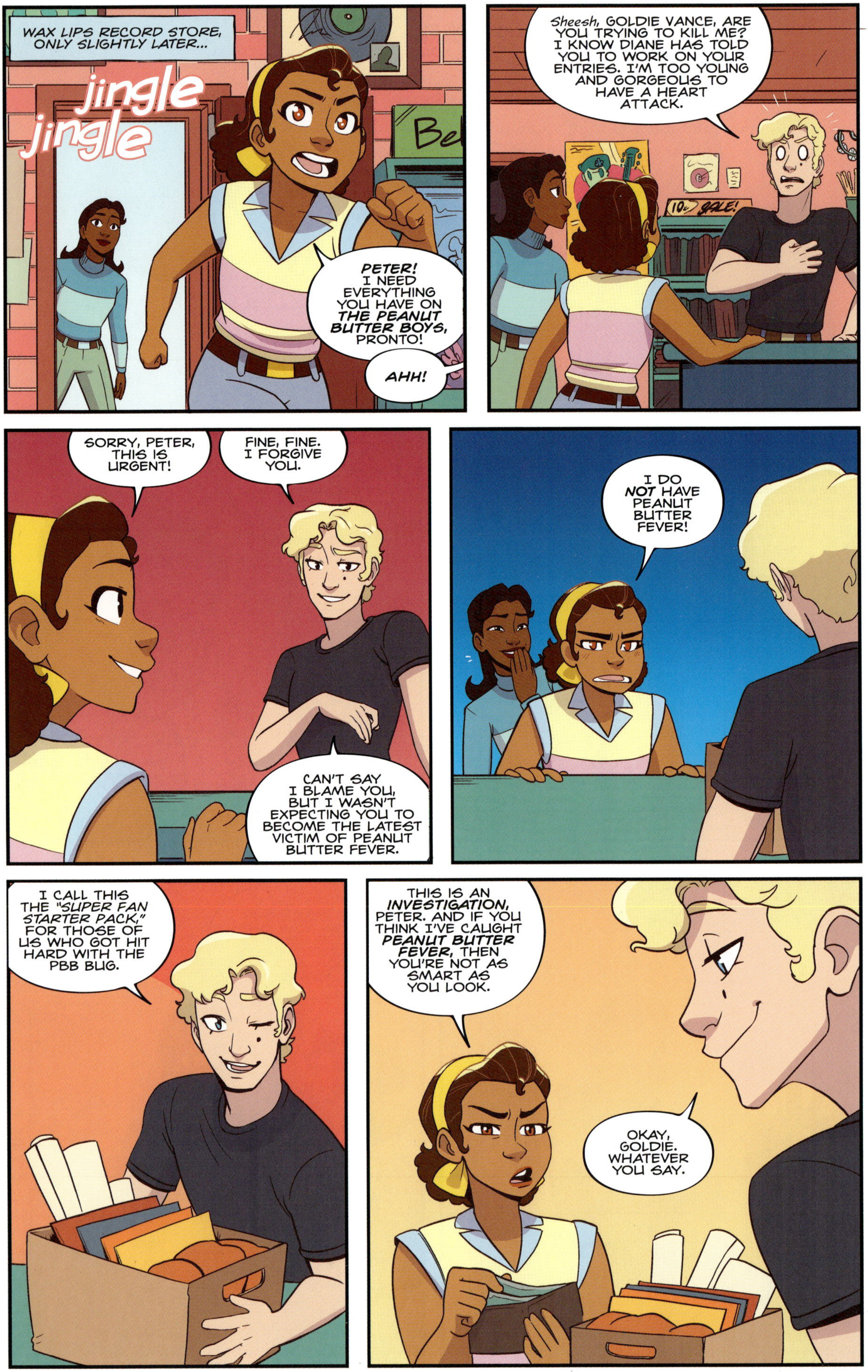
WAX LIPS RECORD STORE, ONLY SLIGHTLY LATER...
jingle jingle
PETER! I NEED EVERYTHING YOU HAVE ON THE PEANUT BUTTER BOYS, PRONTO!
AHH!
Sheesh, GOLDIE VANCE, ARE YOU TRYING TO KILL ME? I KNOW DIANE HAS TOLD YOU TO WORK ON YOUR ENTRIES. I'M TOO YOUNG AND GORGEOUS TO HAVE A HEART ATTACK.
10¢ SALE!
SORRY, PETER, THIS IS URGENT!
FINE, FINE. I FORGIVE YOU.
CAN'T SAY I BLAME YOU, BUT I WASN'T EXPECTING YOU TO BECOME THE LATEST VICTIM OF PEANUT BUTTER FEVER.
I DO NOT HAVE PEANUT BUTTER FEVER!
I CALL THIS THE "SUPER FAN STARTER PACK," FOR THOSE OF US WHO GOT HIT HARD WITH THE PBB BUG.
THIS IS AN INVESTIGATION, PETER. AND IF YOU THINK I'VE CAUGHT PEANUT BUTTER FEVER, THEN YOU'RE NOT AS SMART AS YOU LOOK.
OKAY, GOLDIE. WHATEVER YOU SAY.

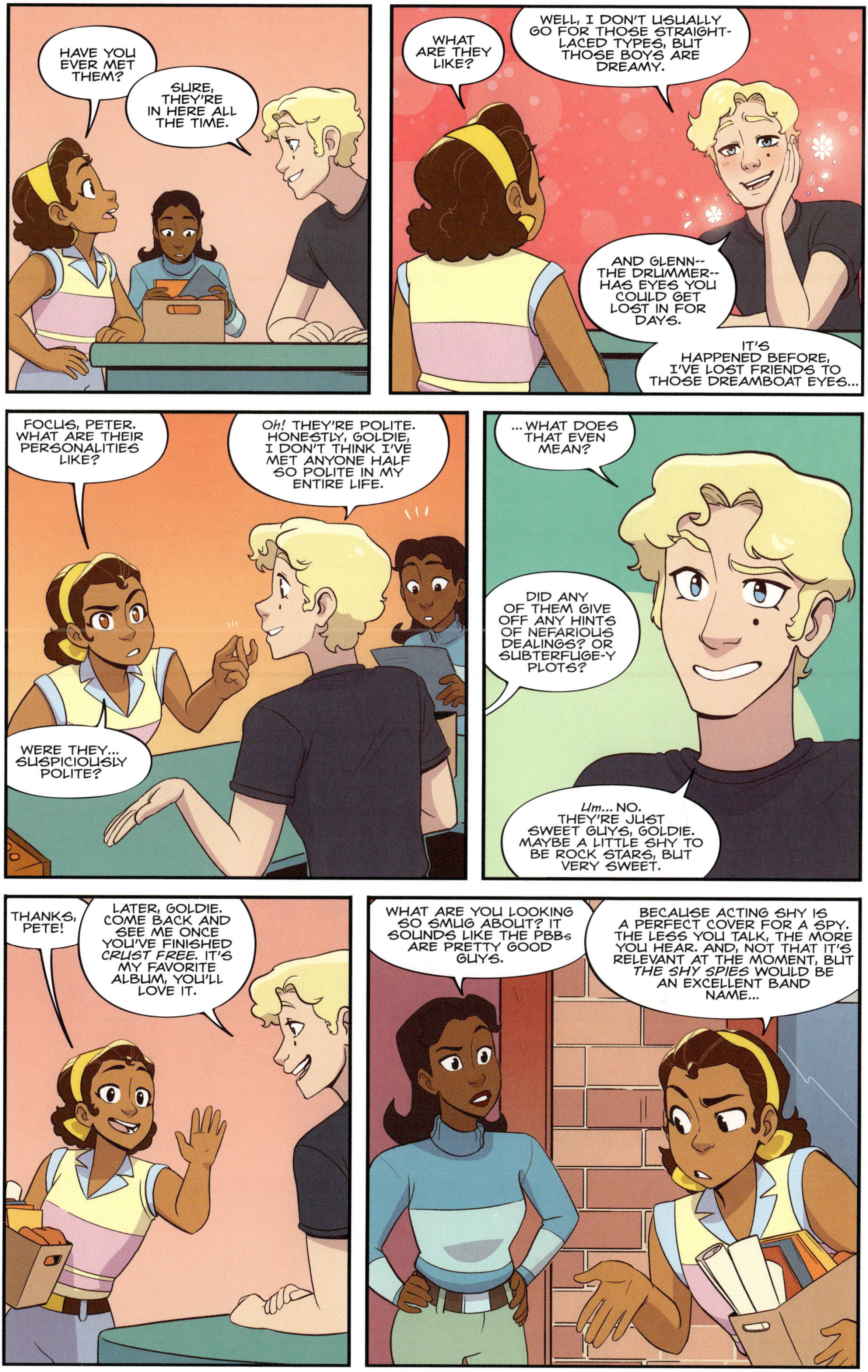
HAVE YOU EVER MET THEM?
SURE, THEY'RE IN HERE ALL THE TIME.
WHAT ARE THEY LIKE?
WELL, I DON'T USUALLY GO FOR THOSE STRAIGHT-LACED TYPES, BUT THOSE BOYS ARE DREAMY.
AND GLENN-- THE DRUMMER-- HAS EYES YOU COULD GET LOST IN FOR DAYS.
IT'S HAPPENED BEFORE, I'VE LOST FRIENDS TO THOSE DREAMBOAT EYES...
FOCUS, PETER. WHAT ARE THEIR PERSONALITIES LIKE?
Oh! THEY'RE POLITE. HONESTLY, GOLDIE, I DON'T THINK I'VE MET ANYONE HALF SO POLITE IN MY ENTIRE LIFE.
WERE THEY... SUSPICIOUSLY POLITE?
...WHAT DOES THAT EVEN MEAN?
DID ANY OF THEM GIVE OFF ANY HINTS OF NEFARIOUS DEALINGS? OR SUBTERFUGE-Y PLOTS?
Um... NO. THEY'RE JUST SWEET GUYS, GOLDIE. MAYBE A LITTLE SHY TO BE ROCK STARS, BUT VERY SWEET.
THANKS, PETE!
LATER, GOLDIE. COME BACK AND SEE ME ONCE YOU'VE FINISHED CRUST FREE. IT'S MY FAVORITE ALBUM, YOU'LL LOVE IT.
WHAT ARE YOU LOOKING SO SMUG ABOUT? IT SOUNDS LIKE THE PBBs ARE PRETTY GOOD GUYS.
BECAUSE ACTING SHY IS A PERFECT COVER FOR A SPY. THE LESS YOU TALK, THE MORE YOU HEAR. AND, NOT THAT IT'S RELEVANT AT THE MOMENT, BUT THE SHY SPIES WOULD BE AN EXCELLENT BAND NAME...

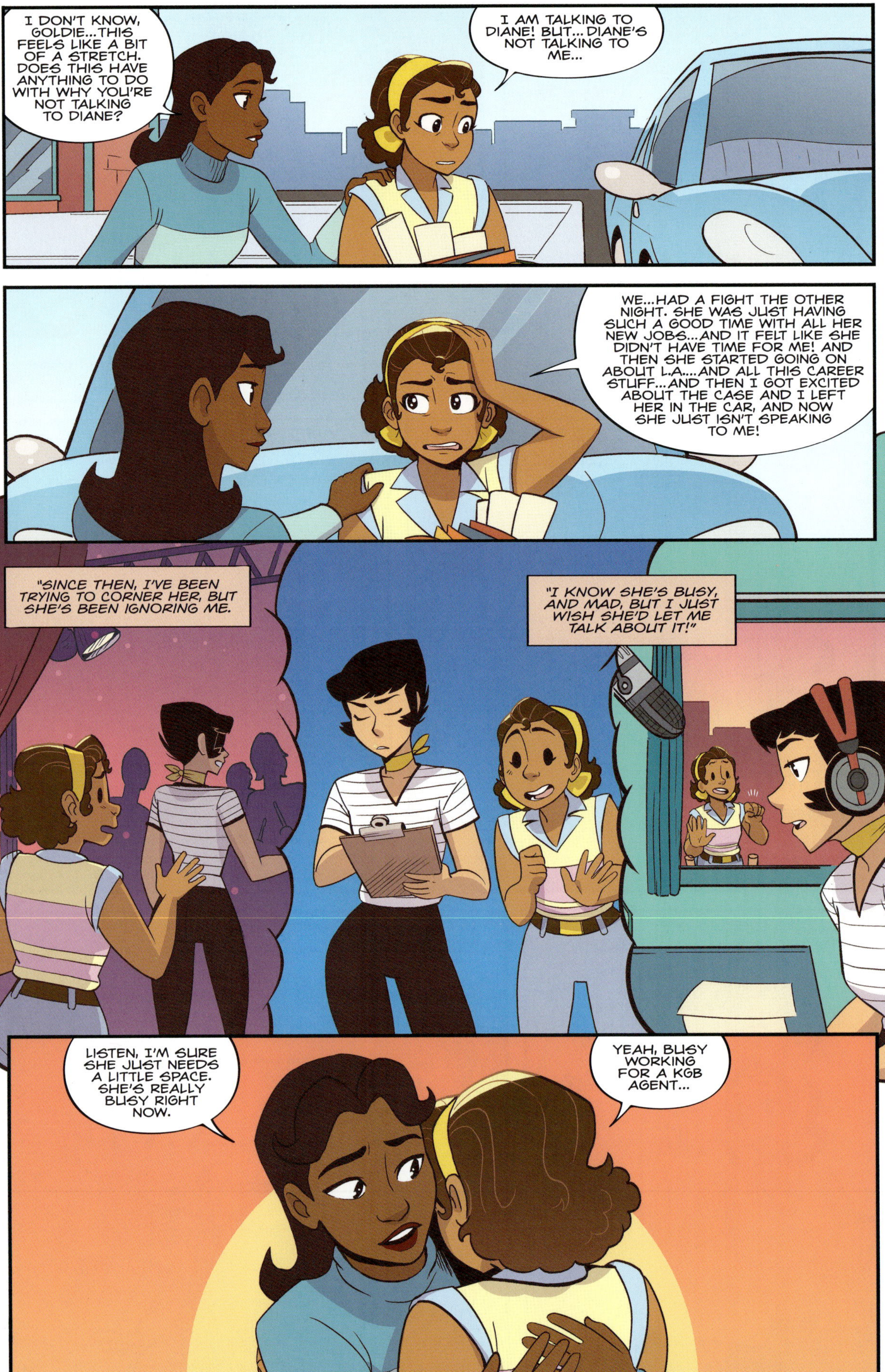
I DON'T KNOW, GOLDIE...THIS FEELS LIKE A BIT OF A STRETCH. DOES THIS HAVE ANYTHING TO DO WITH WHY YOU'RE NOT TALKING TO DIANE?
I AM TALKING TO DIANE! BUT... DIANE'S NOT TALKING TO ME...
WE...HAD A FIGHT THE OTHER NIGHT. SHE WAS JUST HAVING SUCH A GOOD TIME WITH ALL HER NEW JOBS...AND IT FELT LIKE SHE DIDN'T HAVE TIME FOR ME! AND THEN SHE STARTED GOING ON ABOUT L.A....AND ALL THIS CAREER STUFF...AND THEN I GOT EXCITED ABOUT THE CASE AND I LEFT HER IN THE CAR, AND NOW SHE JUST ISN'T SPEAKING TO ME!
"SINCE THEN, I'VE BEEN TRYING TO CORNER HER, BUT SHE'S BEEN IGNORING ME.
"I KNOW SHE'S BUSY, AND MAD, BUT I JUST WISH SHE'D LET ME TALK ABOUT IT!"
LISTEN, I'M SURE SHE JUST NEEDS A LITTLE SPACE. SHE'S REALLY BUSY RIGHT NOW.
YEAH, BUSY WORKING FOR A KGB AGENT...

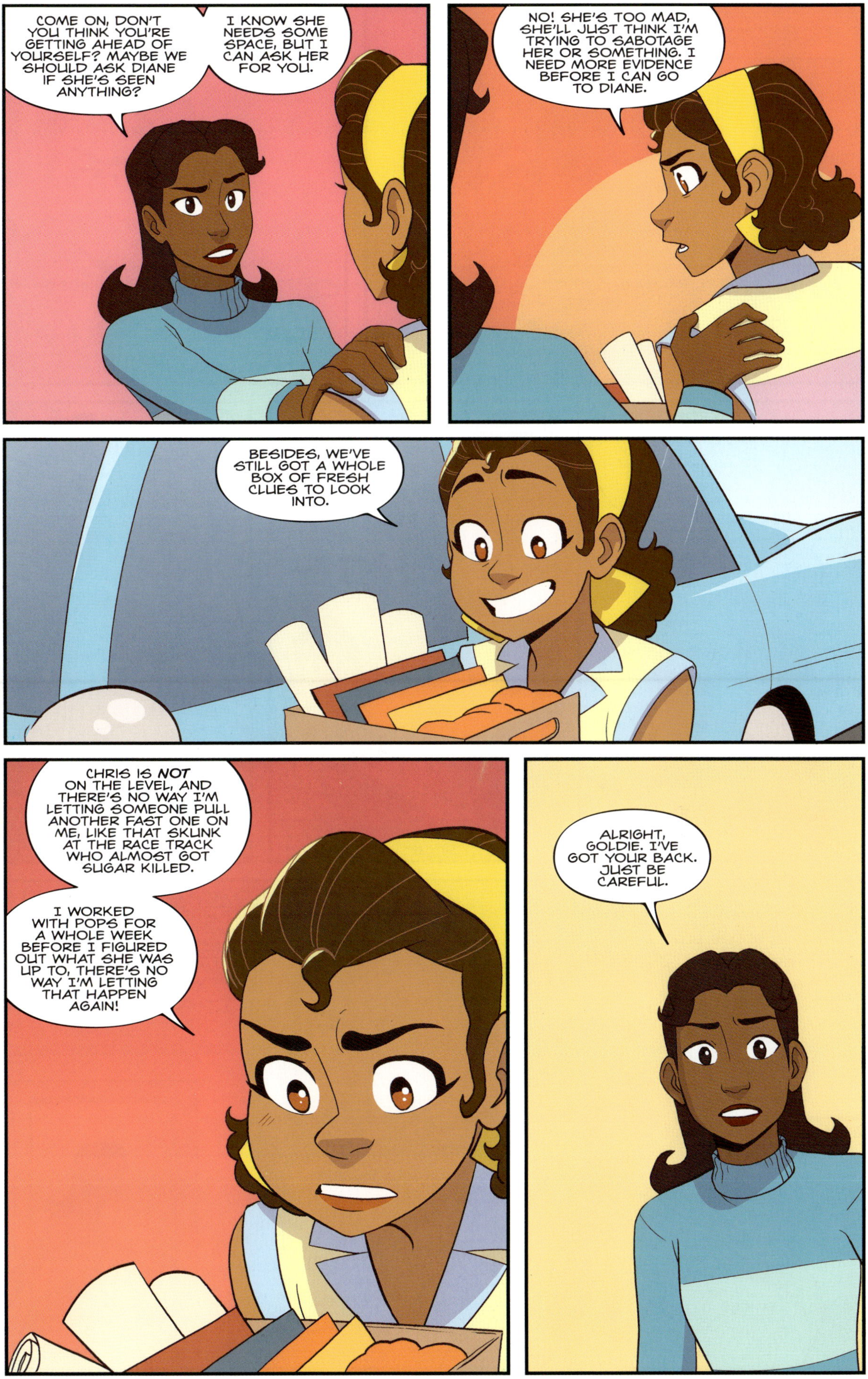
COME ON, DON'T YOU THINK YOU'RE GETTING AHEAD OF YOURSELF? MAYBE WE SHOULD ASK DIANE IF SHE'S SEEN ANYTHING?
I KNOW SHE NEEDS SOME SPACE, BUT I CAN ASK HER FOR YOU.
NO! SHE'S TOO MAD, SHE'LL JUST THINK I'M TRYING TO SABOTAGE HER OR SOMETHING. I NEED MORE EVIDENCE BEFORE I CAN GO TO DIANE.
BESIDES, WE'VE STILL GOT A WHOLE BOX OF FRESH CLUES TO LOOK INTO.
CHRIS IS *NOT* ON THE LEVEL, AND THERE'S NO WAY I'M LETTING SOMEONE PULL ANOTHER FAST ONE ON ME, LIKE THAT SKUNK AT THE RACE TRACK WHO ALMOST GOT SUGAR KILLED.
I WORKED WITH POPS FOR A WHOLE WEEK BEFORE I FIGURED OUT WHAT SHE WAS UP TO, THERE'S NO WAY I'M LETTING THAT HAPPEN AGAIN!
ALRIGHT, GOLDIE. I'VE GOT YOUR BACK. JUST BE CAREFUL.

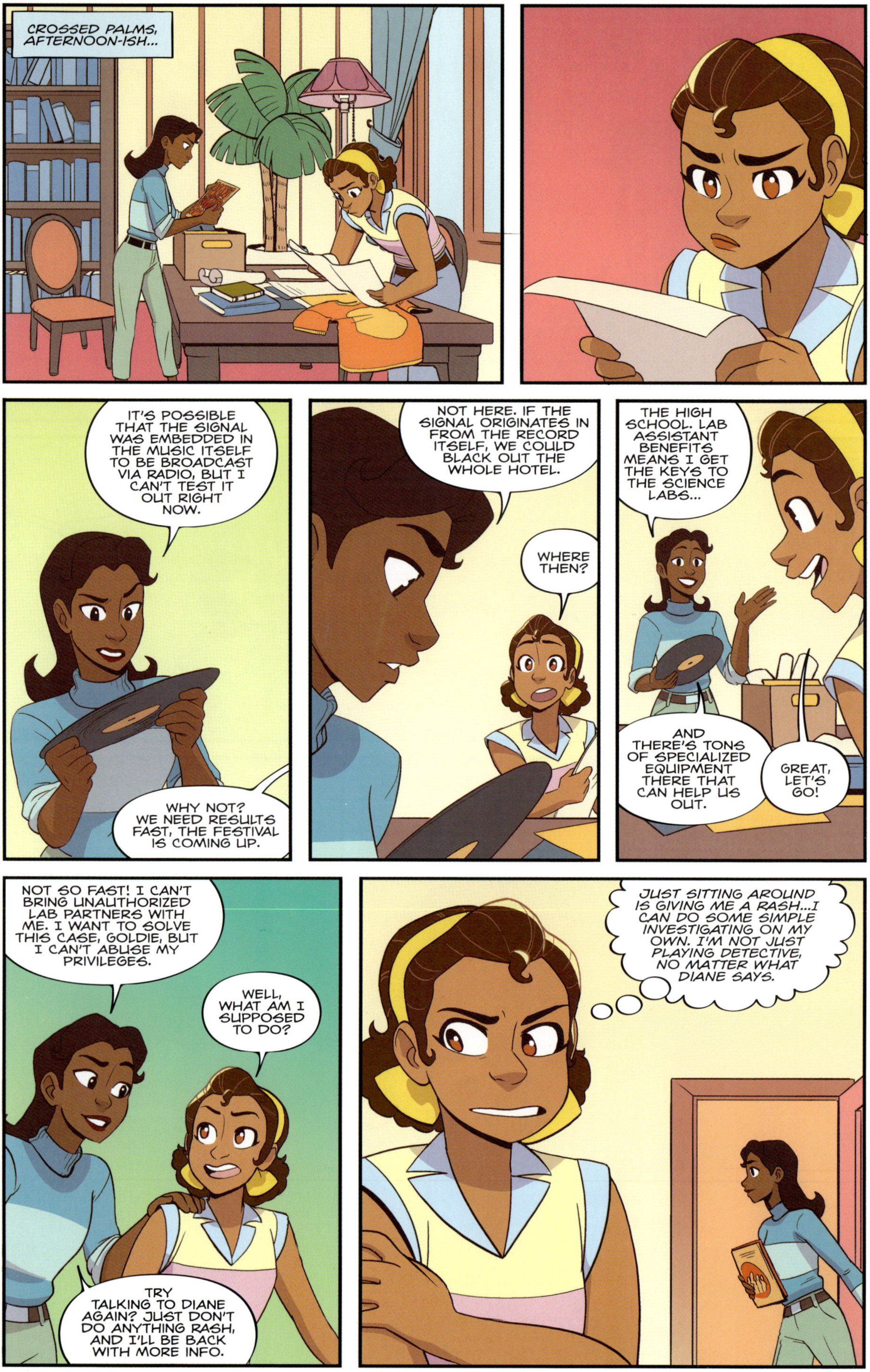
CROSSED PALMS, AFTERNOON-ISH...
IT'S POSSIBLE THAT THE SIGNAL WAS EMBEDDED IN THE MUSIC ITSELF TO BE BROADCAST VIA RADIO, BUT I CAN'T TEST IT OUT RIGHT NOW.
WHY NOT? WE NEED RESULTS FAST, THE FESTIVAL IS COMING UP.
NOT HERE. IF THE SIGNAL ORIGINATES IN FROM THE RECORD ITSELF, WE COULD BLACK OUT THE WHOLE HOTEL.
WHERE THEN?
THE HIGH SCHOOL. LAB ASSISTANT BENEFITS MEANS I GET THE KEYS TO THE SCIENCE LABS...
AND THERE'S TONS OF SPECIALIZED EQUIPMENT THERE THAT CAN HELP US OUT.
GREAT, LET'S GO!
NOT SO FAST! I CAN'T BRING UNAUTHORIZED LAB PARTNERS WITH ME. I WANT TO SOLVE THIS CASE, GOLDIE, BUT I CAN'T ABUSE MY PRIVILEGES.
WELL, WHAT AM I SUPPOSED TO DO?
TRY TALKING TO DIANE AGAIN? JUST DON'T DO ANYTHING RASH, AND I'LL BE BACK WITH MORE INFO.
JUST SITTING AROUND IS GIVING ME A RASH...I CAN DO SOME SIMPLE INVESTIGATING ON MY OWN. I'M NOT JUST PLAYING DETECTIVE, NO MATTER WHAT DIANE SAYS.

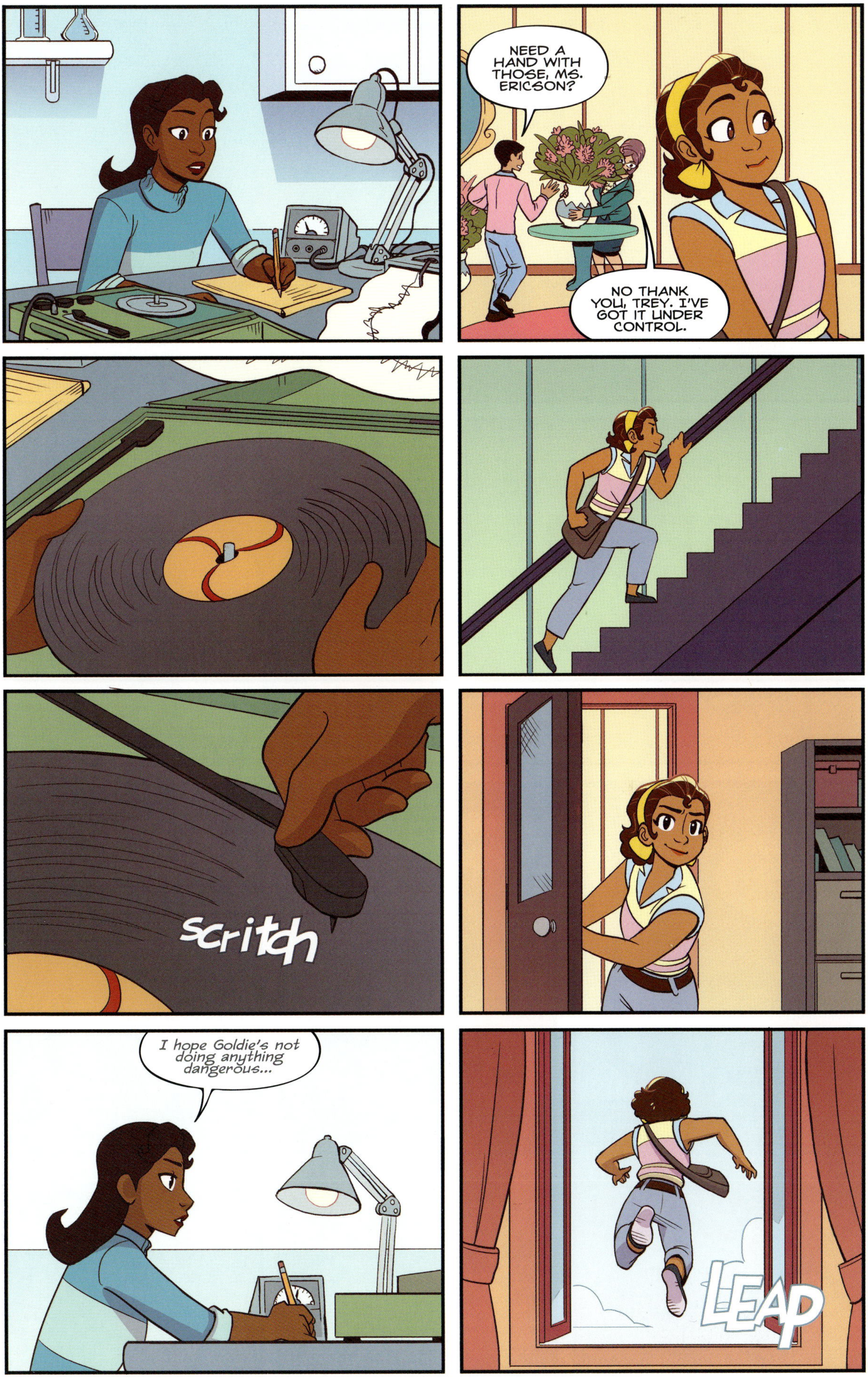
NEED A HAND WITH THOSE, MS. ERICSON?
NO THANK YOU, TREY. I'VE GOT IT UNDER CONTROL.
SCRITCH
I hope Goldie's not doing anything dangerous...
LEAP

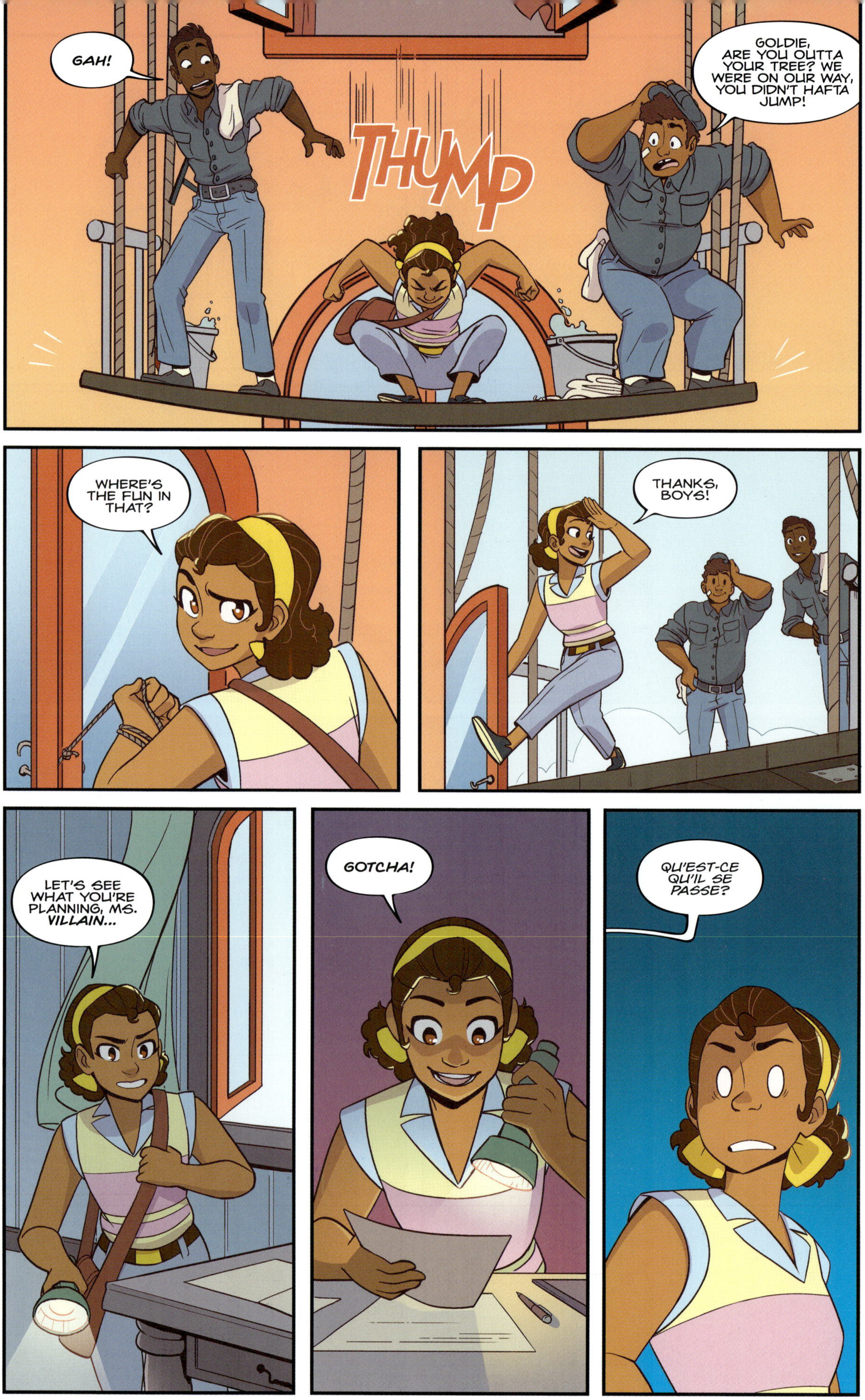
GAH!
THUMP
GOLDIE, ARE YOU OUTTA YOUR TREE? WE WERE ON OUR WAY, YOU DIDN'T HAFTA JUMP!
WHERE'S THE FUN IN THAT?
THANKS, BOYS!
LET'S SEE WHAT YOU'RE PLANNING, MS. *VILLAIN*...
GOTCHA!
*QU'EST-CE QU'IL SE PASSE?*

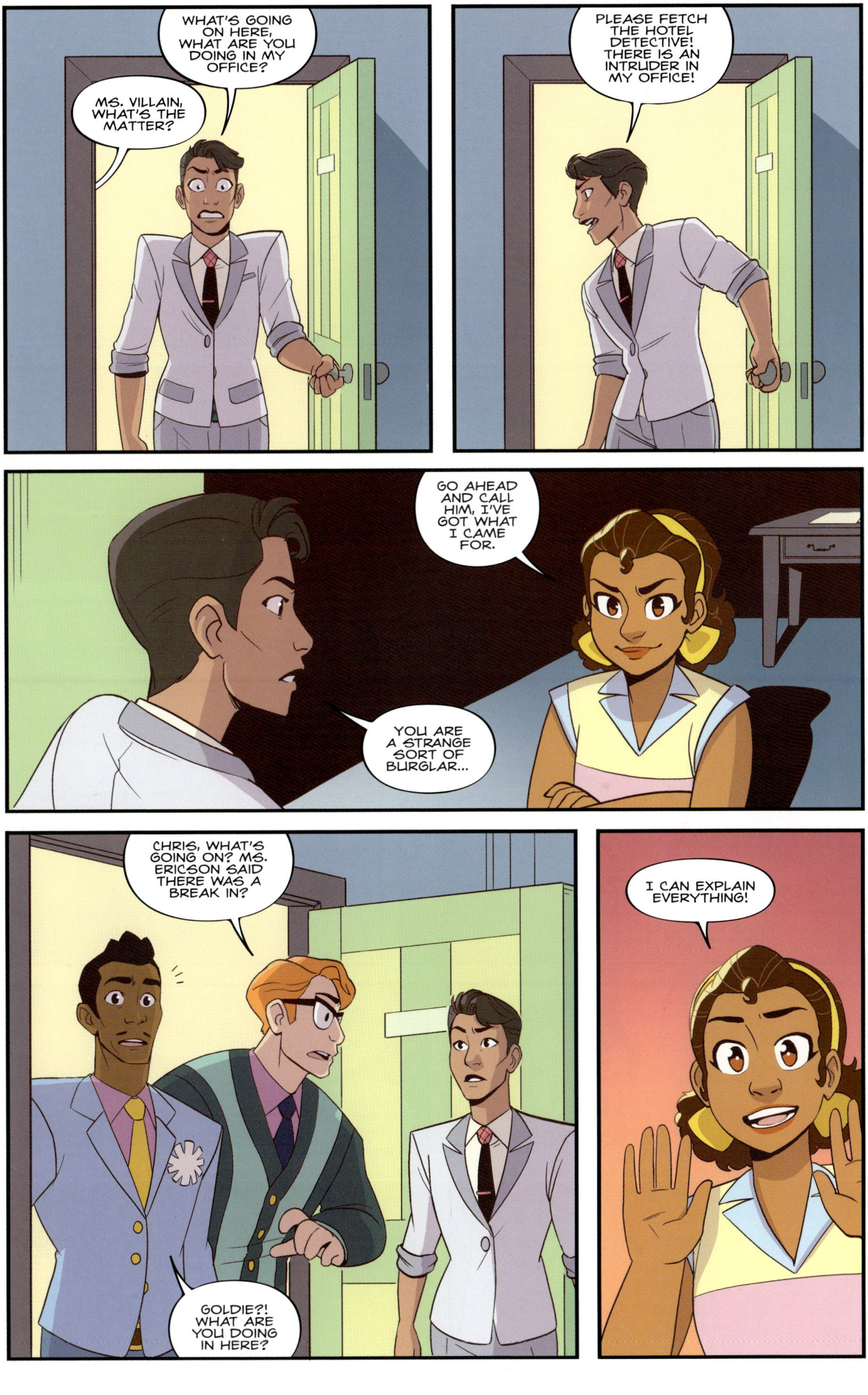

MS. VILLAIN, WHAT'S THE MATTER?
WHAT'S GOING ON HERE, WHAT ARE YOU DOING IN MY OFFICE?
PLEASE FETCH THE HOTEL DETECTIVE! THERE IS AN INTRUDER IN MY OFFICE!
GO AHEAD AND CALL HIM, I'VE GOT WHAT I CAME FOR.
YOU ARE A STRANGE SORT OF BURGLAR...
CHRIS, WHAT'S GOING ON? MS. ERICSON SAID THERE WAS A BREAK IN?
GOLDIE?! WHAT ARE YOU DOING IN HERE?
I CAN EXPLAIN EVERYTHING!

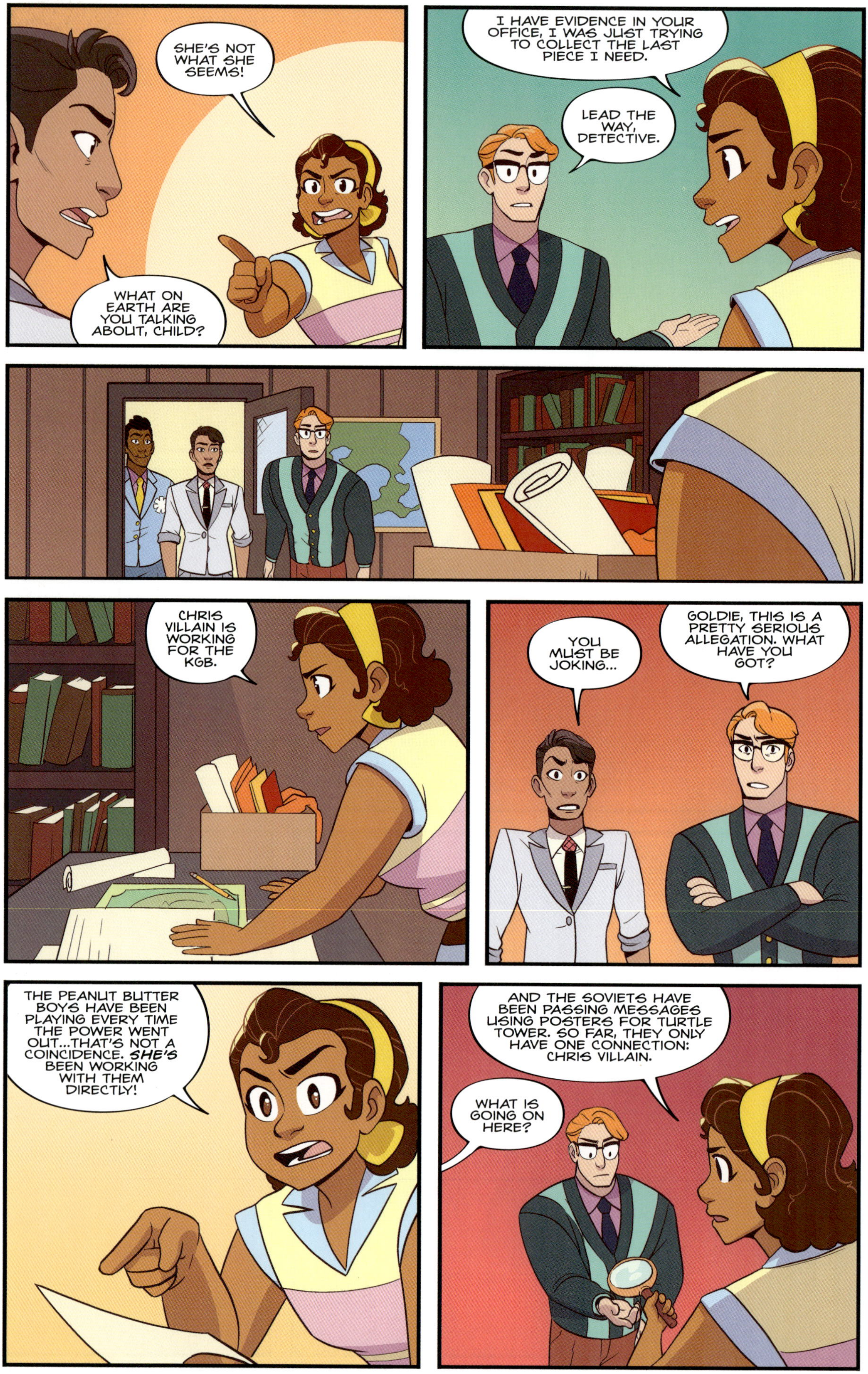
SHE'S NOT WHAT SHE SEEMS!
WHAT ON EARTH ARE YOU TALKING ABOUT, CHILD?
I HAVE EVIDENCE IN YOUR OFFICE, I WAS JUST TRYING TO COLLECT THE LAST PIECE I NEED.
LEAD THE WAY, DETECTIVE.
CHRIS VILLAIN IS WORKING FOR THE KGB.
YOU MUST BE JOKING...
GOLDIE, THIS IS A PRETTY SERIOUS ALLEGATION. WHAT HAVE YOU GOT?
THE PEANUT BUTTER BOYS HAVE BEEN PLAYING EVERY TIME THE POWER WENT OUT...THAT'S NOT A COINCIDENCE. SHE'S BEEN WORKING WITH THEM DIRECTLY!
AND THE SOVIETS HAVE BEEN PASSING MESSAGES USING POSTERS FOR TURTLE TOWER. SO FAR, THEY ONLY HAVE ONE CONNECTION: CHRIS VILLAIN.
WHAT IS GOING ON HERE?

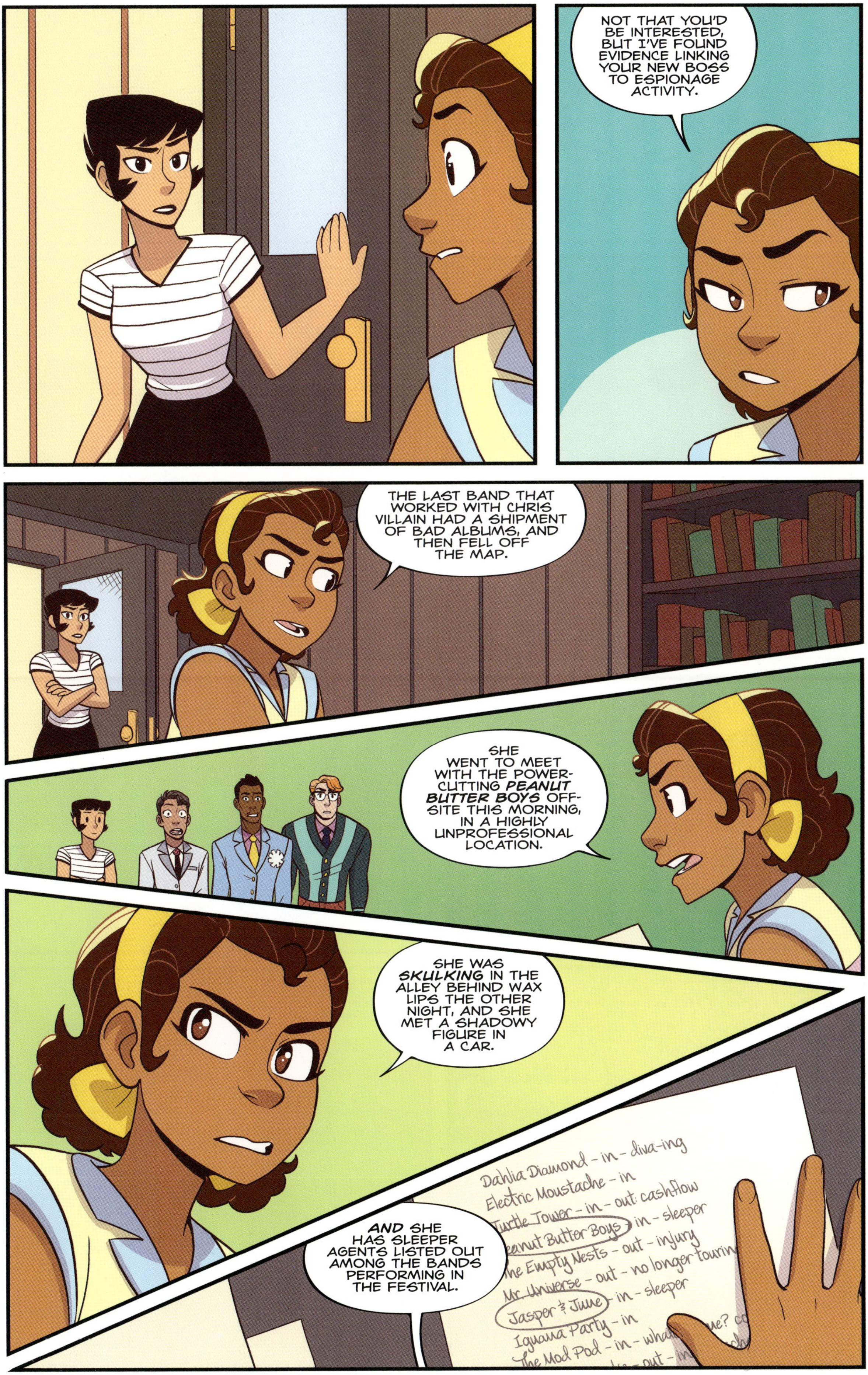

NOT THAT YOU'D BE INTERESTED, BUT I'VE FOUND EVIDENCE LINKING YOUR NEW BOSS TO ESPIONAGE ACTIVITY.
THE LAST BAND THAT WORKED WITH CHRIS VILLAIN HAD A SHIPMENT OF BAD ALBUMS, AND THEN FELL OFF THE MAP.
SHE WENT TO MEET WITH THE POWER-CUTTING ***PEANUT BUTTER BOYS*** OFF-SITE THIS MORNING, IN A HIGHLY UNPROFESSIONAL LOCATION.
SHE WAS ***SKULKING*** IN THE ALLEY BEHIND WAX LIPS THE OTHER NIGHT, AND SHE MET A SHADOWY FIGURE IN A CAR.
***AND*** SHE HAS SLEEPER AGENTS LISTED OUT AMONG THE BANDS PERFORMING IN THE FESTIVAL.
Dahlia Diamond - in - diva-ing
Electric Moustache - in
Turtle Tower - in - out: cashflow
eanut Butter Boys - in - sleeper
he Empty Nests - out - injury
Mr. Universe - out - no longer tourin
Jasper & June - in - sleeper
Iguana Party - in
The Mod Pod - in

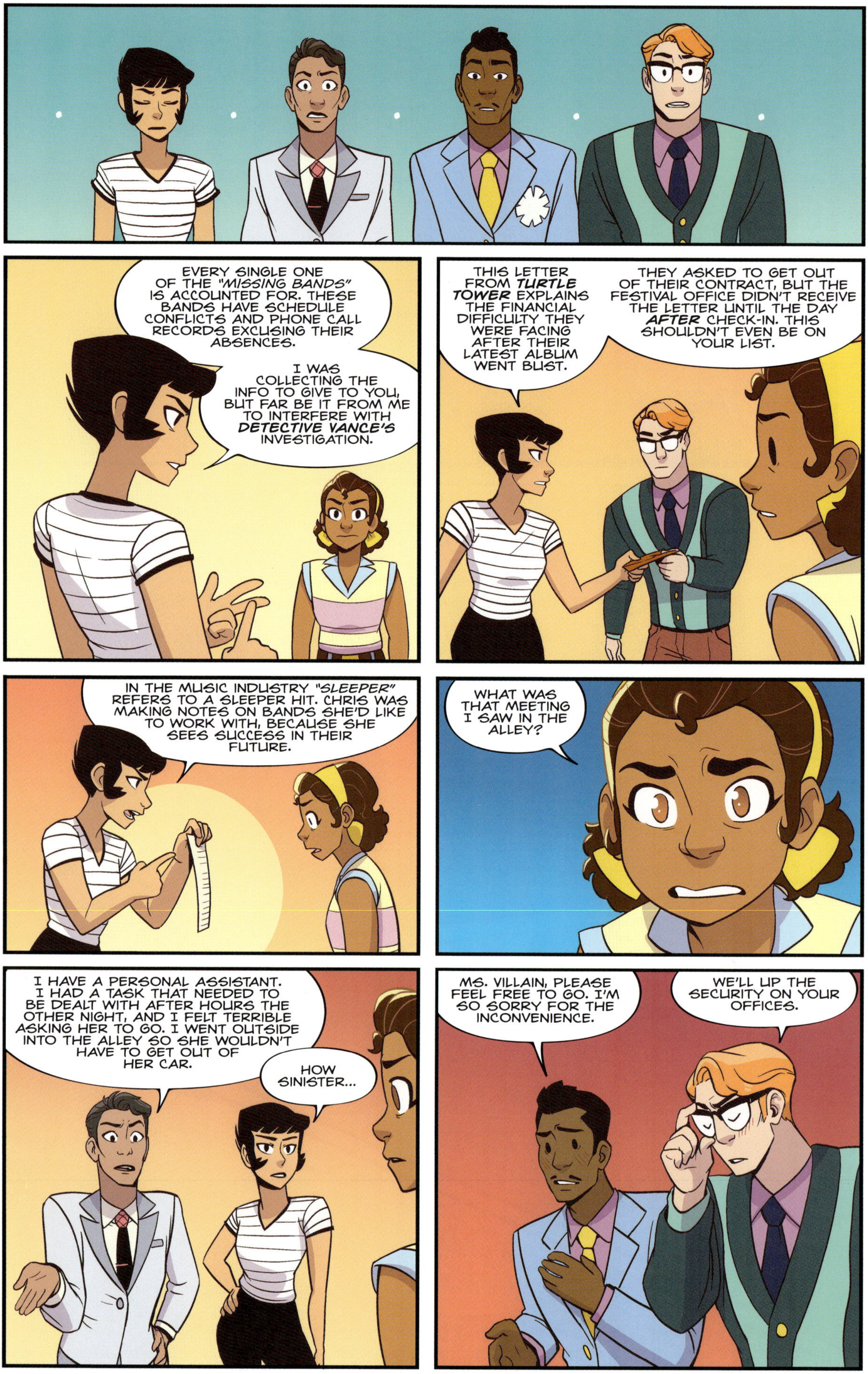
EVERY SINGLE ONE OF THE "MISSING BANDS" IS ACCOUNTED FOR. THESE BANDS HAVE SCHEDULE CONFLICTS AND PHONE CALL RECORDS EXCUSING THEIR ABSENCES.
I WAS COLLECTING THE INFO TO GIVE TO YOU, BUT FAR BE IT FROM ME TO INTERFERE WITH DETECTIVE VANCE'S INVESTIGATION.
THIS LETTER FROM TURTLE TOWER EXPLAINS THE FINANCIAL DIFFICULTY THEY WERE FACING AFTER THEIR LATEST ALBUM WENT BUST.
THEY ASKED TO GET OUT OF THEIR CONTRACT, BUT THE FESTIVAL OFFICE DIDN'T RECEIVE THE LETTER UNTIL THE DAY AFTER CHECK-IN. THIS SHOULDN'T EVEN BE ON YOUR LIST.
IN THE MUSIC INDUSTRY "SLEEPER" REFERS TO A SLEEPER HIT. CHRIS WAS MAKING NOTES ON BANDS SHE'D LIKE TO WORK WITH, BECAUSE SHE SEES SUCCESS IN THEIR FUTURE.
WHAT WAS THAT MEETING I SAW IN THE ALLEY?
I HAVE A PERSONAL ASSISTANT. I HAD A TASK THAT NEEDED TO BE DEALT WITH AFTER HOURS THE OTHER NIGHT, AND I FELT TERRIBLE ASKING HER TO GO. I WENT OUTSIDE INTO THE ALLEY SO SHE WOULDN'T HAVE TO GET OUT OF HER CAR.
HOW SINISTER...
MS. VILLAIN, PLEASE FEEL FREE TO GO. I'M SO SORRY FOR THE INCONVENIENCE.
WE'LL UP THE SECURITY ON YOUR OFFICES.

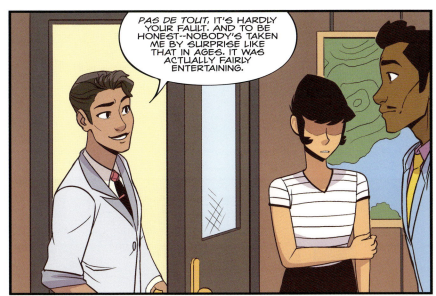
PAS DE TOUT, IT'S HARDLY YOUR FAULT. AND TO BE HONEST--NOBODY'S TAKEN ME BY SURPRISE LIKE THAT IN AGES. IT WAS ACTUALLY FAIRLY ENTERTAINING.

GOLDIE, PLEASE. I APPRECIATE YOUR ENTHUSIASM FOR JUSTICE, BUT YOU NEED TO BE MORE CAREFUL.

I DIDN'T TECHNICALLY BREAK ANY LAWS--

GOLDIE, IT'S NOT JUST ABOUT THE LAW, IT'S ABOUT DOING WHAT'S RIGHT. YOU CAN'T JUST DO WHATEVER YOU WANT BECAUSE I'M HIGHER UP THE CHAIN NOW.

I EXPECT YOU TO RESPECT THE LAW, BUT I ALSO EXPECT YOU TO RESPECT THE BOUNDARIES OF OUR PARTNERS AND OUR GUESTS.

BESIDES, ISN'T FLOUTING THE RULES LIKE THAT EXACTLY WHAT USED TO UPSET YOU SO MUCH ABOUT SUGAR?

I'M GOING TO GO TRY TO SMOOTH THINGS OVER WITH MS. VILLAIN.

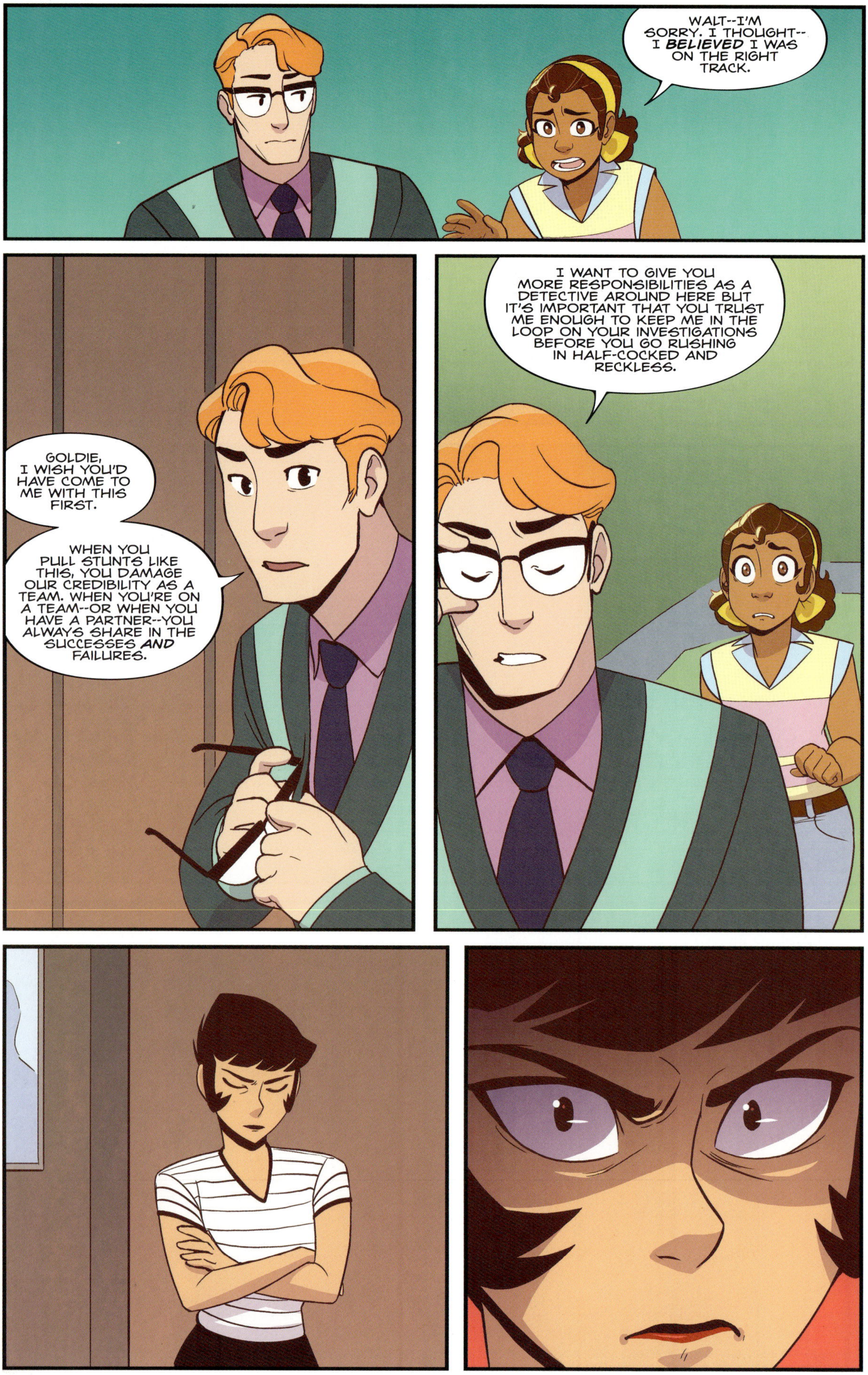
WALT--I'M SORRY. I THOUGHT-- I *BELIEVED* I WAS ON THE RIGHT TRACK.
GOLDIE, I WISH YOU'D HAVE COME TO ME WITH THIS FIRST.
WHEN YOU PULL STUNTS LIKE THIS, YOU DAMAGE OUR CREDIBILITY AS A TEAM. WHEN YOU'RE ON A TEAM--OR WHEN YOU HAVE A PARTNER--YOU ALWAYS SHARE IN THE SUCCESSES *AND* FAILURES.
I WANT TO GIVE YOU MORE RESPONSIBILITIES AS A DETECTIVE AROUND HERE BUT IT'S IMPORTANT THAT YOU TRUST ME ENOUGH TO KEEP ME IN THE LOOP ON YOUR INVESTIGATIONS BEFORE YOU GO RUSHING IN HALF-COCKED AND RECKLESS.

ALRIGHT, GOLDIE. NO MATTER WHAT'S GOING ON BETWEEN US, IT'S NOT OKAY FOR YOU TO ACT LIKE THAT! YOU ACCUSED MY BOSS OF BEING A SPY?!

ON THAT FLIMSY EVIDENCE?!

I'M NOT SURE WHAT'S GOING ON WITH YOU, BUT I'VE NEVER SEEN YOU PUT A CASE IN JEOPARDY LIKE THAT.

DIANE, I--

LISTEN, LET'S JUST TALK AFTER THE FESTIVAL IS OVER. I CAN'T DEAL WITH THIS AND EVERYTHING ELSE RIGHT NOW...

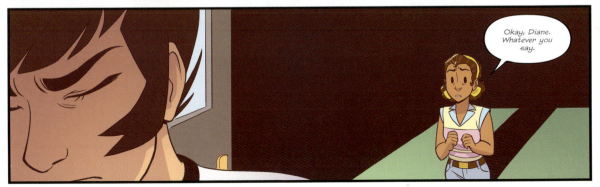

Okay, Diane. Whatever you say.

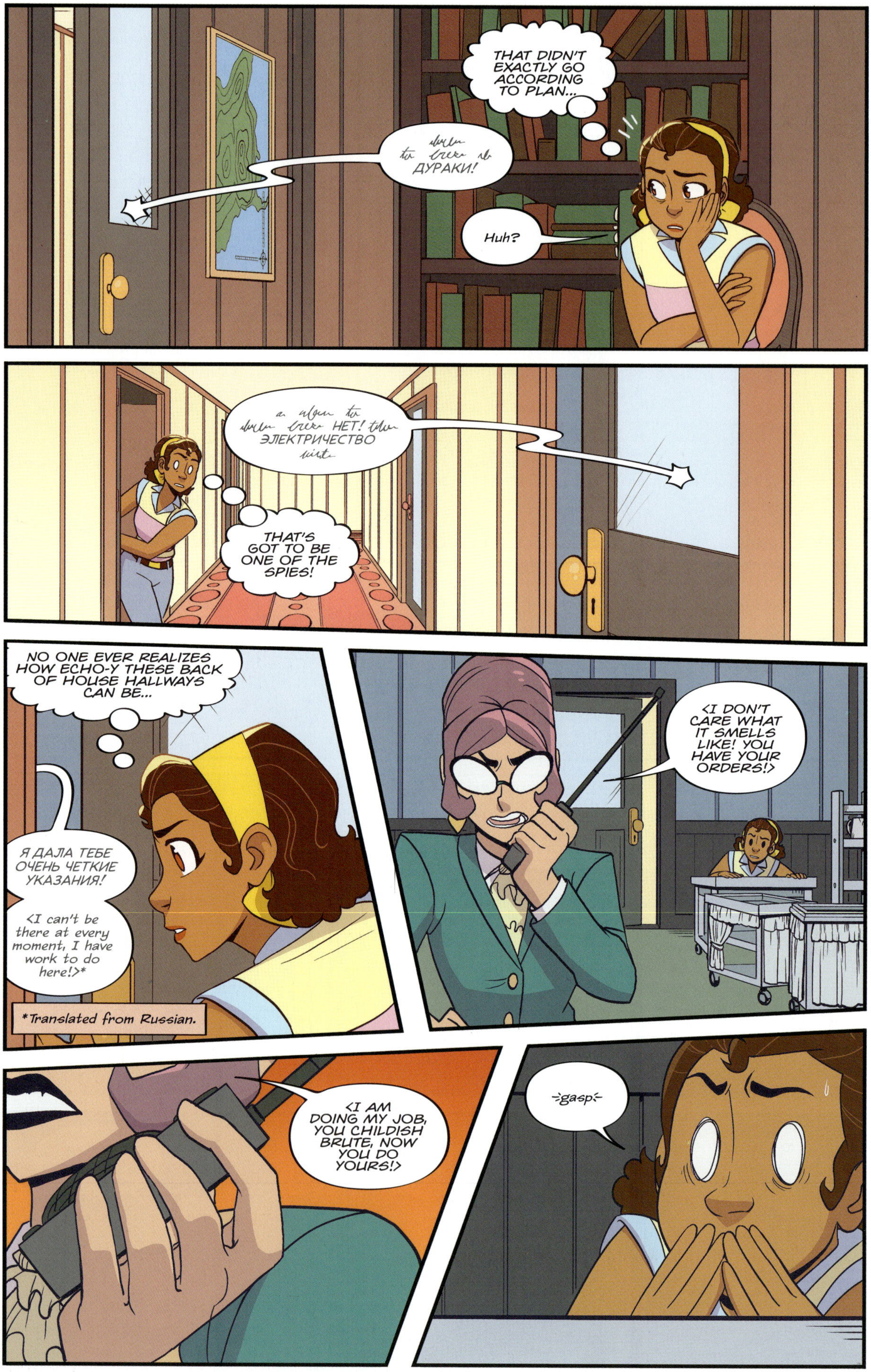
THAT DIDN'T EXACTLY GO ACCORDING TO PLAN...
ДУРАКИ!
Huh?
НЕТ! ЭЛЕКТРИЧЕСТВО
THAT'S GOT TO BE ONE OF THE SPIES!
NO ONE EVER REALIZES HOW ECHO-Y THESE BACK OF HOUSE HALLWAYS CAN BE...
Я ДАЛА ТЕБЕ ОЧЕНЬ ЧЕТКИЕ УКАЗАНИЯ!
<I can't be there at every moment, I have work to do here!>*
*Translated from Russian.
<I DON'T CARE WHAT IT SMELLS LIKE! YOU HAVE YOUR ORDERS!>
<I AM DOING MY JOB, YOU CHILDISH BRUTE, NOW YOU DO YOURS!>
gasp

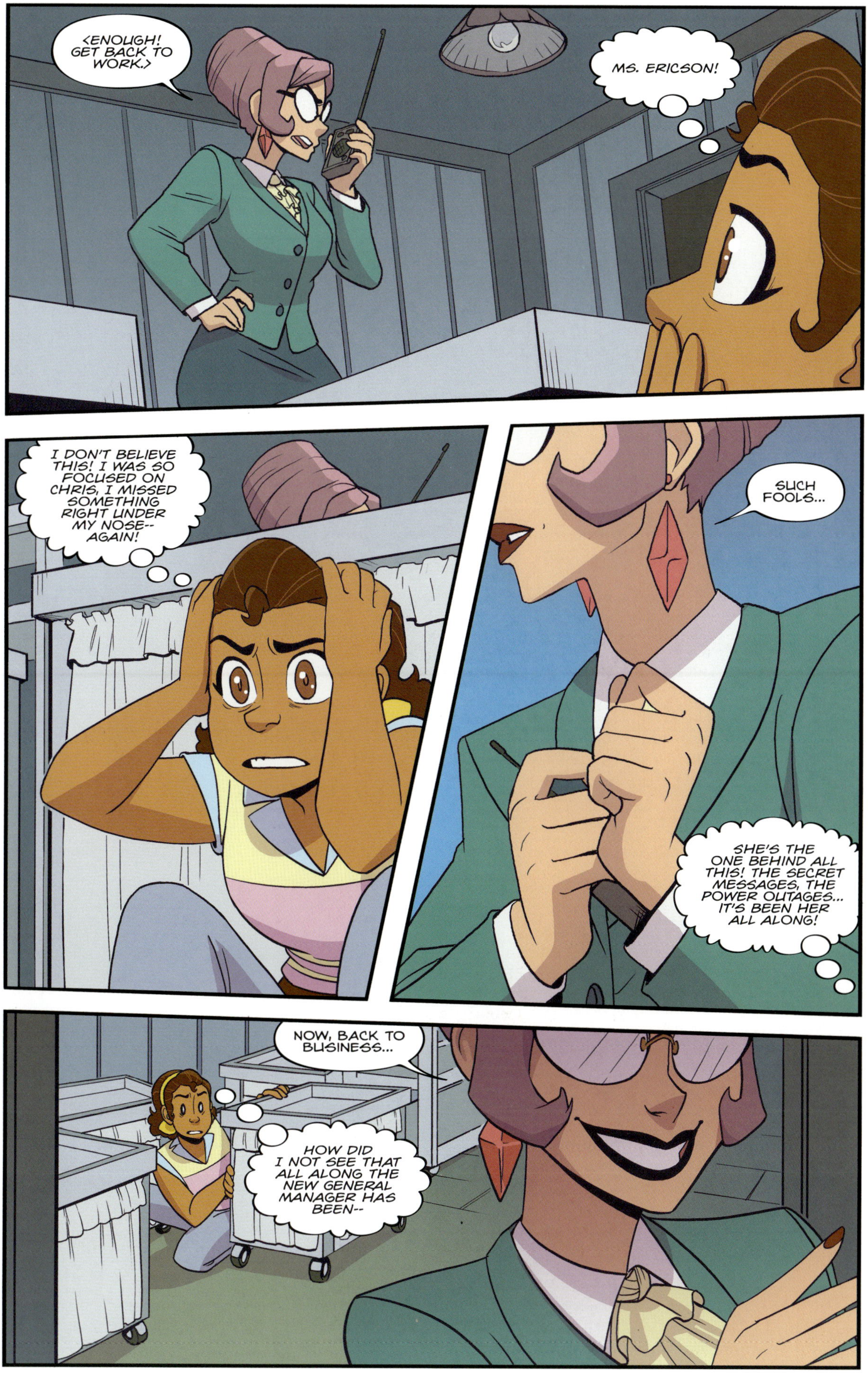
<ENOUGH! GET BACK TO WORK.>
MS. ERICSON!
I DON'T BELIEVE THIS! I WAS SO FOCUSED ON CHRIS, I MISSED SOMETHING RIGHT UNDER MY NOSE-- AGAIN!
SUCH FOOLS...
SHE'S THE ONE BEHIND ALL THIS! THE SECRET MESSAGES, THE POWER OUTAGES... IT'S BEEN HER ALL ALONG!
NOW, BACK TO BUSINESS...
HOW DID I NOT SEE THAT ALL ALONG THE NEW GENERAL MANAGER HAS BEEN--

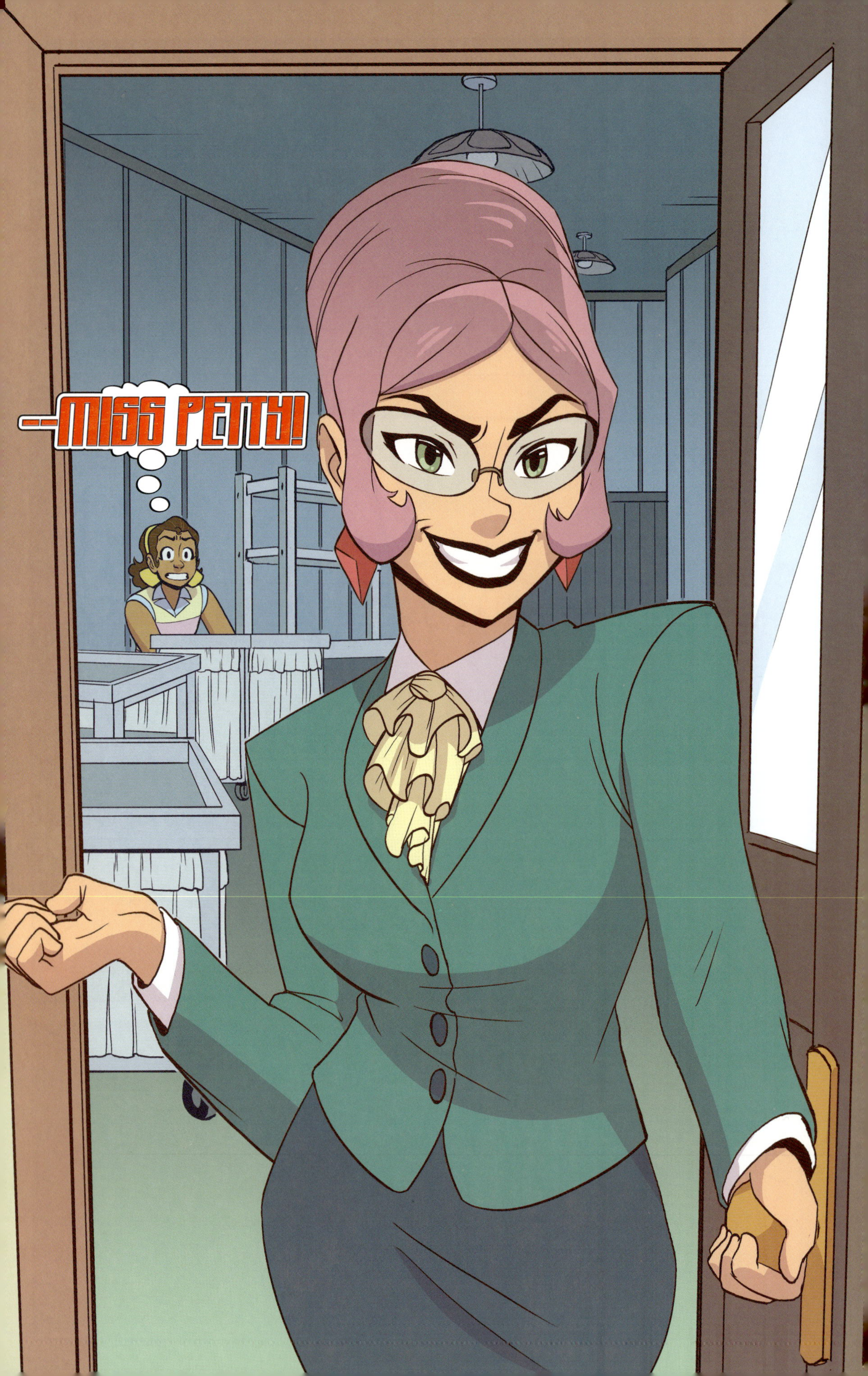
--MISS PETTY!

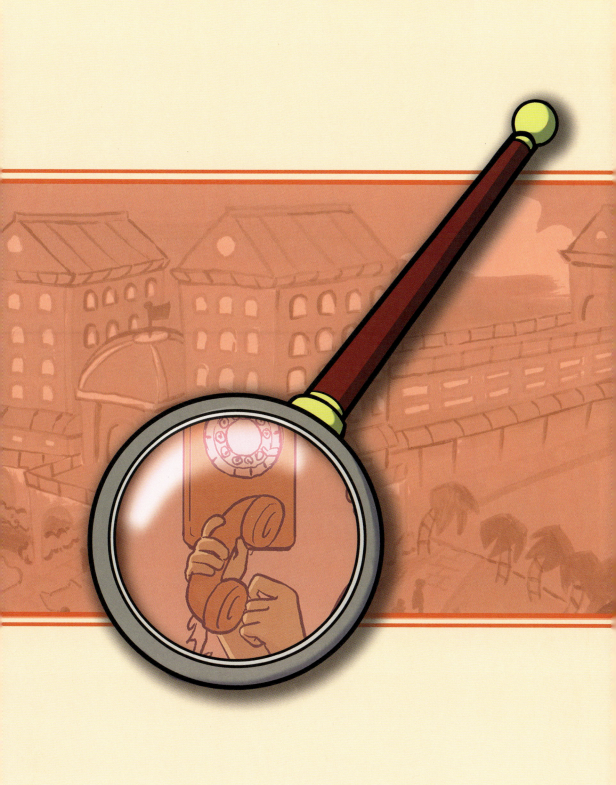

# chapter
# FIFTEEN

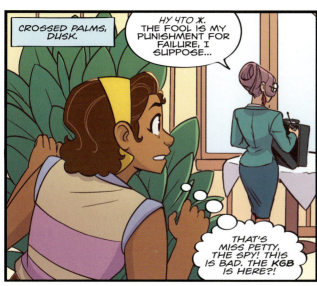

CROSSED PALMS, DUSK.

HУ ЧТО X. THE FOOL IS MY PUNISHMENT FOR FAILURE, I SUPPOSE...

THAT'S MISS PETTY, THE SPY! THIS IS BAD. THE **KGB** IS HERE?!

*Oh NO!*

I CAN'T BELIEVE THIS! SHE WAS UNDER MY NOSE THIS WHOLE TIME-- *AGAIN!* I'VE GOTTA TELL WALT!

WAIT A MINUTE... *FLASH,* I CAN'T TELL WALT *NOW.* NOT AFTER THE STUNT I JUST PULLED, HE'LL NEVER BELIEVE ME! I'M LIKE THE GIRL WHO CRIED KGB, *ARGH!*

AND I DID IT ALL TO MYSELF! IF I HADN'T BEEN SO FOCUSED ON CHRIS AND ACTUALLY *DONE* MY JOB I WOULDN'T HAVE MISSED THIS.

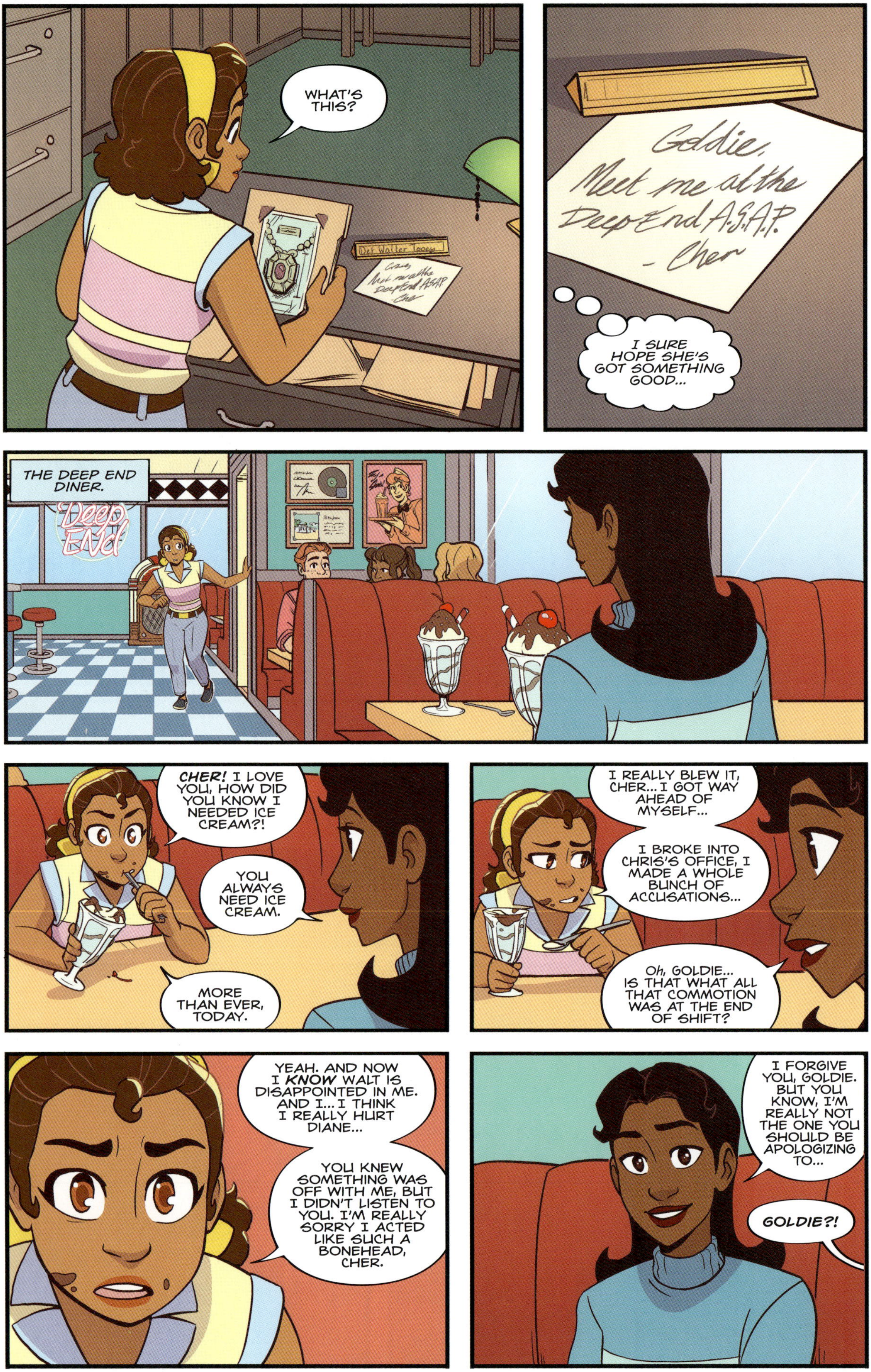
WHAT'S THIS?
Goldie, Meet me at the Deep End A.S.A.P. - Cher
I SURE HOPE SHE'S GOT SOMETHING GOOD...
THE DEEP END DINER.
Deep End
CHER! I LOVE YOU, HOW DID YOU KNOW I NEEDED ICE CREAM?!
YOU ALWAYS NEED ICE CREAM.
MORE THAN EVER, TODAY.
I REALLY BLEW IT, CHER... I GOT WAY AHEAD OF MYSELF...
I BROKE INTO CHRIS'S OFFICE, I MADE A WHOLE BUNCH OF ACCUSATIONS...
Oh, GOLDIE... IS THAT WHAT ALL THAT COMMOTION WAS AT THE END OF SHIFT?
YEAH. AND NOW I KNOW WALT IS DISAPPOINTED IN ME. AND I... I THINK I REALLY HURT DIANE...
YOU KNEW SOMETHING WAS OFF WITH ME, BUT I DIDN'T LISTEN TO YOU. I'M REALLY SORRY I ACTED LIKE SUCH A BONEHEAD, CHER.
I FORGIVE YOU, GOLDIE. BUT YOU KNOW, I'M REALLY NOT THE ONE YOU SHOULD BE APOLOGIZING TO...
GOLDIE?!

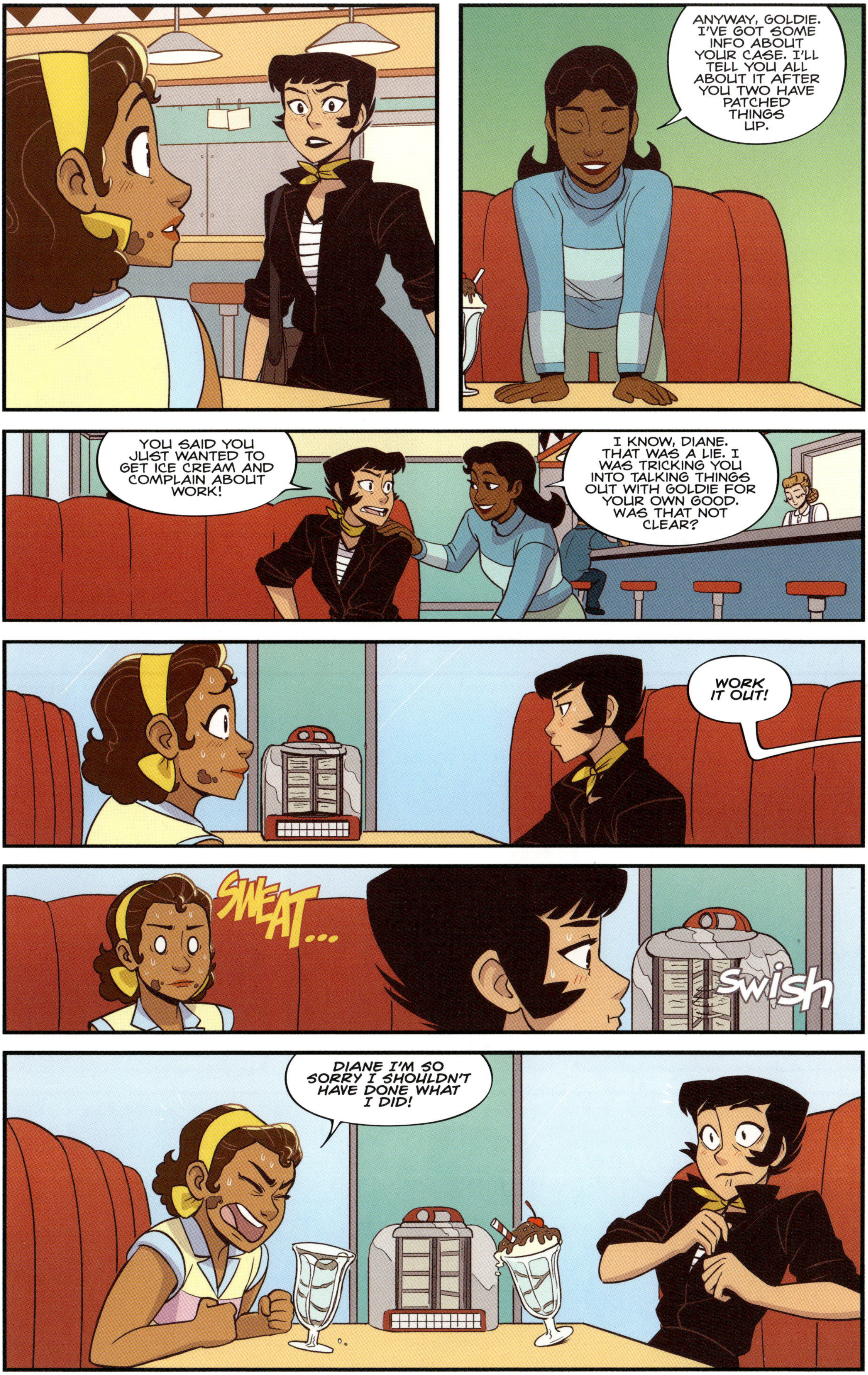
ANYWAY, GOLDIE. I'VE GOT SOME INFO ABOUT YOUR CASE. I'LL TELL YOU ALL ABOUT IT AFTER YOU TWO HAVE PATCHED THINGS UP.
YOU SAID YOU JUST WANTED TO GET ICE CREAM AND COMPLAIN ABOUT WORK!
I KNOW, DIANE. THAT WAS A LIE. I WAS TRICKING YOU INTO TALKING THINGS OUT WITH GOLDIE FOR YOUR OWN GOOD. WAS THAT NOT CLEAR?
WORK IT OUT!
SWEAT...
SWISH
DIANE I'M SO SORRY I SHOULDN'T HAVE DONE WHAT I DID!

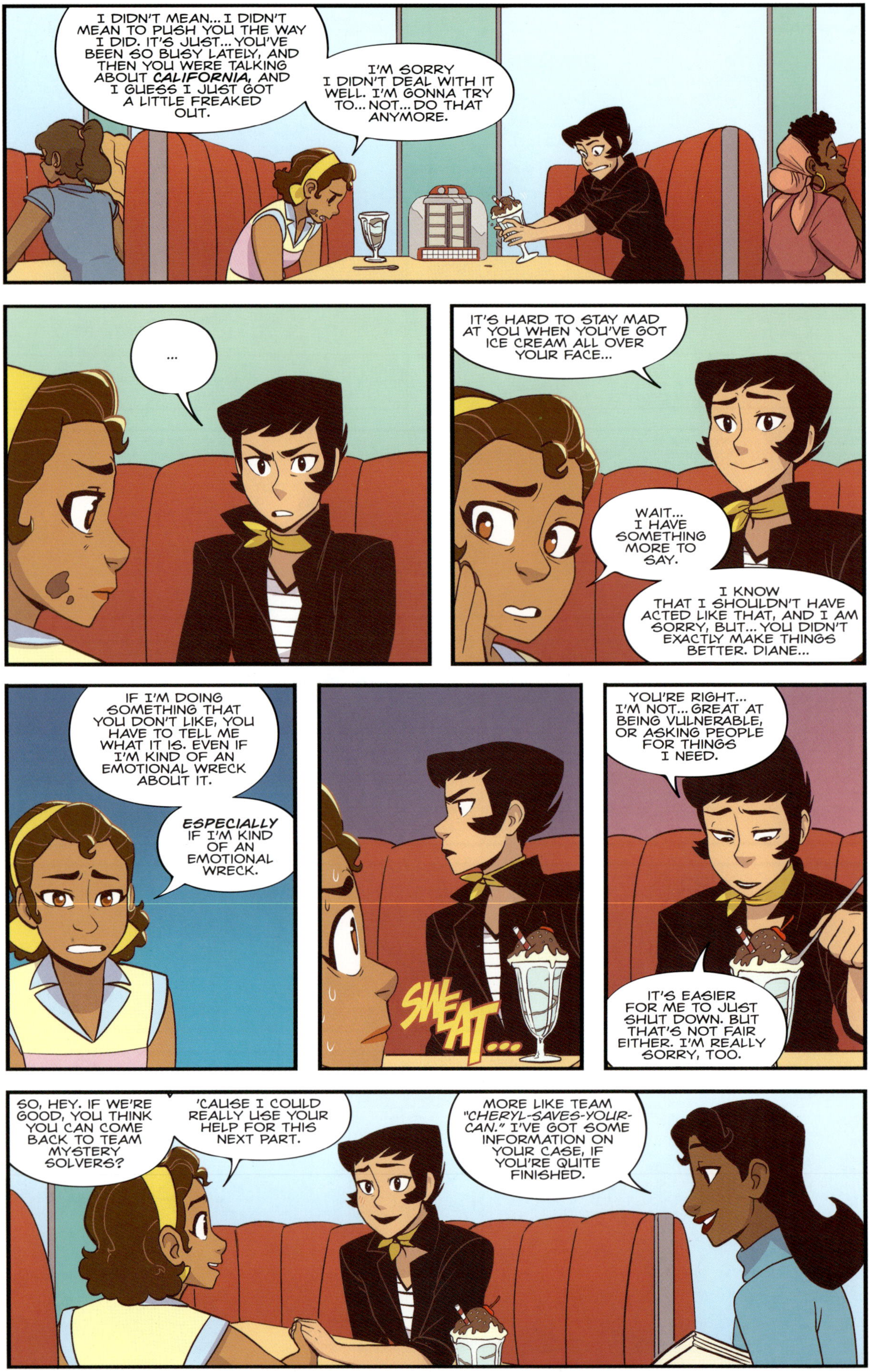
I DIDN'T MEAN... I DIDN'T MEAN TO PUSH YOU THE WAY I DID. IT'S JUST... YOU'VE BEEN SO BUSY LATELY, AND THEN YOU WERE TALKING ABOUT **CALIFORNIA,** AND I GUESS I JUST GOT A LITTLE FREAKED OUT.
I'M SORRY I DIDN'T DEAL WITH IT WELL. I'M GONNA TRY TO... NOT... DO THAT ANYMORE.
...
IT'S HARD TO STAY MAD AT YOU WHEN YOU'VE GOT ICE CREAM ALL OVER YOUR FACE...
WAIT... I HAVE SOMETHING MORE TO SAY.
I KNOW THAT I SHOULDN'T HAVE ACTED LIKE THAT, AND I AM SORRY, BUT... YOU DIDN'T EXACTLY MAKE THINGS BETTER. DIANE...
IF I'M DOING SOMETHING THAT YOU DON'T LIKE, YOU HAVE TO TELL ME WHAT IT IS. EVEN IF I'M KIND OF AN EMOTIONAL WRECK ABOUT IT.
***ESPECIALLY*** IF I'M KIND OF AN EMOTIONAL WRECK.
SWEAT...
YOU'RE RIGHT... I'M NOT... GREAT AT BEING VULNERABLE, OR ASKING PEOPLE FOR THINGS I NEED.
IT'S EASIER FOR ME TO JUST SHUT DOWN. BUT THAT'S NOT FAIR EITHER. I'M REALLY SORRY, TOO.
SO, HEY. IF WE'RE GOOD, YOU THINK YOU CAN COME BACK TO TEAM MYSTERY SOLVERS?
'CAUSE I COULD REALLY USE YOUR HELP FOR THIS NEXT PART.
MORE LIKE TEAM *"CHERYL-SAVES-YOUR-CAN."* I'VE GOT SOME INFORMATION ON YOUR CASE, IF YOU'RE QUITE FINISHED.

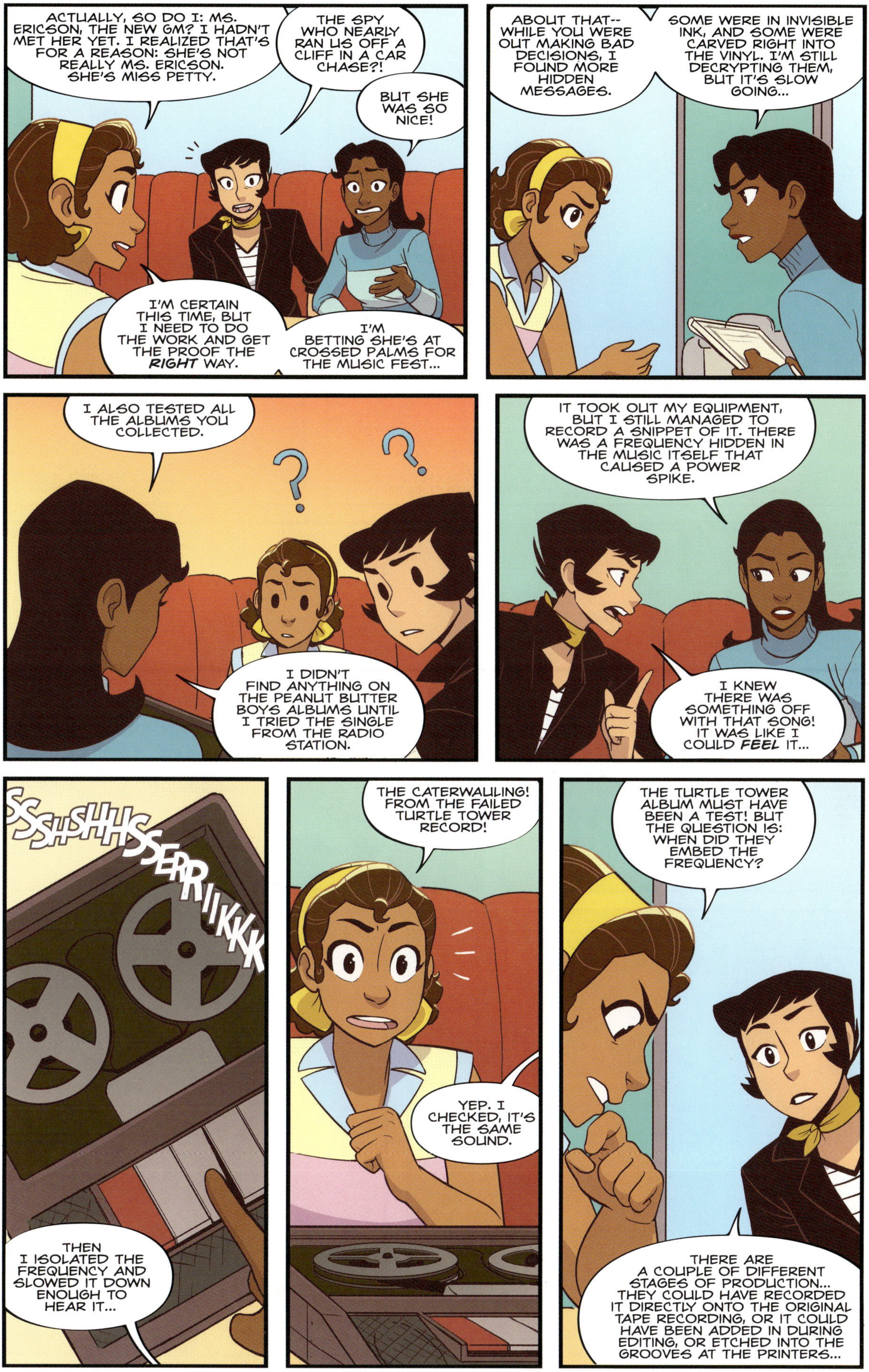
ACTUALLY, SO DO I: MS. ERICSON, THE NEW GM? I HADN'T MET HER YET. I REALIZED THAT'S FOR A REASON: SHE'S NOT REALLY MS. ERICSON. SHE'S MISS PETTY.
THE SPY WHO NEARLY RAN US OFF A CLIFF IN A CAR CHASE?!
BUT SHE WAS SO NICE!
I'M CERTAIN THIS TIME, BUT I NEED TO DO THE WORK AND GET THE PROOF THE *RIGHT* WAY.
I'M BETTING SHE'S AT CROSSED PALMS FOR THE MUSIC FEST...
ABOUT THAT-- WHILE YOU WERE OUT MAKING BAD DECISIONS, I FOUND MORE HIDDEN MESSAGES.
SOME WERE IN INVISIBLE INK, AND SOME WERE CARVED RIGHT INTO THE VINYL. I'M STILL DECRYPTING THEM, BUT IT'S SLOW GOING...
I ALSO TESTED ALL THE ALBUMS YOU COLLECTED.
I DIDN'T FIND ANYTHING ON THE PEANUT BUTTER BOYS ALBUMS UNTIL I TRIED THE SINGLE FROM THE RADIO STATION.
IT TOOK OUT MY EQUIPMENT, BUT I STILL MANAGED TO RECORD A SNIPPET OF IT. THERE WAS A FREQUENCY HIDDEN IN THE MUSIC ITSELF THAT CAUSED A POWER SPIKE.
I KNEW THERE WAS SOMETHING OFF WITH THAT SONG! IT WAS LIKE I COULD *FEEL* IT...
SSSHSHHSSERRIIKKK
THEN I ISOLATED THE FREQUENCY AND SLOWED IT DOWN ENOUGH TO HEAR IT...
THE CATERWAULING! FROM THE FAILED TURTLE TOWER RECORD!
YEP. I CHECKED, IT'S THE SAME SOUND.
THE TURTLE TOWER ALBUM MUST HAVE BEEN A TEST! BUT THE QUESTION IS: WHEN DID THEY EMBED THE FREQUENCY?
THERE ARE A COUPLE OF DIFFERENT STAGES OF PRODUCTION... THEY COULD HAVE RECORDED IT DIRECTLY ONTO THE ORIGINAL TAPE RECORDING, OR IT COULD HAVE BEEN ADDED IN DURING EDITING, OR ETCHED INTO THE GROOVES AT THE PRINTERS...

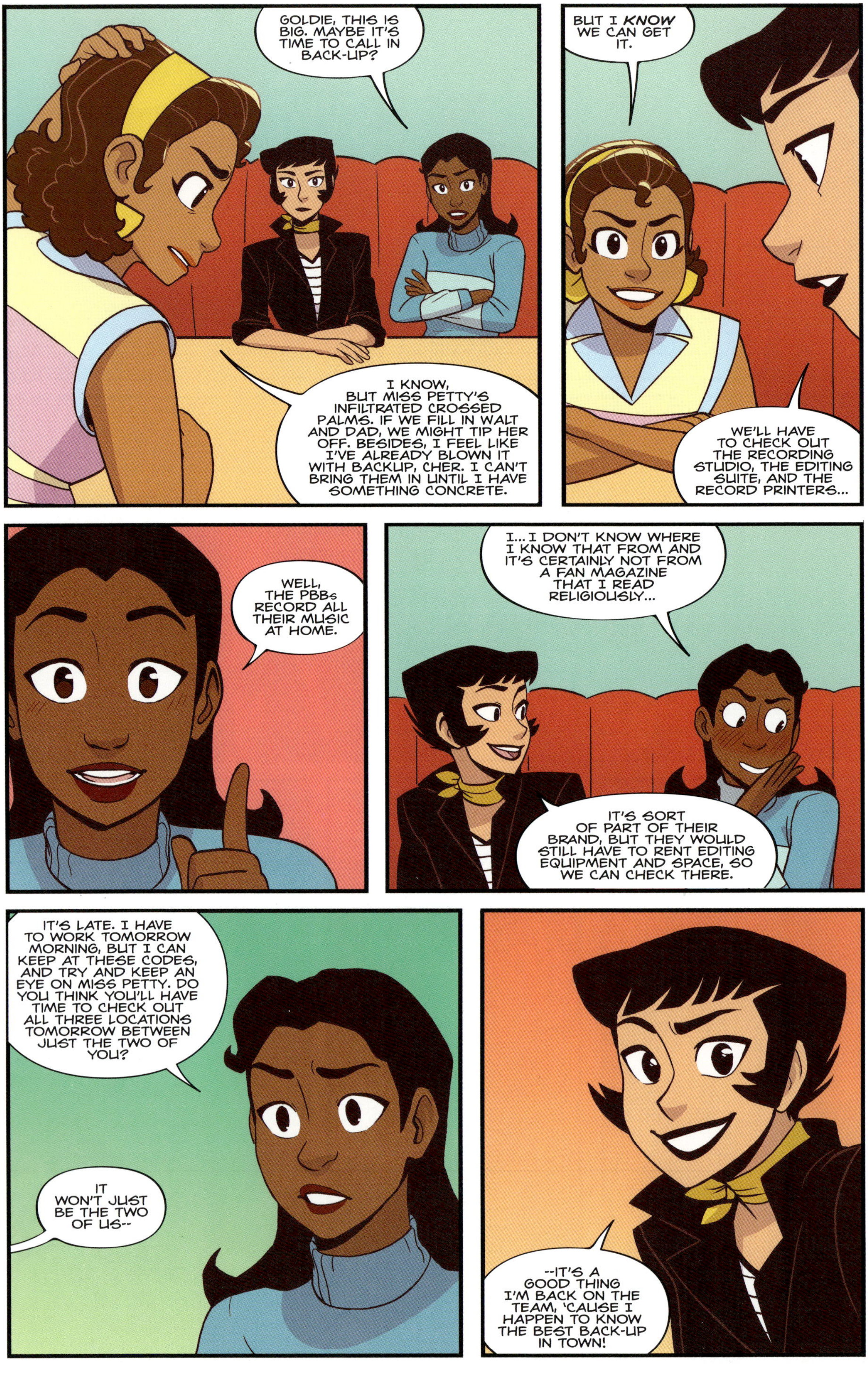
GOLDIE, THIS IS BIG. MAYBE IT'S TIME TO CALL IN BACK-UP?
I KNOW, BUT MISS PETTY'S INFILTRATED CROSSED PALMS. IF WE FILL IN WALT AND DAD, WE MIGHT TIP HER OFF. BESIDES, I FEEL LIKE I'VE ALREADY BLOWN IT WITH BACKUP, CHER. I CAN'T BRING THEM IN UNTIL I HAVE SOMETHING CONCRETE.
BUT I *KNOW* WE CAN GET IT.
WE'LL HAVE TO CHECK OUT THE RECORDING STUDIO, THE EDITING SUITE, AND THE RECORD PRINTERS...
WELL, THE PBBs RECORD ALL THEIR MUSIC AT HOME.
I... I DON'T KNOW WHERE I KNOW THAT FROM AND IT'S CERTAINLY NOT FROM A FAN MAGAZINE THAT I READ RELIGIOUSLY...
IT'S SORT OF PART OF THEIR BRAND, BUT THEY WOULD STILL HAVE TO RENT EDITING EQUIPMENT AND SPACE, SO WE CAN CHECK THERE.
IT'S LATE. I HAVE TO WORK TOMORROW MORNING, BUT I CAN KEEP AT THESE CODES, AND TRY AND KEEP AN EYE ON MISS PETTY. DO YOU THINK YOU'LL HAVE TIME TO CHECK OUT ALL THREE LOCATIONS TOMORROW BETWEEN JUST THE TWO OF YOU?
IT WON'T JUST BE THE TWO OF US--
--IT'S A GOOD THING I'M BACK ON THE TEAM, 'CAUSE I HAPPEN TO KNOW THE BEST BACK-UP IN TOWN!

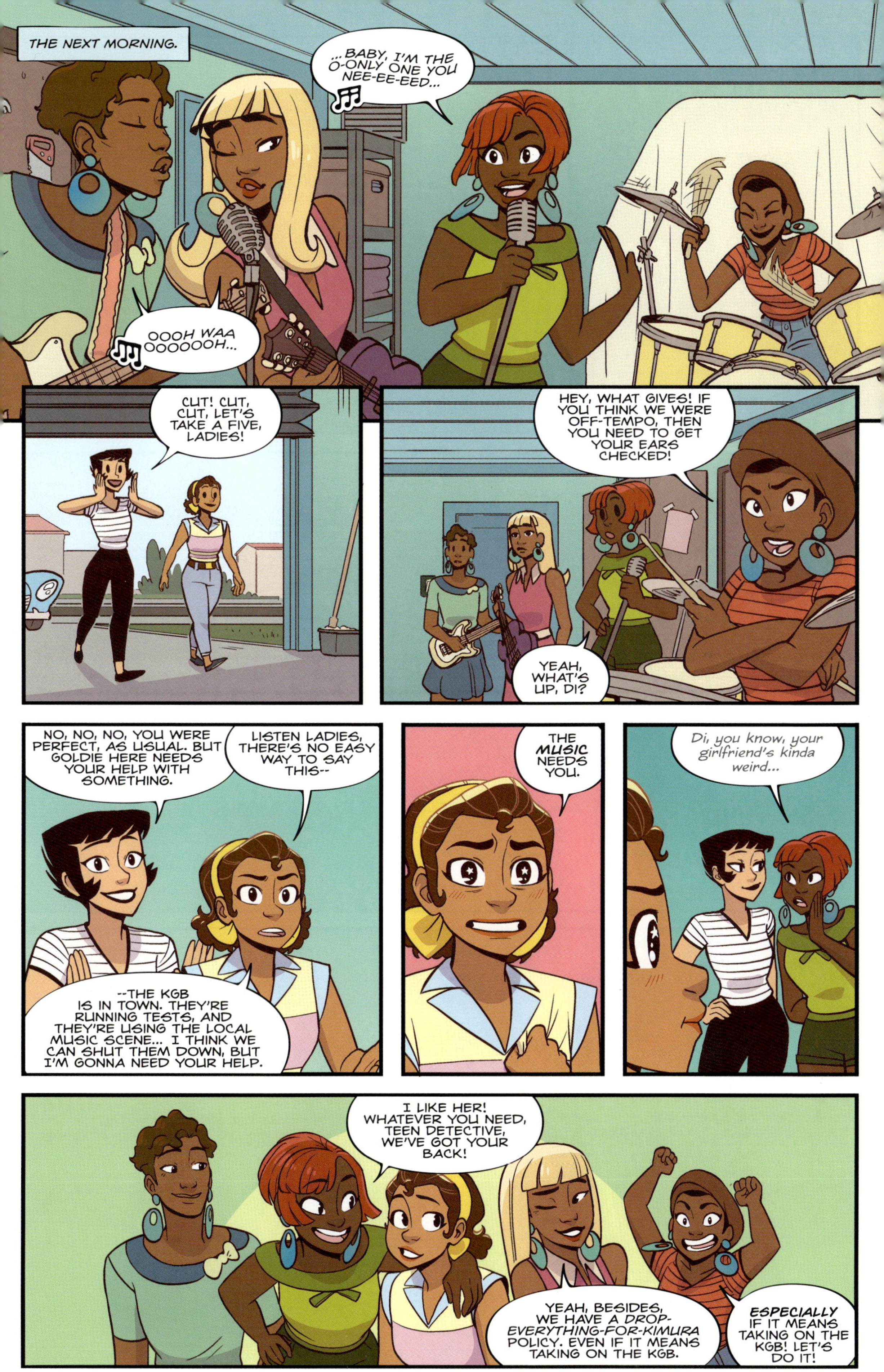
THE NEXT MORNING.
...BABY, I'M THE O-ONLY ONE YOU NEE-EE-EED...
OOOH WAA OOOOOOH...
CUT! CUT, CUT, LET'S TAKE A FIVE, LADIES!
HEY, WHAT GIVES! IF YOU THINK WE WERE OFF-TEMPO, THEN YOU NEED TO GET YOUR EARS CHECKED!
YEAH, WHAT'S UP, DI?
NO, NO, NO, YOU WERE PERFECT, AS USUAL. BUT GOLDIE HERE NEEDS YOUR HELP WITH SOMETHING.
LISTEN LADIES, THERE'S NO EASY WAY TO SAY THIS--
--THE KGB IS IN TOWN. THEY'RE RUNNING TESTS, AND THEY'RE USING THE LOCAL MUSIC SCENE... I THINK WE CAN SHUT THEM DOWN, BUT I'M GONNA NEED YOUR HELP.
THE MUSIC NEEDS YOU.
Di, you know, your girlfriend's kinda weird...
I LIKE HER! WHATEVER YOU NEED, TEEN DETECTIVE, WE'VE GOT YOUR BACK!
YEAH, BESIDES, WE HAVE A DROP-EVERYTHING-FOR-KIMURA POLICY. EVEN IF IT MEANS TAKING ON THE KGB.
ESPECIALLY IF IT MEANS TAKING ON THE KGB! LET'S DO IT!

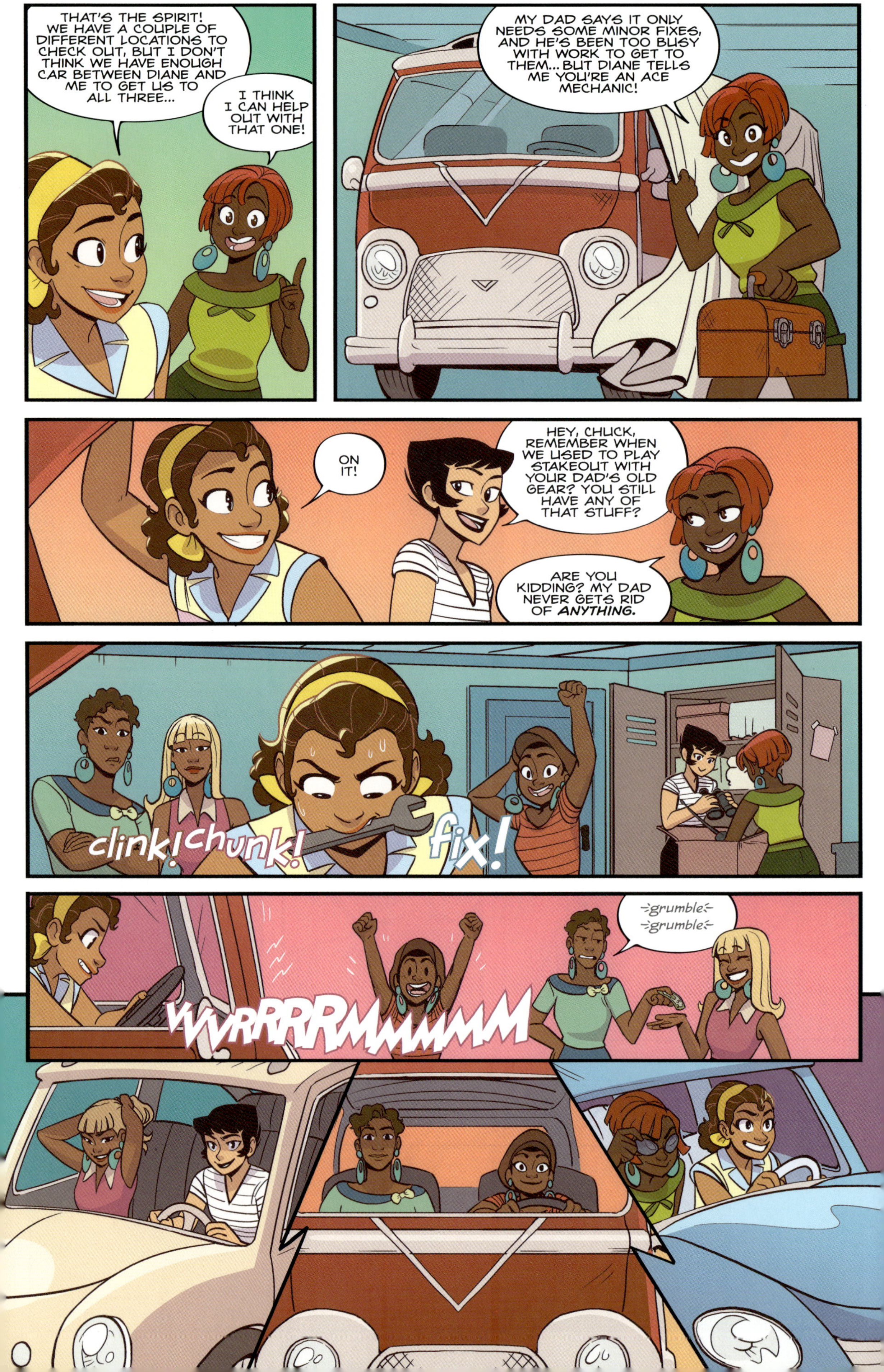
THAT'S THE SPIRIT! WE HAVE A COUPLE OF DIFFERENT LOCATIONS TO CHECK OUT, BUT I DON'T THINK WE HAVE ENOUGH CAR BETWEEN DIANE AND ME TO GET US TO ALL THREE...
I THINK I CAN HELP OUT WITH THAT ONE!
MY DAD SAYS IT ONLY NEEDS SOME MINOR FIXES, AND HE'S BEEN TOO BUSY WITH WORK TO GET TO THEM... BUT DIANE TELLS ME YOU'RE AN ACE MECHANIC!
ON IT!
HEY, CHUCK, REMEMBER WHEN WE USED TO PLAY STAKEOUT WITH YOUR DAD'S OLD GEAR? YOU STILL HAVE ANY OF THAT STUFF?
ARE YOU KIDDING? MY DAD NEVER GETS RID OF ANYTHING.
clink! chunk! fix!
WVRRRRMMMMMM
grumble grumble

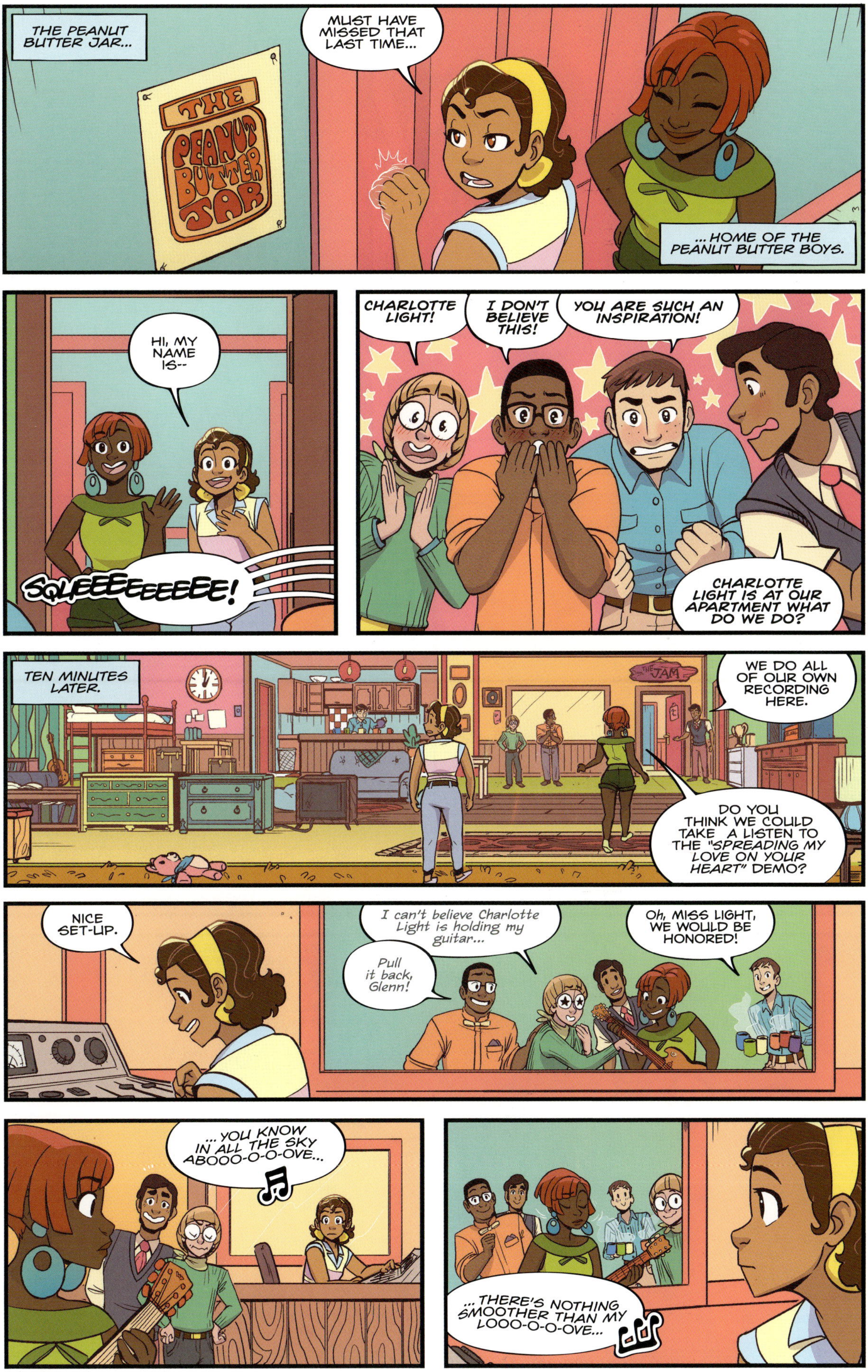
THE PEANUT BUTTER JAR...
MUST HAVE MISSED THAT LAST TIME...
THE PEANUT BUTTER JAR
...HOME OF THE PEANUT BUTTER BOYS.
HI, MY NAME IS--
SQUEEEEEEEEEE!
CHARLOTTE LIGHT!
I DON'T BELIEVE THIS!
YOU ARE SUCH AN INSPIRATION!
CHARLOTTE LIGHT IS AT OUR APARTMENT WHAT DO WE DO?
TEN MINUTES LATER.
THE JAM
WE DO ALL OF OUR OWN RECORDING HERE.
DO YOU THINK WE COULD TAKE A LISTEN TO THE "SPREADING MY LOVE ON YOUR HEART" DEMO?
NICE SET-UP.
I can't believe Charlotte Light is holding my guitar...
Pull it back, Glenn!
Oh, MISS LIGHT, WE WOULD BE HONORED!
...YOU KNOW IN ALL THE SKY ABOOO-O-O-OVE...
...THERE'S NOTHING SMOOTHER THAN MY LOOO-O-O-OVE...

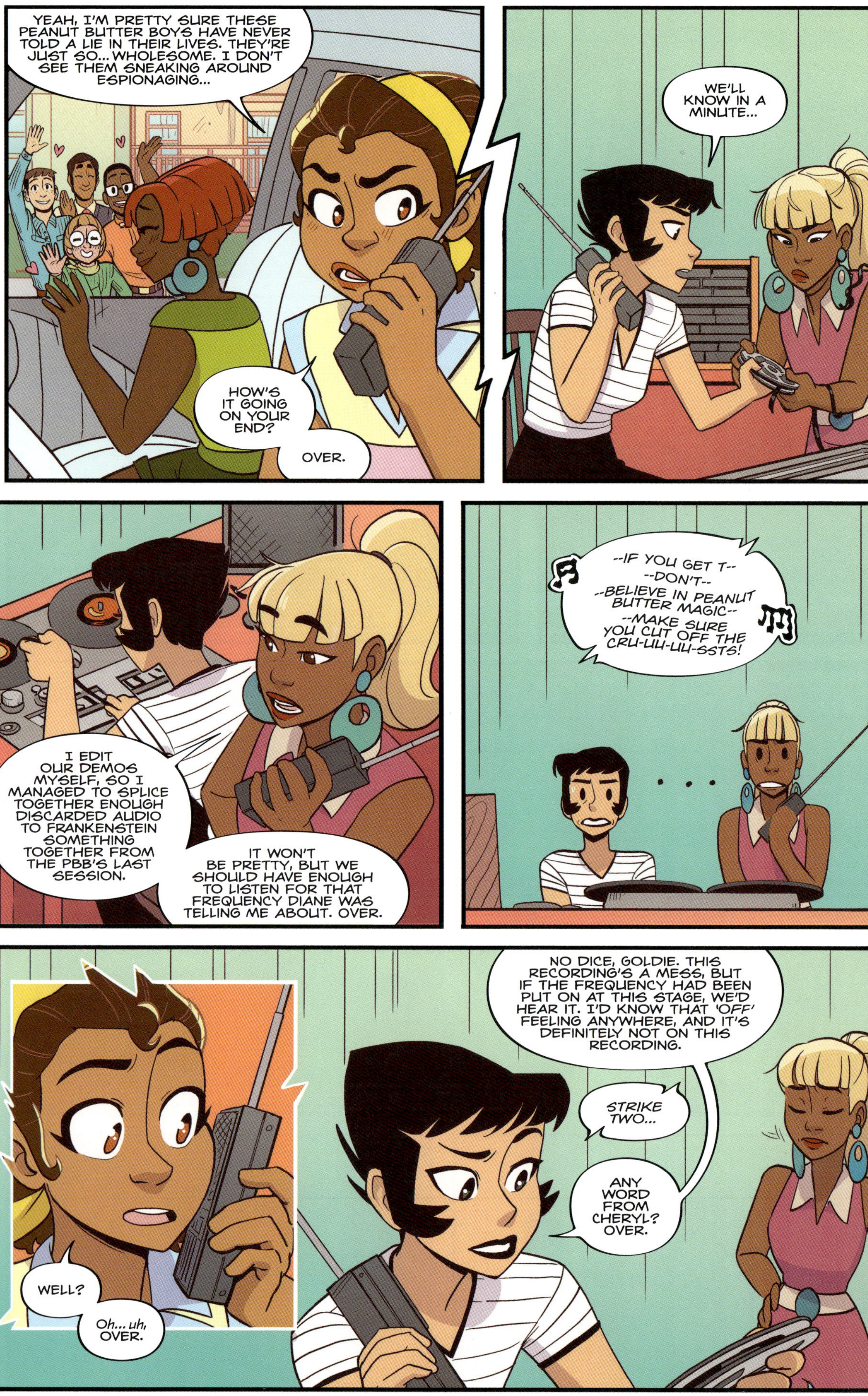
YEAH, I'M PRETTY SURE THESE PEANUT BUTTER BOYS HAVE NEVER TOLD A LIE IN THEIR LIVES. THEY'RE JUST SO... WHOLESOME. I DON'T SEE THEM SNEAKING AROUND ESPIONAGING...
HOW'S IT GOING ON YOUR END?
OVER.
WE'LL KNOW IN A MINUTE...
I EDIT OUR DEMOS MYSELF, SO I MANAGED TO SPLICE TOGETHER ENOUGH DISCARDED AUDIO TO FRANKENSTEIN SOMETHING TOGETHER FROM THE PBB'S LAST SESSION.
IT WON'T BE PRETTY, BUT WE SHOULD HAVE ENOUGH TO LISTEN FOR THAT FREQUENCY DIANE WAS TELLING ME ABOUT. OVER.
--IF YOU GET T--
--DON'T--
--BELIEVE IN PEANUT BUTTER MAGIC--
--MAKE SURE YOU CUT OFF THE CRU-UU-UU-SSTS!
...
NO DICE, GOLDIE. THIS RECORDING'S A MESS, BUT IF THE FREQUENCY HAD BEEN PUT ON AT THIS STAGE, WE'D HEAR IT. I'D KNOW THAT 'OFF' FEELING ANYWHERE, AND IT'S DEFINITELY NOT ON THIS RECORDING.
STRIKE TWO...
ANY WORD FROM CHERYL? OVER.
WELL?
Oh... uh, OVER.

"NOT YET... I HOPE SHE'S HAVING BETTER LUCK THAN WE ARE... OVER AND OUT."

MEANWHILE, AT STATELY CROSSED PALMS RESORT...

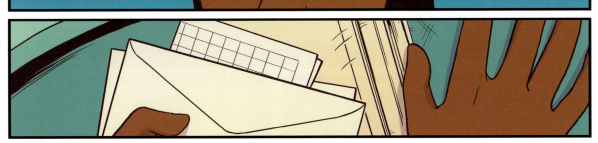

MISS LEBEAUX, I HAVE AN ERRAND TO RUN, BUT I TRUST THAT YOU HAVE THINGS UNDER CONTR--*WHAT IS THAT??*

*Tsk, tsk.* MISS LEBEAUX, CROSSWORD PUZZLES ON DUTY? I EXPECT BETTER FROM YOU, DEAR.

⊰*Phew*⊱

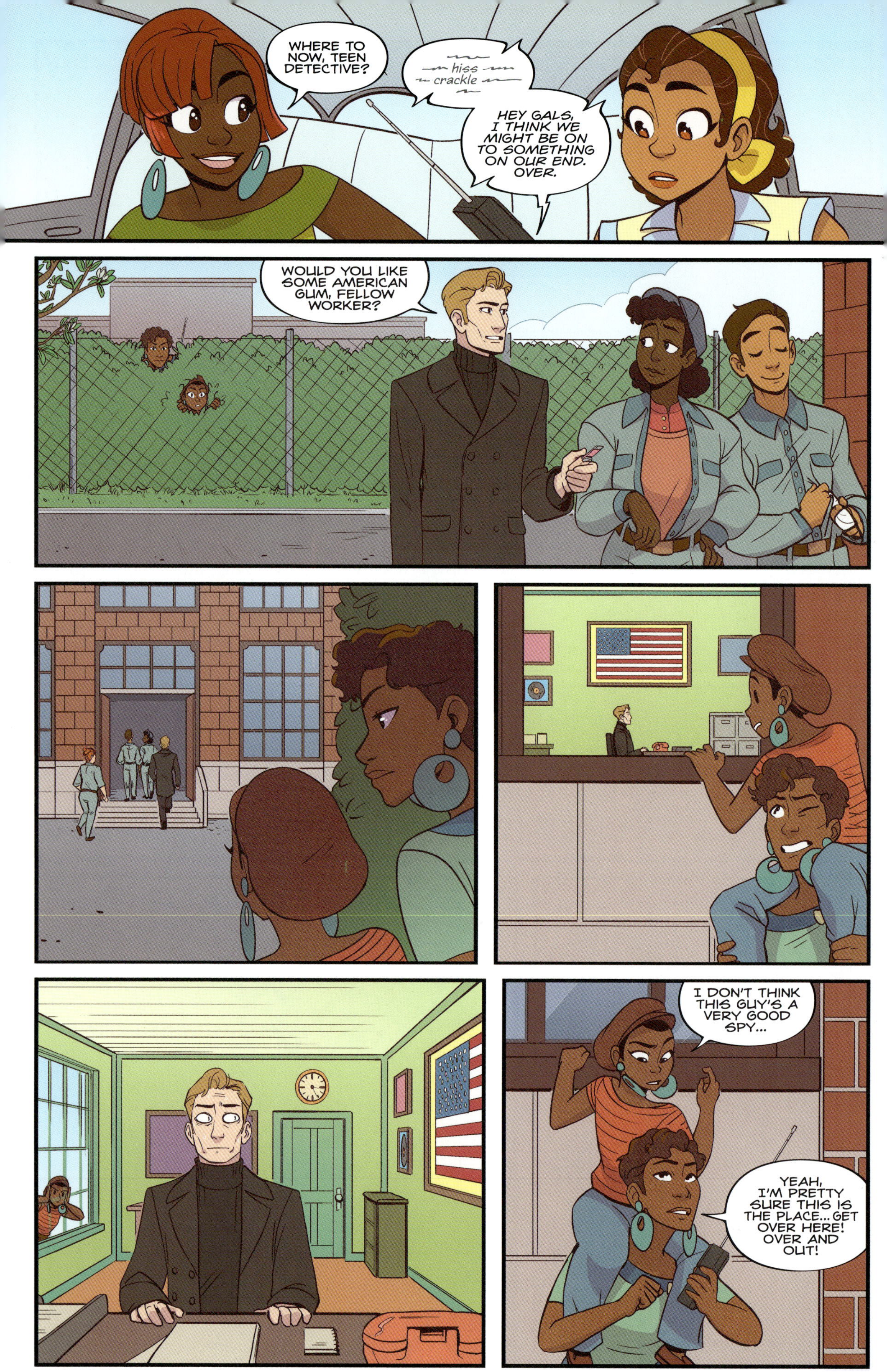
WHERE TO NOW, TEEN DETECTIVE?
hiss crackle
HEY GALS, I THINK WE MIGHT BE ON TO SOMETHING ON OUR END. OVER.
WOULD YOU LIKE SOME AMERICAN GUM, FELLOW WORKER?
I DON'T THINK THIS GUY'S A VERY GOOD SPY...
YEAH, I'M PRETTY SURE THIS IS THE PLACE... GET OVER HERE! OVER AND OUT!

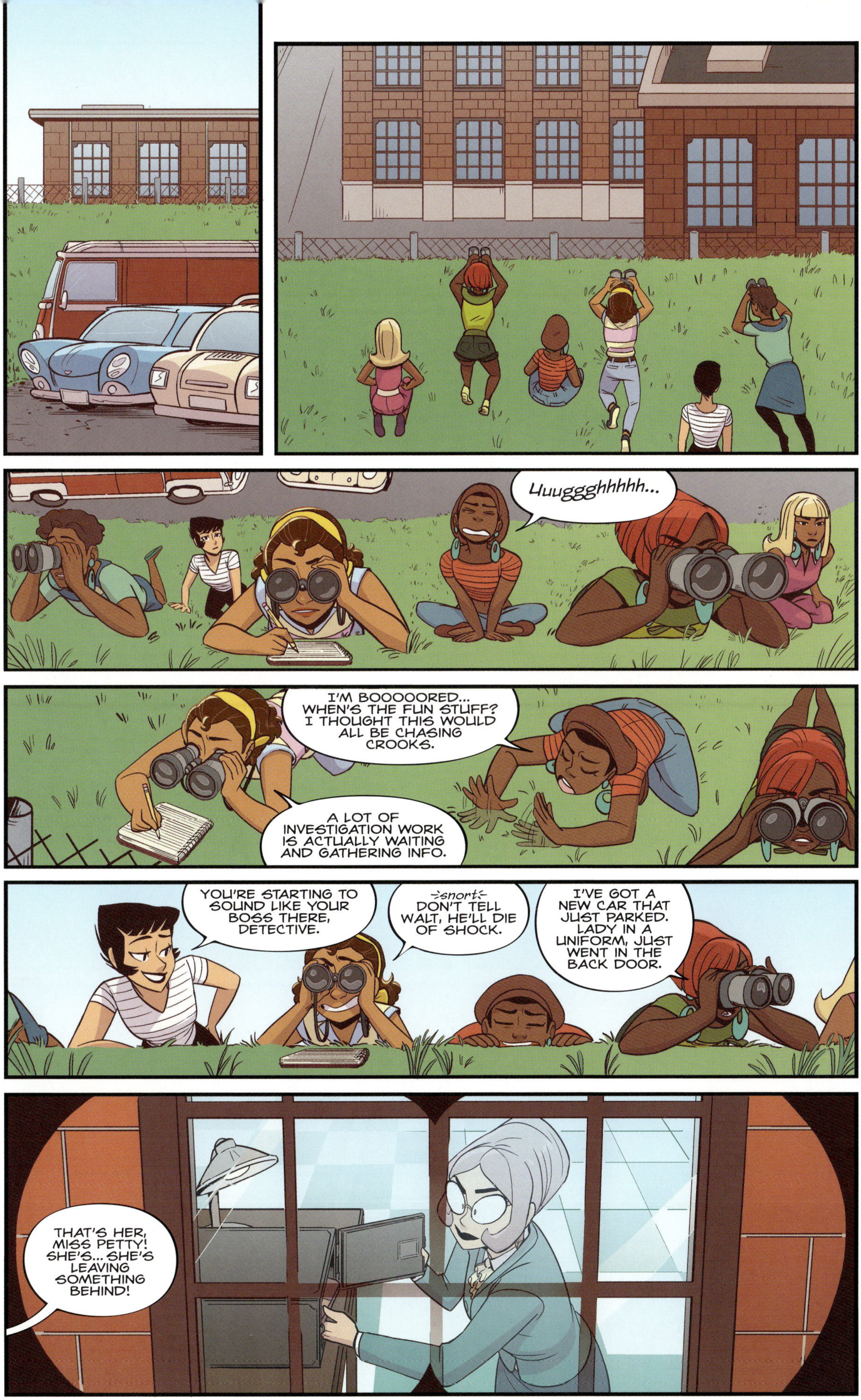
Uuuggghhhhh...
I'M BOOOOORED... WHEN'S THE FUN STUFF? I THOUGHT THIS WOULD ALL BE CHASING CROOKS.
A LOT OF INVESTIGATION WORK IS ACTUALLY WAITING AND GATHERING INFO.
YOU'RE STARTING TO SOUND LIKE YOUR BOSS THERE, DETECTIVE.
-snort- DON'T TELL WALT, HE'LL DIE OF SHOCK.
I'VE GOT A NEW CAR THAT JUST PARKED. LADY IN A UNIFORM, JUST WENT IN THE BACK DOOR.
THAT'S HER, MISS PETTY! SHE'S... SHE'S LEAVING SOMETHING BEHIND!

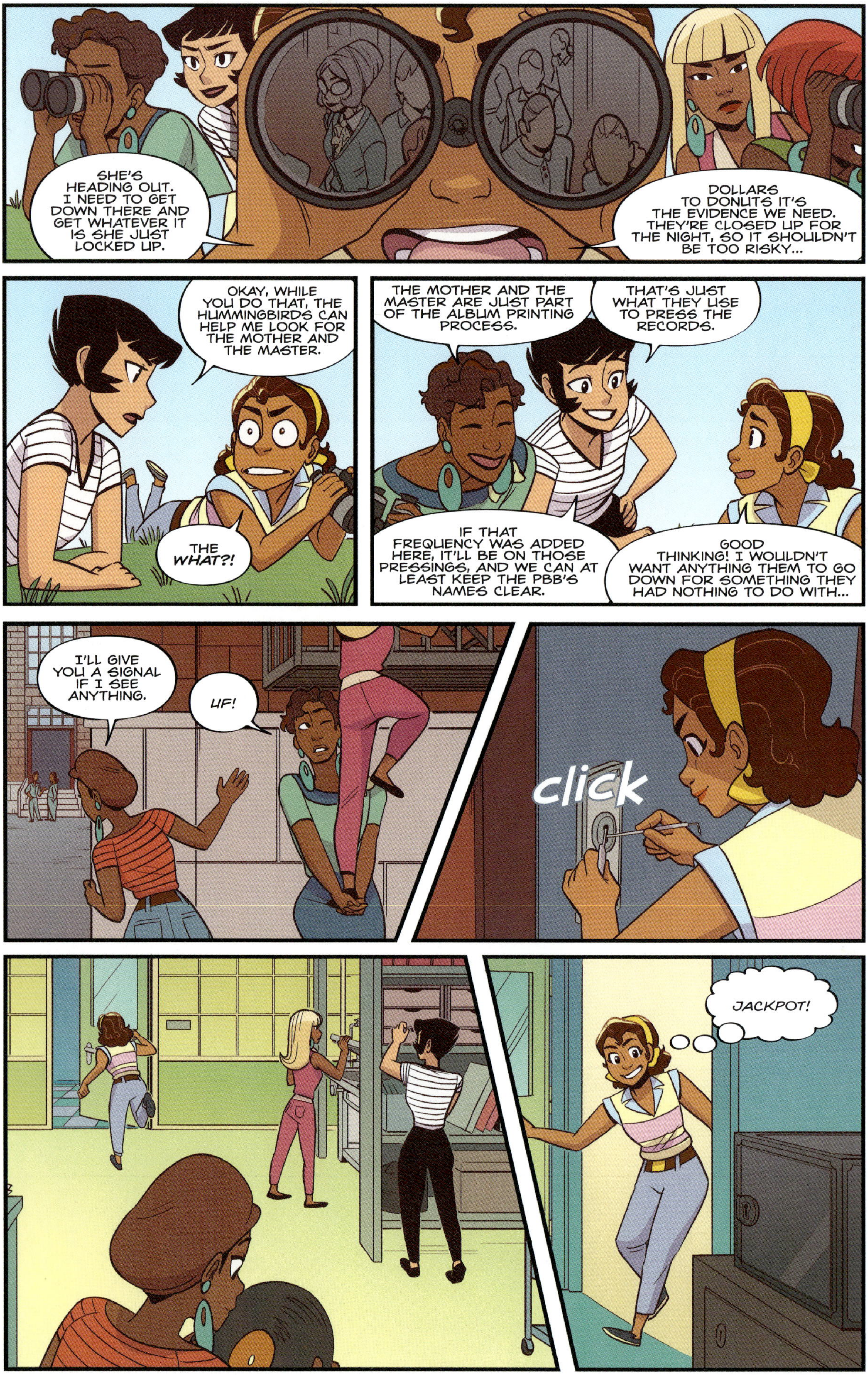
SHE'S HEADING OUT. I NEED TO GET DOWN THERE AND GET WHATEVER IT IS SHE JUST LOCKED UP.
DOLLARS TO DONUTS IT'S THE EVIDENCE WE NEED. THEY'RE CLOSED UP FOR THE NIGHT, SO IT SHOULDN'T BE TOO RISKY...
OKAY, WHILE YOU DO THAT, THE HUMMINGBIRDS CAN HELP ME LOOK FOR THE MOTHER AND THE MASTER.
THE *WHAT?!*
THE MOTHER AND THE MASTER ARE JUST PART OF THE ALBUM PRINTING PROCESS.
THAT'S JUST WHAT THEY USE TO PRESS THE RECORDS.
IF THAT FREQUENCY WAS ADDED HERE, IT'LL BE ON THOSE PRESSINGS, AND WE CAN AT LEAST KEEP THE PBB'S NAMES CLEAR.
GOOD THINKING! I WOULDN'T WANT ANYTHING THEM TO GO DOWN FOR SOMETHING THEY HAD NOTHING TO DO WITH...
I'LL GIVE YOU A SIGNAL IF I SEE ANYTHING.
UF!
click
JACKPOT!

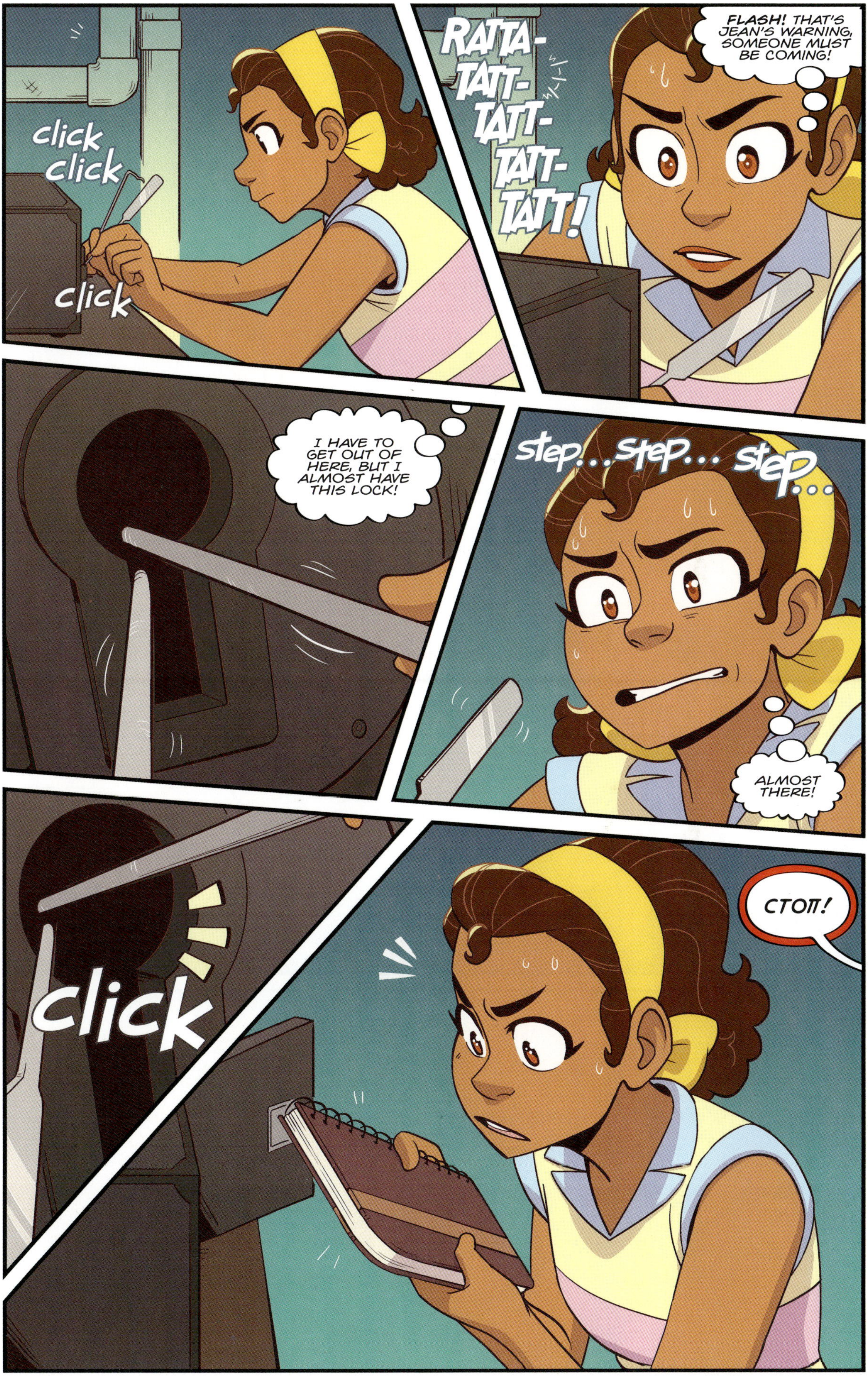
click click
click
RATTA-TATT-TATT-TATT-TATT!
FLASH! THAT'S JEAN'S WARNING, SOMEONE MUST BE COMING!
I HAVE TO GET OUT OF HERE, BUT I ALMOST HAVE THIS LOCK!
step... step... step...
ALMOST THERE!
click
СТОП!

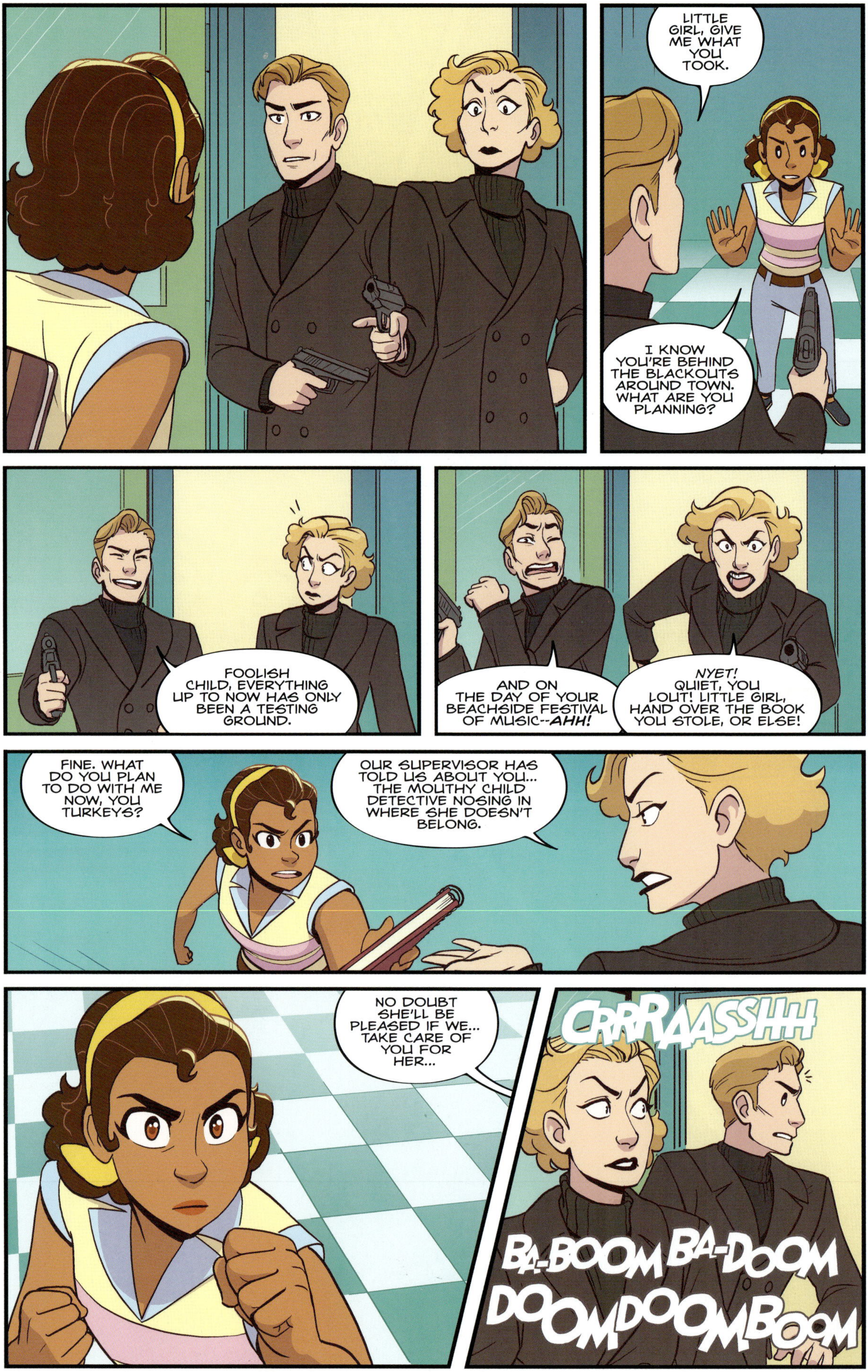
LITTLE GIRL, GIVE ME WHAT YOU TOOK.
I KNOW YOU'RE BEHIND THE BLACKOUTS AROUND TOWN. WHAT ARE YOU PLANNING?
FOOLISH CHILD, EVERYTHING UP TO NOW HAS ONLY BEEN A TESTING GROUND.
AND ON THE DAY OF YOUR BEACHSIDE FESTIVAL OF MUSIC--*AHH!*
*NYET!* QUIET, YOU LOUT! LITTLE GIRL, HAND OVER THE BOOK YOU STOLE, OR ELSE!
FINE. WHAT DO YOU PLAN TO DO WITH ME NOW, YOU TURKEYS?
OUR SUPERVISOR HAS TOLD US ABOUT YOU... THE MOUTHY CHILD DETECTIVE NOSING IN WHERE SHE DOESN'T BELONG.
NO DOUBT SHE'LL BE PLEASED IF WE... TAKE CARE OF YOU FOR HER...
CRRRAASSHHH
BA-BOOM BA-DOOM
DOOMDOOMBOOM

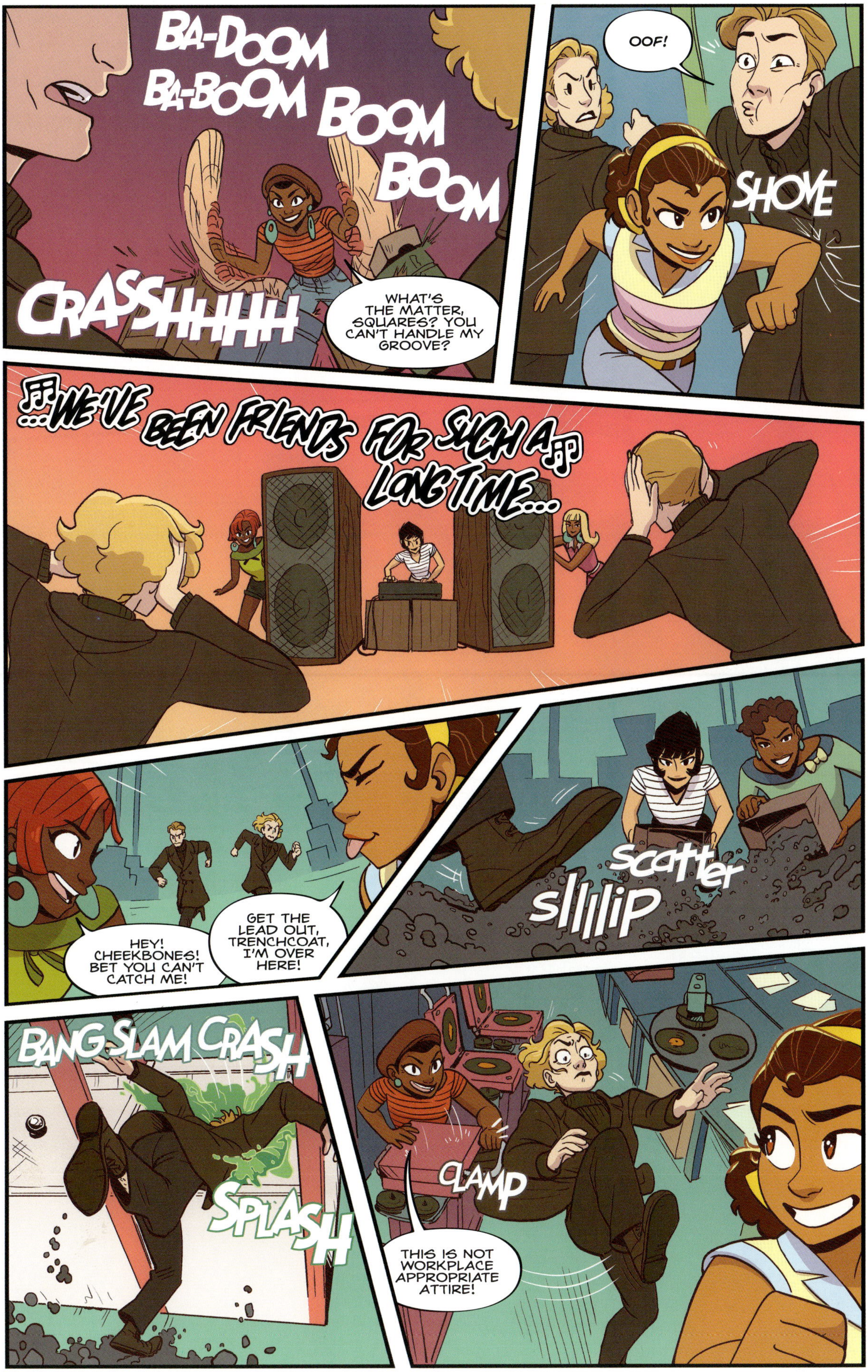
BA-DOOM
BA-BOOM BOOM
BOOM
CRASSHHHHH
WHAT'S THE MATTER, SQUARES? YOU CAN'T HANDLE MY GROOVE?
OOF!
SHOVE
...WE'VE BEEN FRIENDS FOR SUCH A LONG TIME...
HEY! CHEEKBONES! BET YOU CAN'T CATCH ME!
GET THE LEAD OUT, TRENCHCOAT, I'M OVER HERE!
scatter
sllllip
BANG SLAM CRASH
SPLASH
CLAMP
THIS IS NOT WORKPLACE APPROPRIATE ATTIRE!

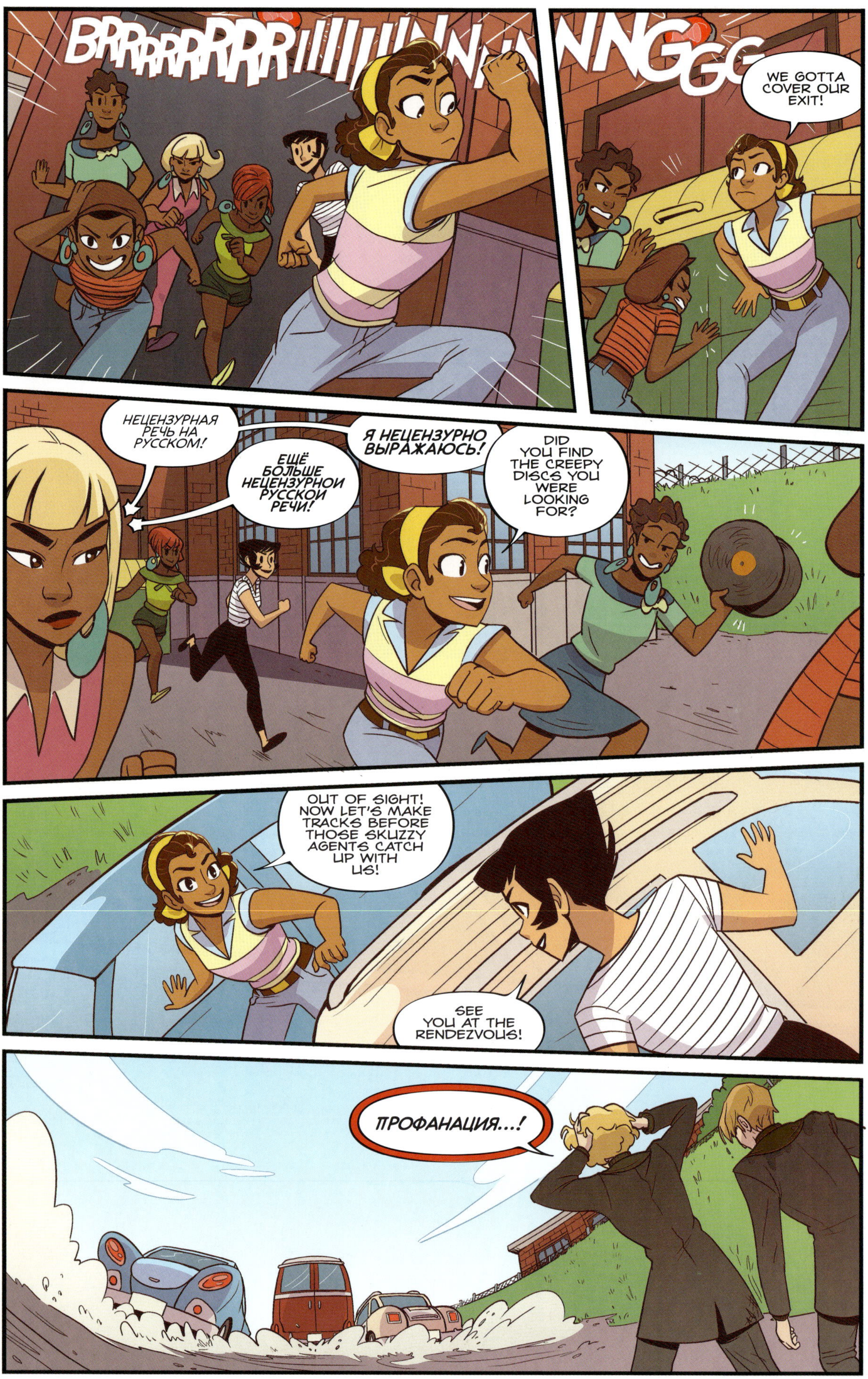
BRRRRRRRRIIIIIIIINNNNNGGG
WE GOTTA COVER OUR EXIT!
НЕЦЕНЗУРНАЯ РЕЧЬ НА РУССКОМ!
Я НЕЦЕНЗУРНО ВЫРАЖАЮСЬ!
ЕЩЁ БОЛЬШЕ НЕЦЕНЗУРНОИ РУССКОИ РЕЧИ!
DID YOU FIND THE CREEPY DISCS YOU WERE LOOKING FOR?
OUT OF SIGHT! NOW LET'S MAKE TRACKS BEFORE THOSE SKUZZY AGENTS CATCH UP WITH US!
SEE YOU AT THE RENDEZVOUS!
ПРОФАНАЦИЯ...!

DeepEN
GREAT WORK, TEAM!
THE MOTHER AND THE MASTER SHOULD BE THE EVIDENCE WE NEED TO KEEP THE PBBs IN THE CLEAR.
WELL, THAT'S ONE PROBLEM SOLVED. IT'S JUST TOO BAD YOU HAD TO GIVE UP THAT NOTEBOOK, GOLDIE!
OR, DID I?
I SWITCHED IT OUT FOR MY NOTES, THE NOTEBOOKS LOOK SO SIMILAR, THEY PROBABLY WON'T NOTICE FOR A BIT.
THAT'S NOT ALL. I MANAGED TO DECODE THE MESSAGE. THE SOVIETS ARE PLANNING A MASSIVE COMMUNICATIONS TEST AT THE FESTIVAL TOMORROW.
IF THEY SUCCEED, IT COULD CAUSE A MASSIVE BLACKOUT!
CHERYL, YOU ARE AN INCREDIBLE SCIENTIST, AND BEAUTIFUL FRIEND! CAN I OWE YOU ANOTHER FAVOR?
YES, BUT YOU'RE WALKING MY DOG FOR A MONTH AFTER THIS.
PERFECT. BRING MY DAD AND WALT TO THE MERMAID CLUB IN AN HOUR. I HAVE A NEW PLAN.
WHAT DO YOU SAY, YOU UP FOR A LITTLE MORE ESPIONAGE OF OUR OWN?
YOU KNOW YOU CAN COUNT ON US, TEEN DETECTIVE!
THERE'S NO WAY WE'RE LETTING SOMETHING STOP THE FESTIVAL, TOO MANY BANDS HAVE BEEN WORKING FOR TOO LONG...
DIANE, I NEED A SPECIAL FAVOR FROM YOU...

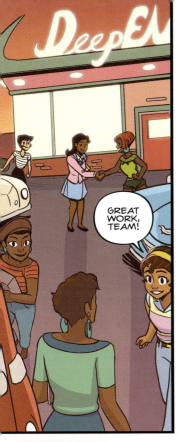

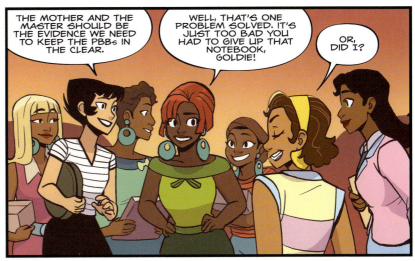

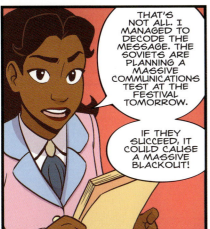

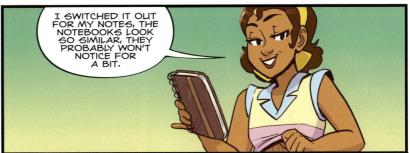

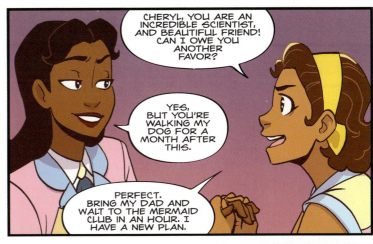

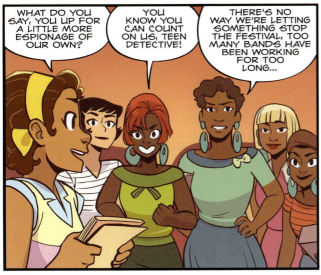

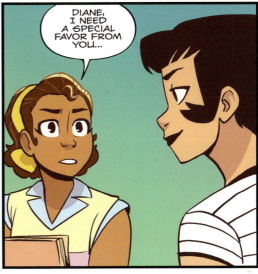

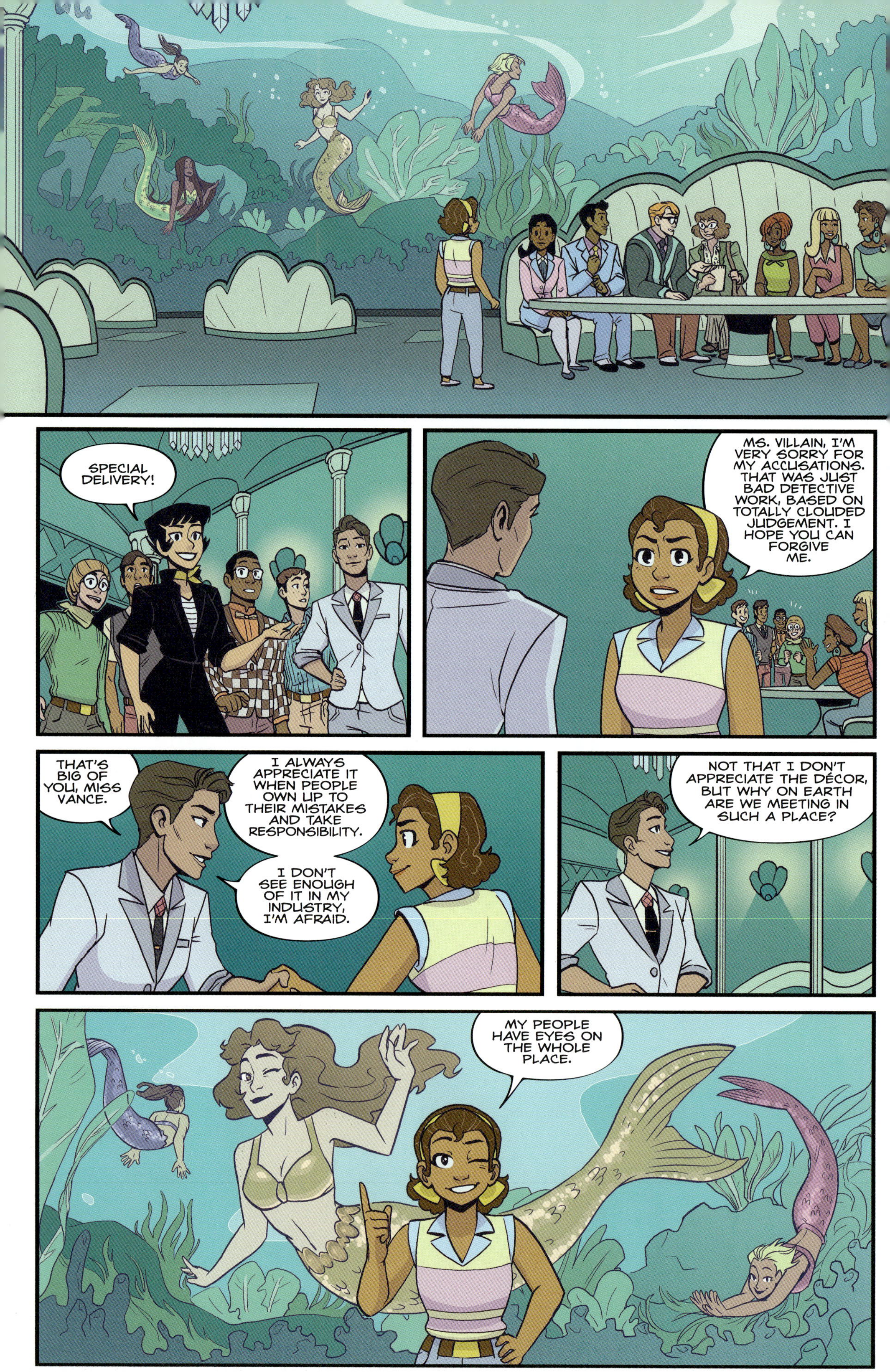
SPECIAL DELIVERY!
MS. VILLAIN, I'M VERY SORRY FOR MY ACCUSATIONS. THAT WAS JUST BAD DETECTIVE WORK, BASED ON TOTALLY CLOUDED JUDGEMENT. I HOPE YOU CAN FORGIVE ME.
THAT'S BIG OF YOU, MISS VANCE.
I ALWAYS APPRECIATE IT WHEN PEOPLE OWN UP TO THEIR MISTAKES AND TAKE RESPONSIBILITY.
I DON'T SEE ENOUGH OF IT IN MY INDUSTRY, I'M AFRAID.
NOT THAT I DON'T APPRECIATE THE DÉCOR, BUT WHY ON EARTH ARE WE MEETING IN SUCH A PLACE?
MY PEOPLE HAVE EYES ON THE WHOLE PLACE.

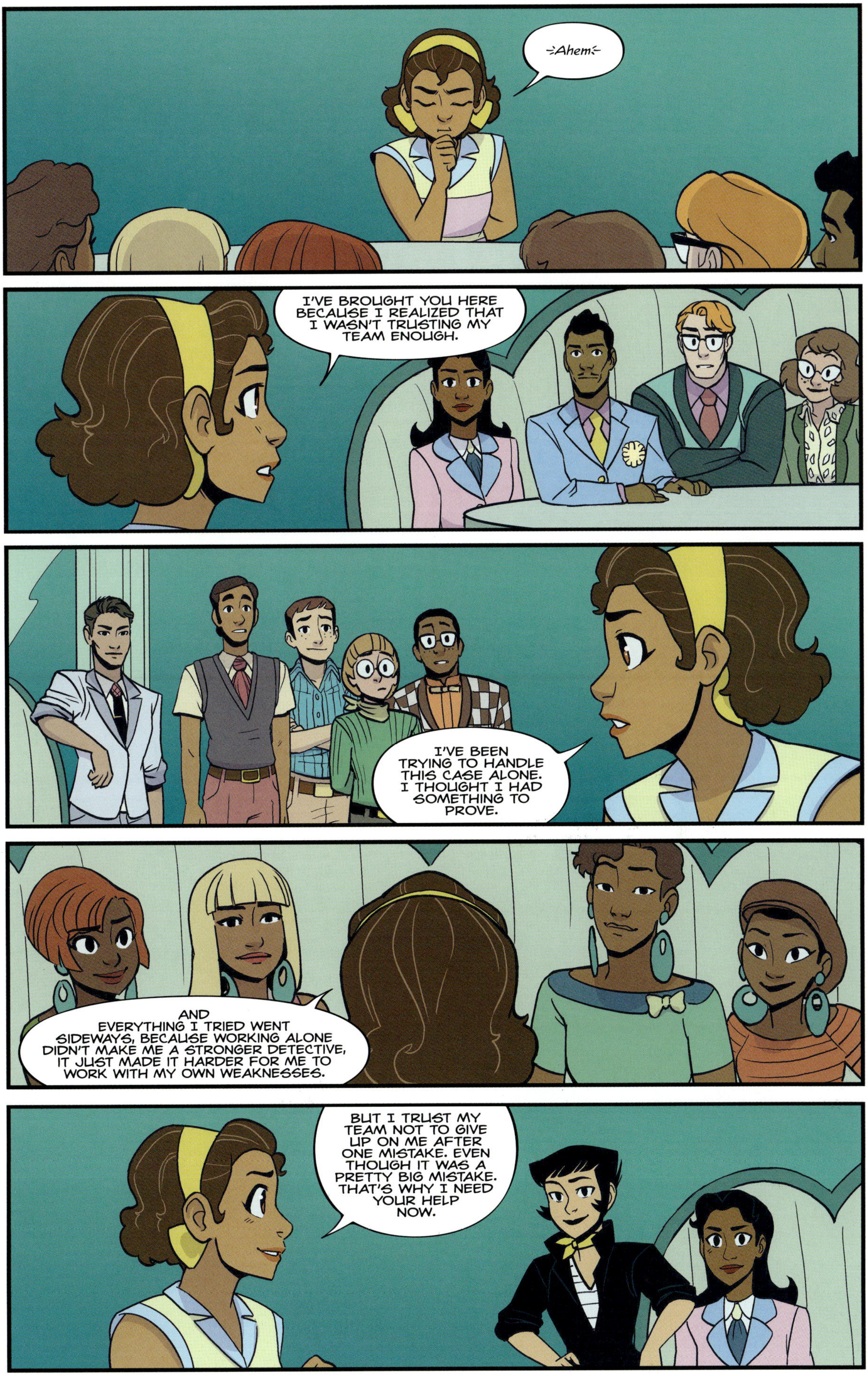

-Ahem-
I'VE BROUGHT YOU HERE BECAUSE I REALIZED THAT I WASN'T TRUSTING MY TEAM ENOUGH.
I'VE BEEN TRYING TO HANDLE THIS CASE ALONE. I THOUGHT I HAD SOMETHING TO PROVE.
AND EVERYTHING I TRIED WENT SIDEWAYS, BECAUSE WORKING ALONE DIDN'T MAKE ME A STRONGER DETECTIVE, IT JUST MADE IT HARDER FOR ME TO WORK WITH MY OWN WEAKNESSES.
BUT I TRUST MY TEAM NOT TO GIVE UP ON ME AFTER ONE MISTAKE. EVEN THOUGH IT WAS A PRETTY BIG MISTAKE. THAT'S WHY I NEED YOUR HELP NOW.

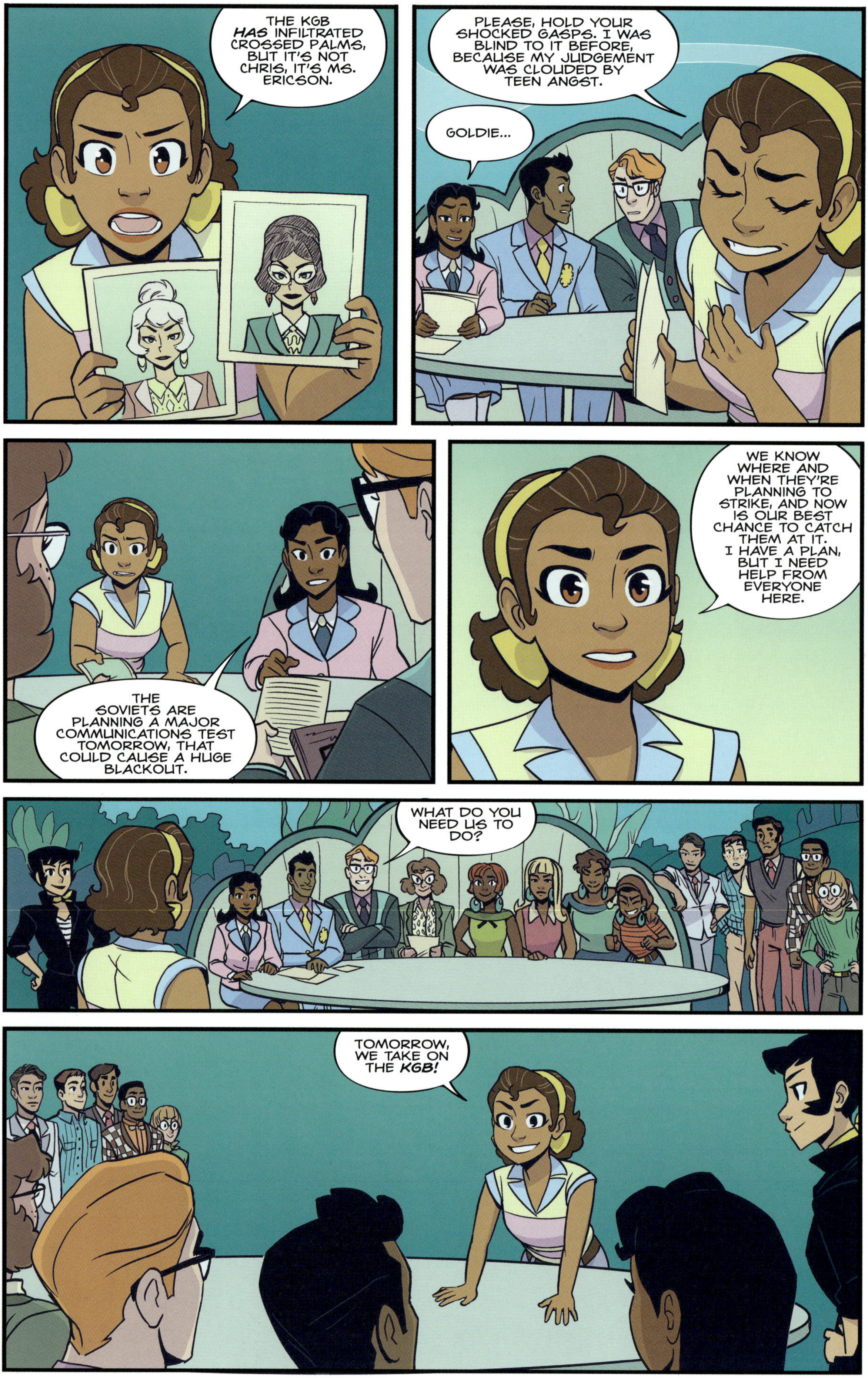
THE KGB *HAS* INFILTRATED CROSSED PALMS, BUT IT'S NOT CHRIS, IT'S MS. ERICSON.
PLEASE, HOLD YOUR SHOCKED GASPS. I WAS BLIND TO IT BEFORE, BECAUSE MY JUDGEMENT WAS CLOUDED BY TEEN ANGST.
GOLDIE...
THE SOVIETS ARE PLANNING A MAJOR COMMUNICATIONS TEST TOMORROW, THAT COULD CAUSE A HUGE BLACKOUT.
WE KNOW WHERE AND WHEN THEY'RE PLANNING TO STRIKE, AND NOW IS OUR BEST CHANCE TO CATCH THEM AT IT. I HAVE A PLAN, BUT I NEED HELP FROM EVERYONE HERE.
WHAT DO YOU NEED US TO DO?
TOMORROW, WE TAKE ON THE *KGB!*

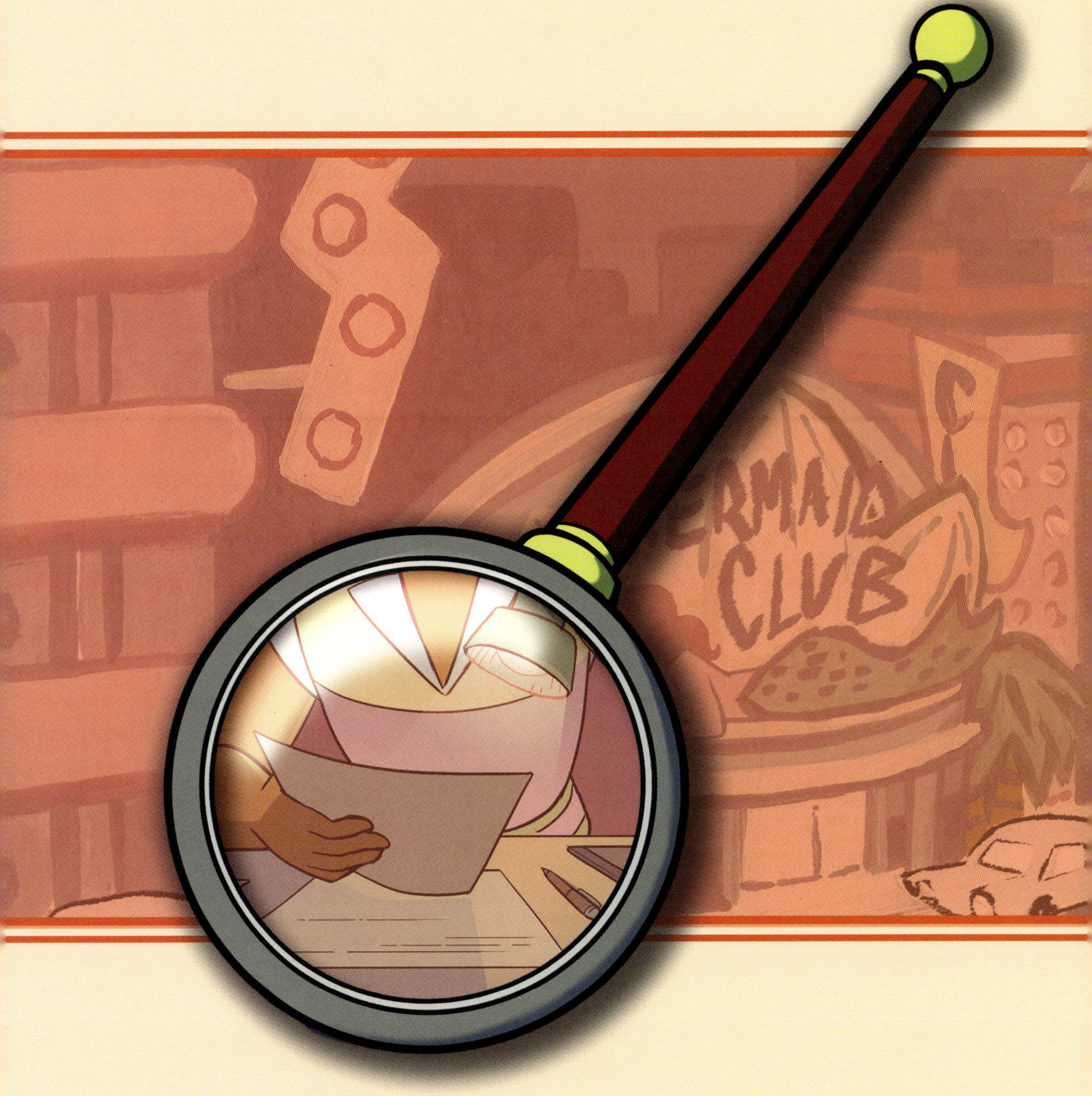
ERMAID
CLUB

chapter

# SIXTEEN

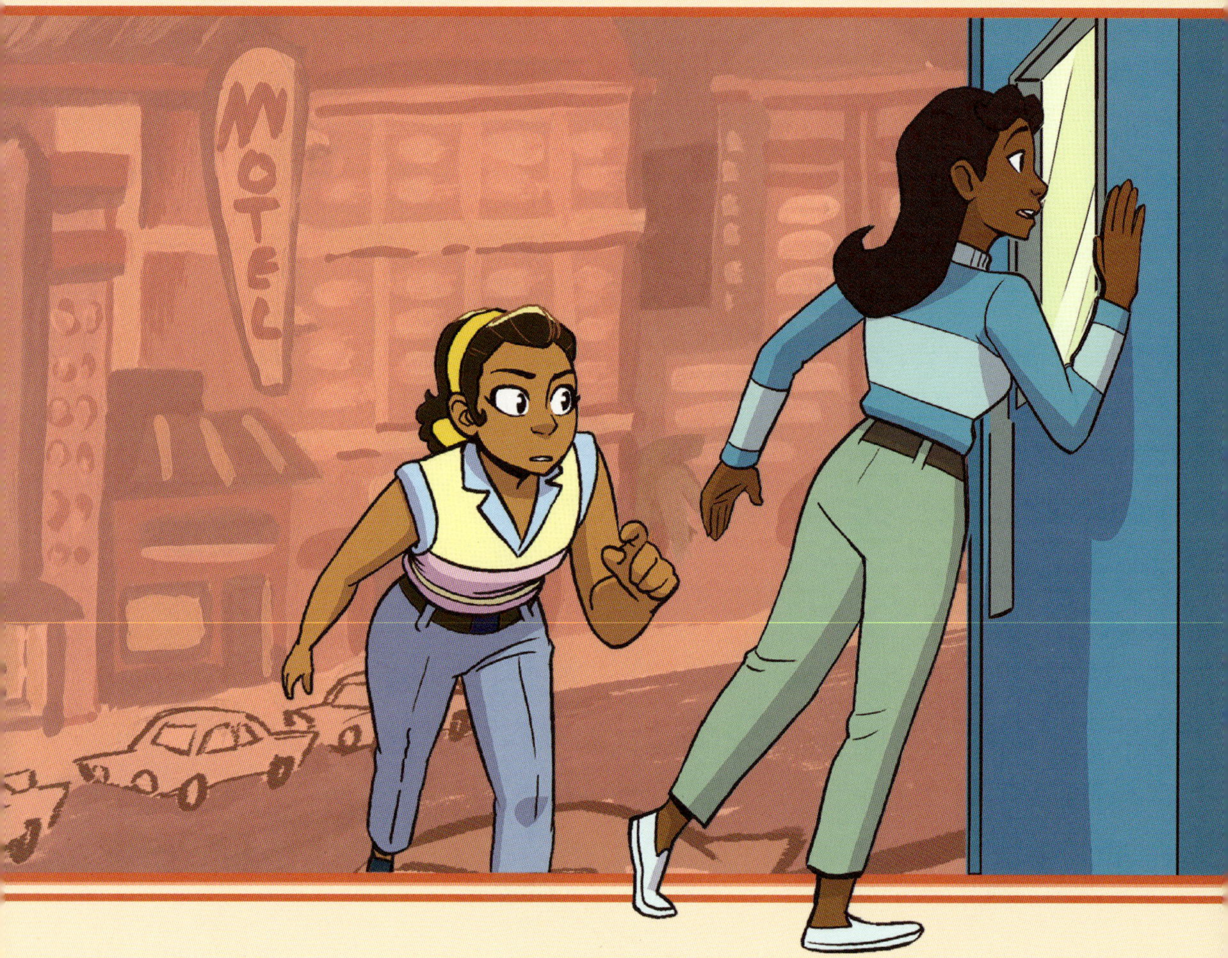
MOTEL

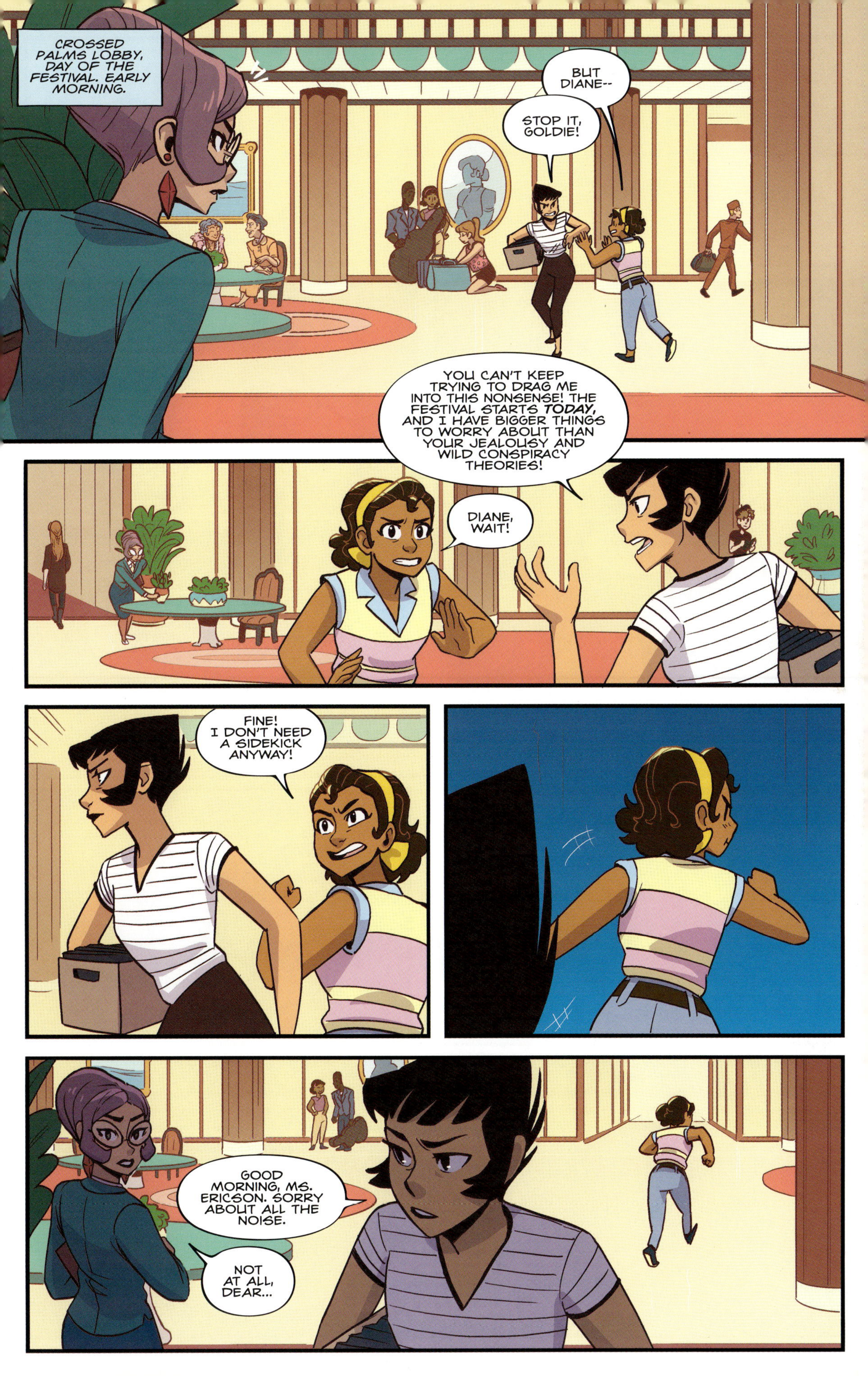
CROSSED PALMS LOBBY, DAY OF THE FESTIVAL. EARLY MORNING.
BUT DIANE--
STOP IT, GOLDIE!
YOU CAN'T KEEP TRYING TO DRAG ME INTO THIS NONSENSE! THE FESTIVAL STARTS TODAY, AND I HAVE BIGGER THINGS TO WORRY ABOUT THAN YOUR JEALOUSY AND WILD CONSPIRACY THEORIES!
DIANE, WAIT!
FINE! I DON'T NEED A SIDEKICK ANYWAY!
GOOD MORNING, MS. ERICSON. SORRY ABOUT ALL THE NOISE.
NOT AT ALL, DEAR...

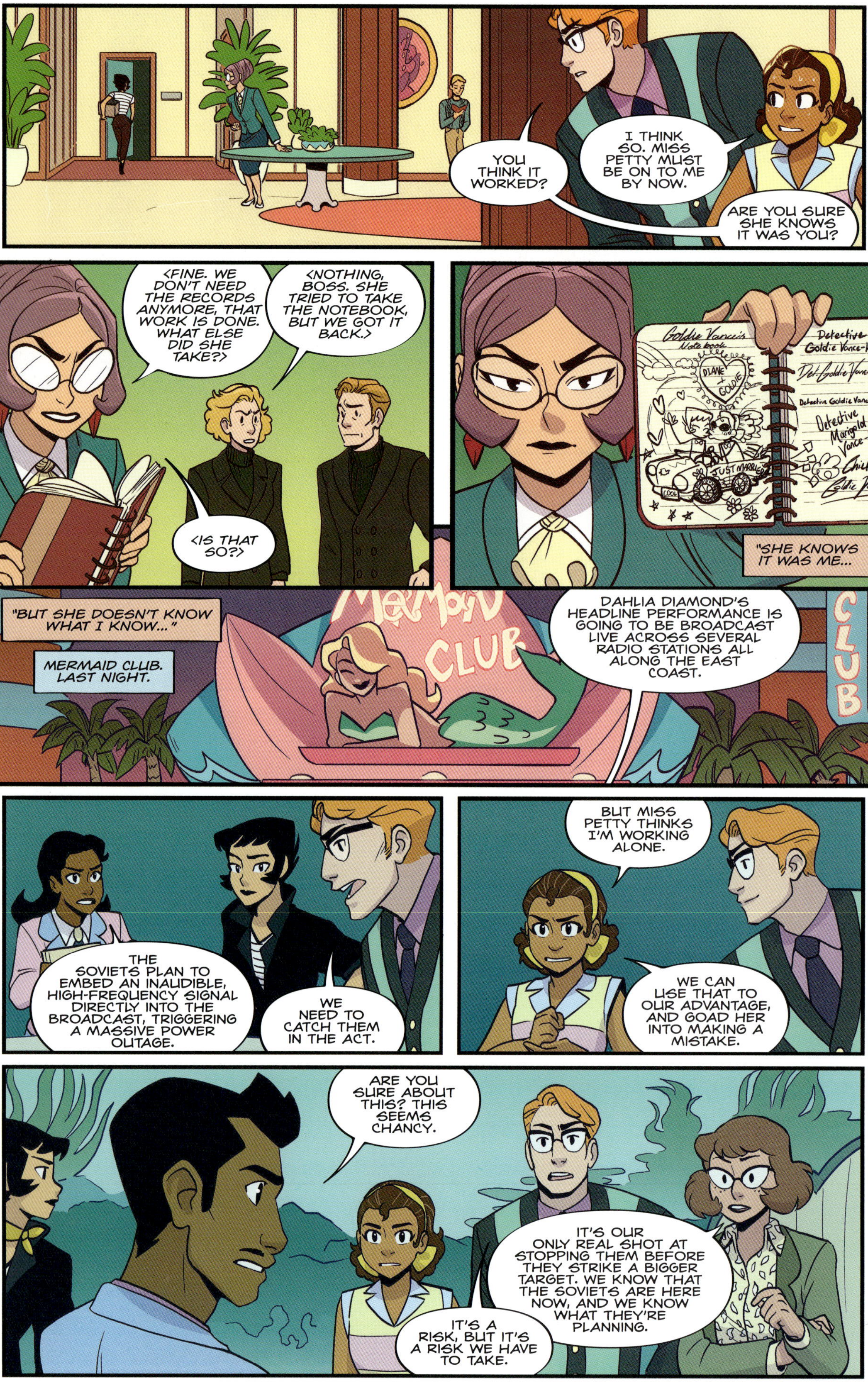

YOU THINK IT WORKED?
I THINK SO. MISS PETTY MUST BE ON TO ME BY NOW.
ARE YOU SURE SHE KNOWS IT WAS YOU?
<FINE. WE DON'T NEED THE RECORDS ANYMORE, THAT WORK IS DONE. WHAT ELSE DID SHE TAKE?>
<NOTHING, BOSS. SHE TRIED TO TAKE THE NOTEBOOK, BUT WE GOT IT BACK.>
<IS THAT SO?>
Goldie Vance's Note book
DIANE
GOLDIE
JUST MARRIED
"SHE KNOWS IT WAS ME...
"BUT SHE DOESN'T KNOW WHAT I KNOW..."
MERMAID CLUB. LAST NIGHT.
MERMAID CLUB
CLUB
DAHLIA DIAMOND'S HEADLINE PERFORMANCE IS GOING TO BE BROADCAST LIVE ACROSS SEVERAL RADIO STATIONS ALL ALONG THE EAST COAST.
THE SOVIETS PLAN TO EMBED AN INAUDIBLE, HIGH-FREQUENCY SIGNAL DIRECTLY INTO THE BROADCAST, TRIGGERING A MASSIVE POWER OUTAGE.
WE NEED TO CATCH THEM IN THE ACT.
BUT MISS PETTY THINKS I'M WORKING ALONE.
WE CAN USE THAT TO OUR ADVANTAGE, AND GOAD HER INTO MAKING A MISTAKE.
ARE YOU SURE ABOUT THIS? THIS SEEMS CHANCY.
IT'S OUR ONLY REAL SHOT AT STOPPING THEM BEFORE THEY STRIKE A BIGGER TARGET. WE KNOW THAT THE SOVIETS ARE HERE NOW, AND WE KNOW WHAT THEY'RE PLANNING.
IT'S A RISK, BUT IT'S A RISK WE HAVE TO TAKE.

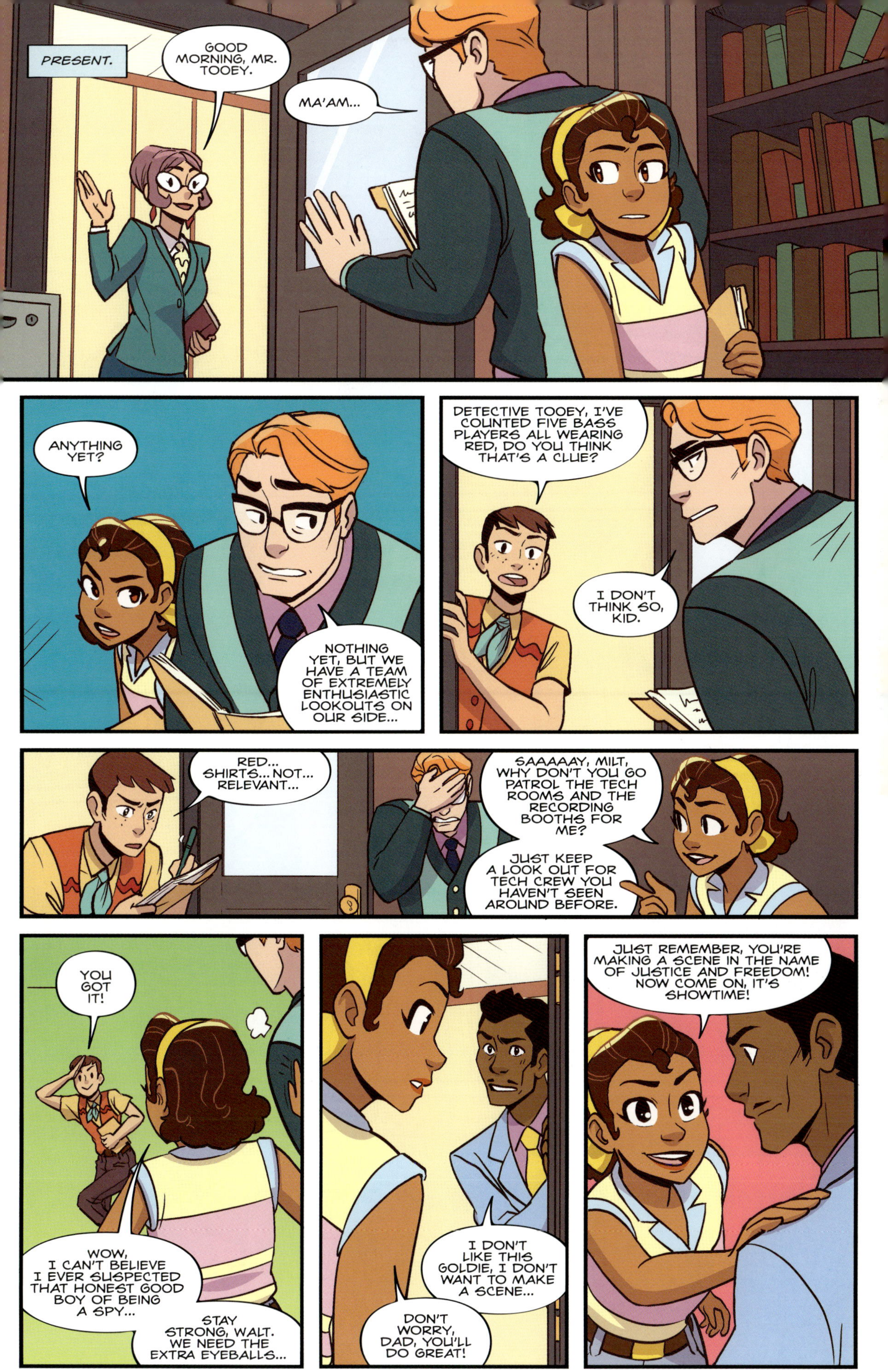
PRESENT.
GOOD MORNING, MR. TOOEY.
MA'AM...
ANYTHING YET?
NOTHING YET, BUT WE HAVE A TEAM OF EXTREMELY ENTHUSIASTIC LOOKOUTS ON OUR SIDE...
DETECTIVE TOOEY, I'VE COUNTED FIVE BASS PLAYERS ALL WEARING RED, DO YOU THINK THAT'S A CLUE?
I DON'T THINK SO, KID.
RED... SHIRTS... NOT... RELEVANT...
SAAAAAY, MILT, WHY DON'T YOU GO PATROL THE TECH ROOMS AND THE RECORDING BOOTHS FOR ME?
JUST KEEP A LOOK OUT FOR TECH CREW YOU HAVEN'T SEEN AROUND BEFORE.
YOU GOT IT!
WOW, I CAN'T BELIEVE I EVER SUSPECTED THAT HONEST GOOD BOY OF BEING A SPY...
STAY STRONG, WALT. WE NEED THE EXTRA EYEBALLS...
I DON'T LIKE THIS GOLDIE, I DON'T WANT TO MAKE A SCENE...
DON'T WORRY, DAD, YOU'LL DO GREAT!
JUST REMEMBER, YOU'RE MAKING A SCENE IN THE NAME OF JUSTICE AND FREEDOM! NOW COME ON, IT'S SHOWTIME!

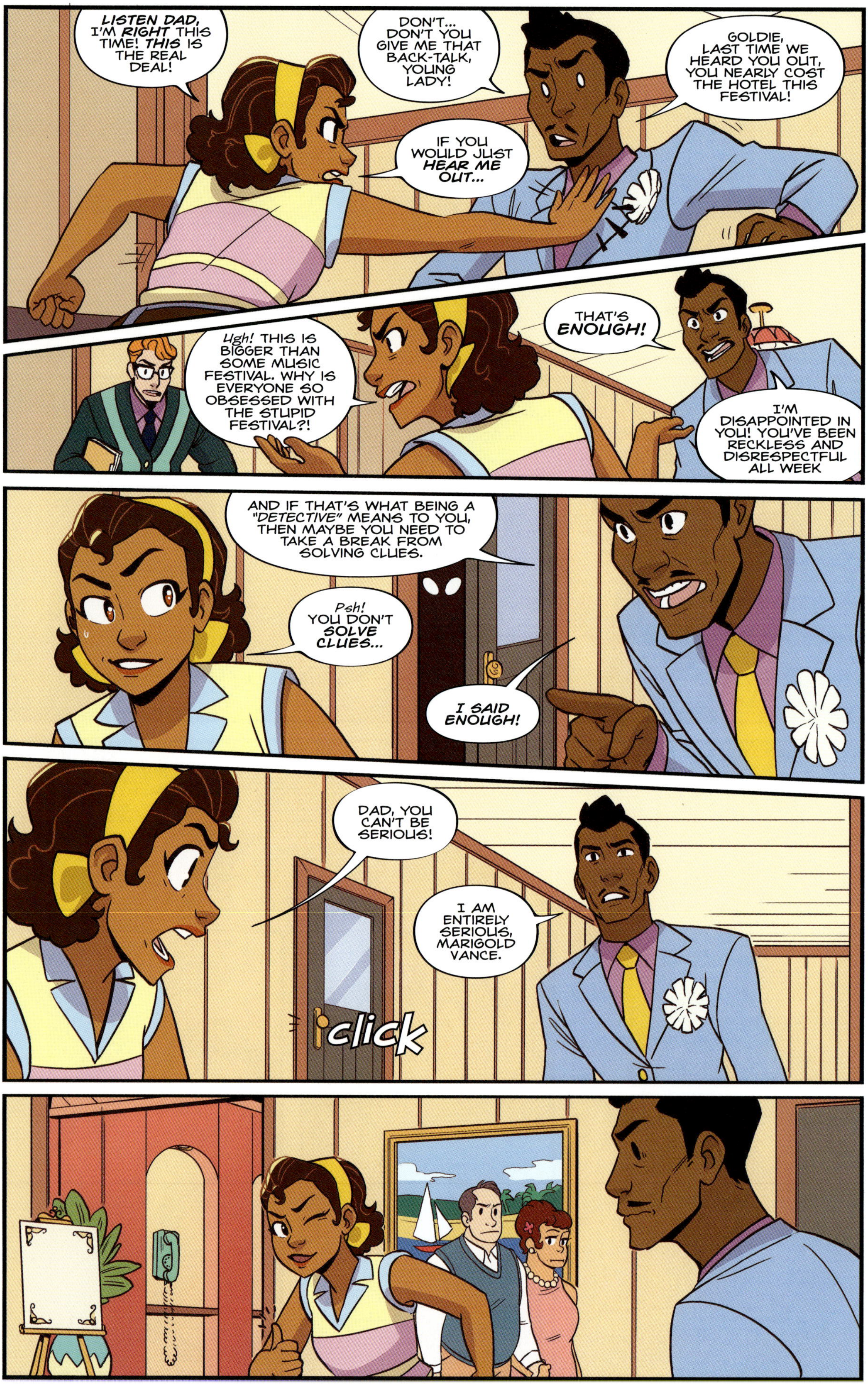
LISTEN DAD, I'M RIGHT THIS TIME! THIS IS THE REAL DEAL!
DON'T... DON'T YOU GIVE ME THAT BACK-TALK, YOUNG LADY!
IF YOU WOULD JUST HEAR ME OUT...
GOLDIE, LAST TIME WE HEARD YOU OUT, YOU NEARLY COST THE HOTEL THIS FESTIVAL!
Ugh! THIS IS BIGGER THAN SOME MUSIC FESTIVAL. WHY IS EVERYONE SO OBSESSED WITH THE STUPID FESTIVAL?!
THAT'S ENOUGH!
I'M DISAPPOINTED IN YOU! YOU'VE BEEN RECKLESS AND DISRESPECTFUL ALL WEEK
AND IF THAT'S WHAT BEING A "DETECTIVE" MEANS TO YOU, THEN MAYBE YOU NEED TO TAKE A BREAK FROM SOLVING CLUES.
Psh! YOU DON'T SOLVE CLUES...
I SAID ENOUGH!
DAD, YOU CAN'T BE SERIOUS!
I AM ENTIRELY SERIOUS, MARIGOLD VANCE.
click

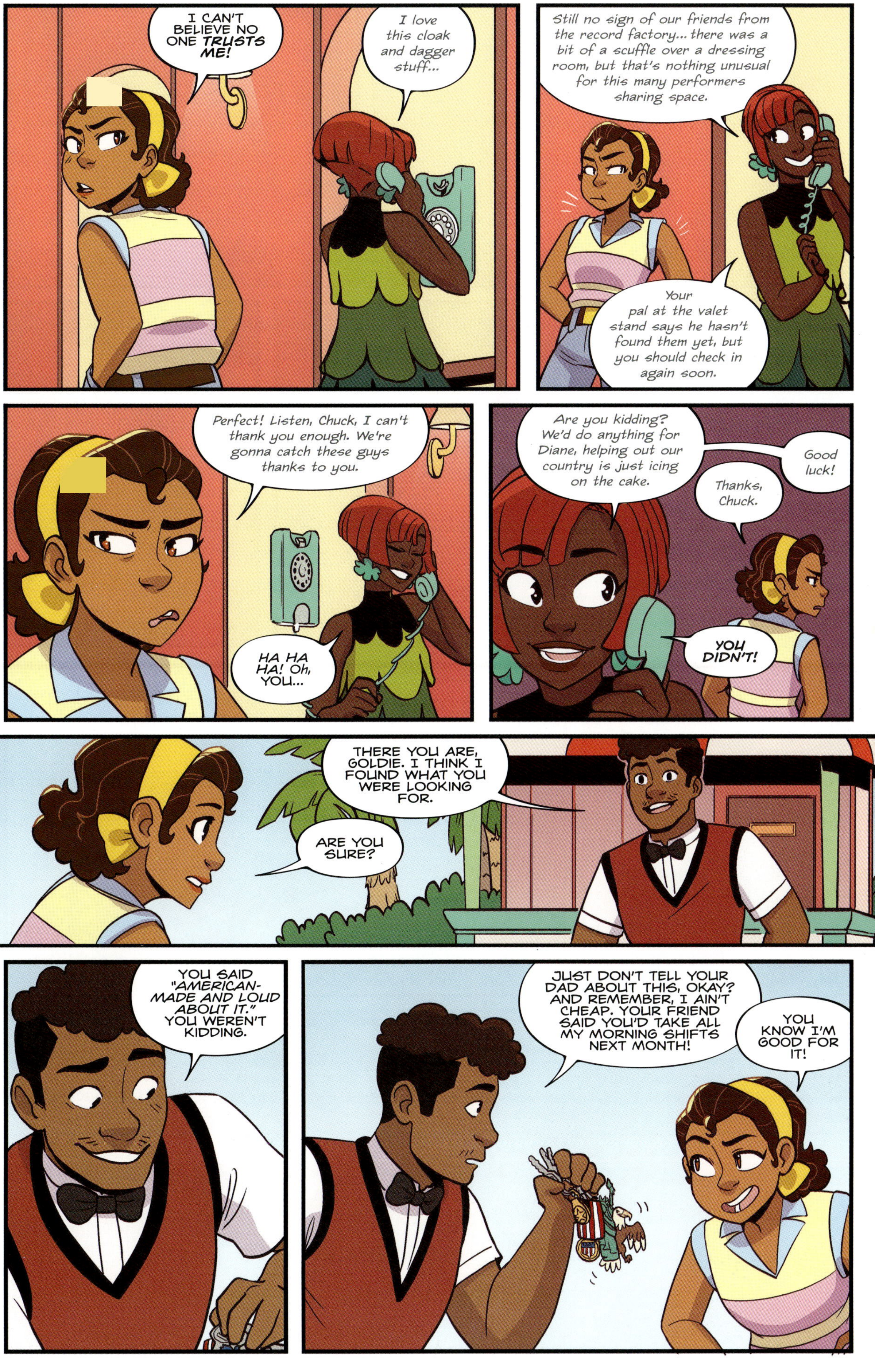
I CAN'T BELIEVE NO ONE TRUSTS ME!
I love this cloak and dagger stuff...
Still no sign of our friends from the record factory... there was a bit of a scuffle over a dressing room, but that's nothing unusual for this many performers sharing space.
Your pal at the valet stand says he hasn't found them yet, but you should check in again soon.
Perfect! Listen, Chuck, I can't thank you enough. We're gonna catch these guys thanks to you.
HA HA HA! Oh, YOU...
Are you kidding? We'd do anything for Diane, helping out our country is just icing on the cake.
Thanks, Chuck.
Good luck!
YOU DIDN'T!
THERE YOU ARE, GOLDIE. I THINK I FOUND WHAT YOU WERE LOOKING FOR.
ARE YOU SURE?
YOU SAID "AMERICAN-MADE AND LOUD ABOUT IT." YOU WEREN'T KIDDING.
JUST DON'T TELL YOUR DAD ABOUT THIS, OKAY? AND REMEMBER, I AIN'T CHEAP. YOUR FRIEND SAID YOU'D TAKE ALL MY MORNING SHIFTS NEXT MONTH!
YOU KNOW I'M GOOD FOR IT!

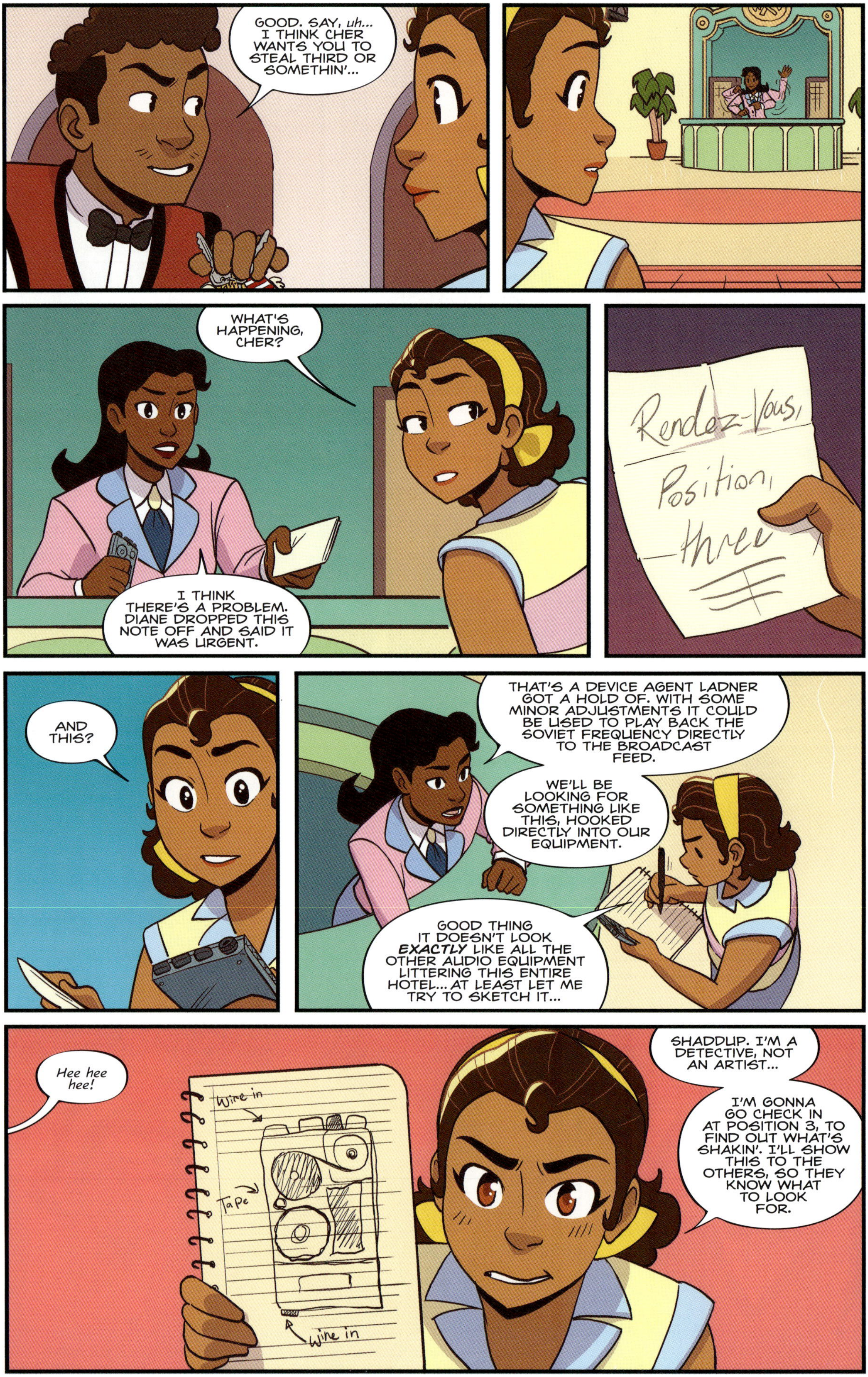

GOOD. SAY, uh... I THINK CHER WANTS YOU TO STEAL THIRD OR SOMETHIN'...
WHAT'S HAPPENING, CHER?
I THINK THERE'S A PROBLEM. DIANE DROPPED THIS NOTE OFF AND SAID IT WAS URGENT.
Rendez-Vous, Position, three
AND THIS?
THAT'S A DEVICE AGENT LADNER GOT A HOLD OF. WITH SOME MINOR ADJUSTMENTS IT COULD BE USED TO PLAY BACK THE SOVIET FREQUENCY DIRECTLY TO THE BROADCAST FEED.
WE'LL BE LOOKING FOR SOMETHING LIKE THIS, HOOKED DIRECTLY INTO OUR EQUIPMENT.
GOOD THING IT DOESN'T LOOK EXACTLY LIKE ALL THE OTHER AUDIO EQUIPMENT LITTERING THIS ENTIRE HOTEL... AT LEAST LET ME TRY TO SKETCH IT...
Hee hee hee!
Wire in
Tape
Wire in
SHADDUP. I'M A DETECTIVE, NOT AN ARTIST...
I'M GONNA GO CHECK IN AT POSITION 3, TO FIND OUT WHAT'S SHAKIN'. I'LL SHOW THIS TO THE OTHERS, SO THEY KNOW WHAT TO LOOK FOR.

♫♪♪♪♫

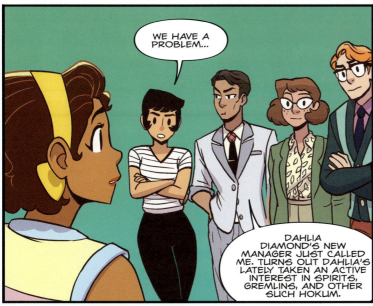

WE HAVE A PROBLEM...

APPARENTLY, SHE'S HEARD SOME RUMORS THAT THIS FESTIVAL IS CURSED.

SHE'S REFUSING TO PERFORM.

DAHLIA DIAMOND'S NEW MANAGER JUST CALLED ME. TURNS OUT DAHLIA'S LATELY TAKEN AN ACTIVE INTEREST IN SPIRITS, GREMLINS, AND OTHER SUCH HOKUM.

THIS IS BAD...

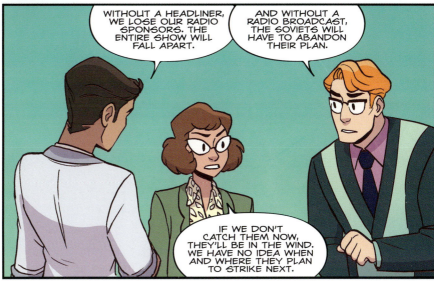

WITHOUT A HEADLINER, WE LOSE OUR RADIO SPONSORS. THE ENTIRE SHOW WILL FALL APART.

AND WITHOUT A RADIO BROADCAST, THE SOVIETS WILL HAVE TO ABANDON THEIR PLAN.

IF WE DON'T CATCH THEM NOW, THEY'LL BE IN THE WIND. WE HAVE NO IDEA WHEN AND WHERE THEY PLAN TO STRIKE NEXT.

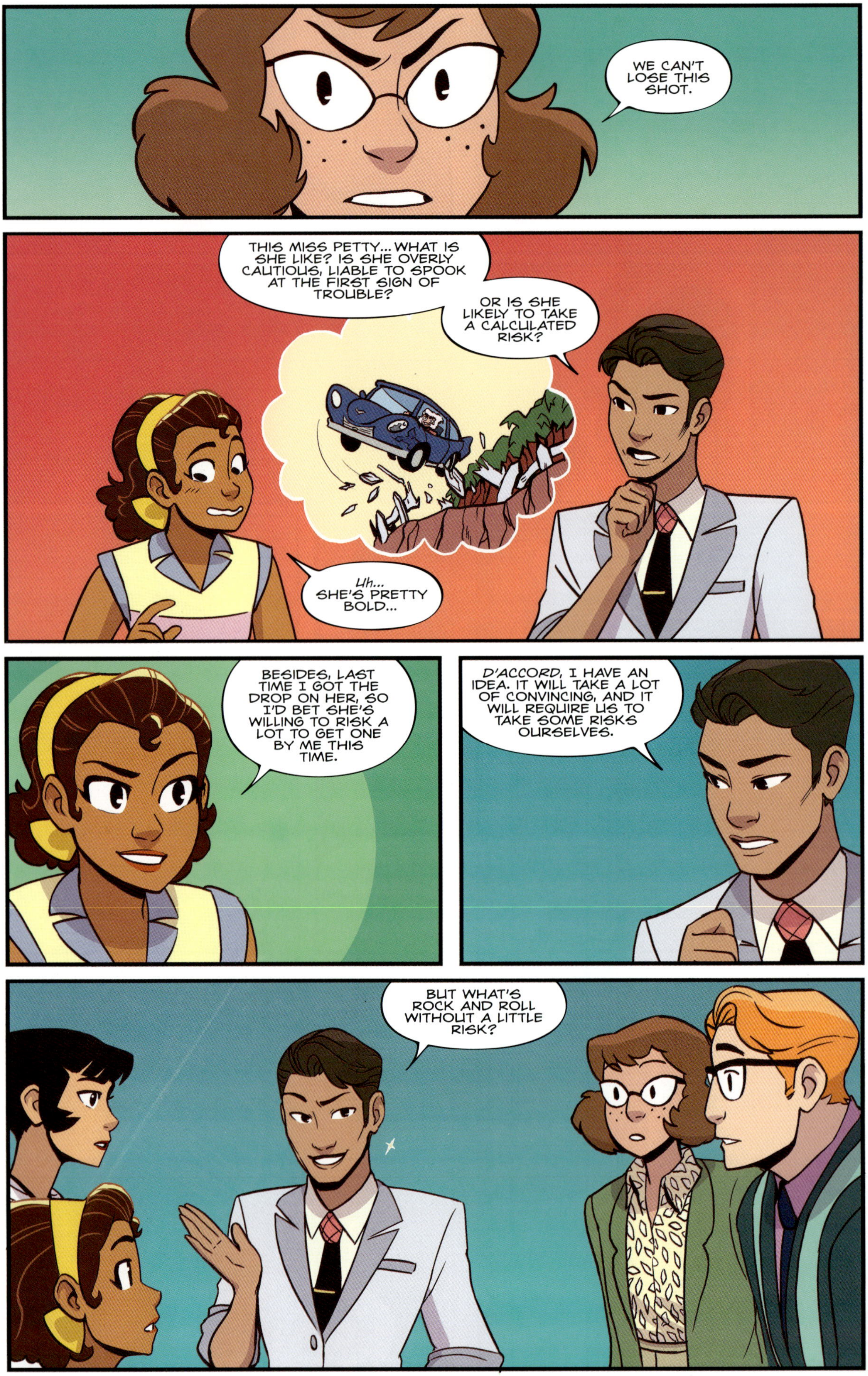
WE CAN'T LOSE THIS SHOT.
THIS MISS PETTY... WHAT IS SHE LIKE? IS SHE OVERLY CAUTIOUS, LIABLE TO SPOOK AT THE FIRST SIGN OF TROUBLE?
OR IS SHE LIKELY TO TAKE A CALCULATED RISK?
Uh... SHE'S PRETTY BOLD...
BESIDES, LAST TIME I GOT THE DROP ON HER, SO I'D BET SHE'S WILLING TO RISK A LOT TO GET ONE BY ME THIS TIME.
D'ACCORD, I HAVE AN IDEA. IT WILL TAKE A LOT OF CONVINCING, AND IT WILL REQUIRE US TO TAKE SOME RISKS OURSELVES.
BUT WHAT'S ROCK AND ROLL WITHOUT A LITTLE RISK?

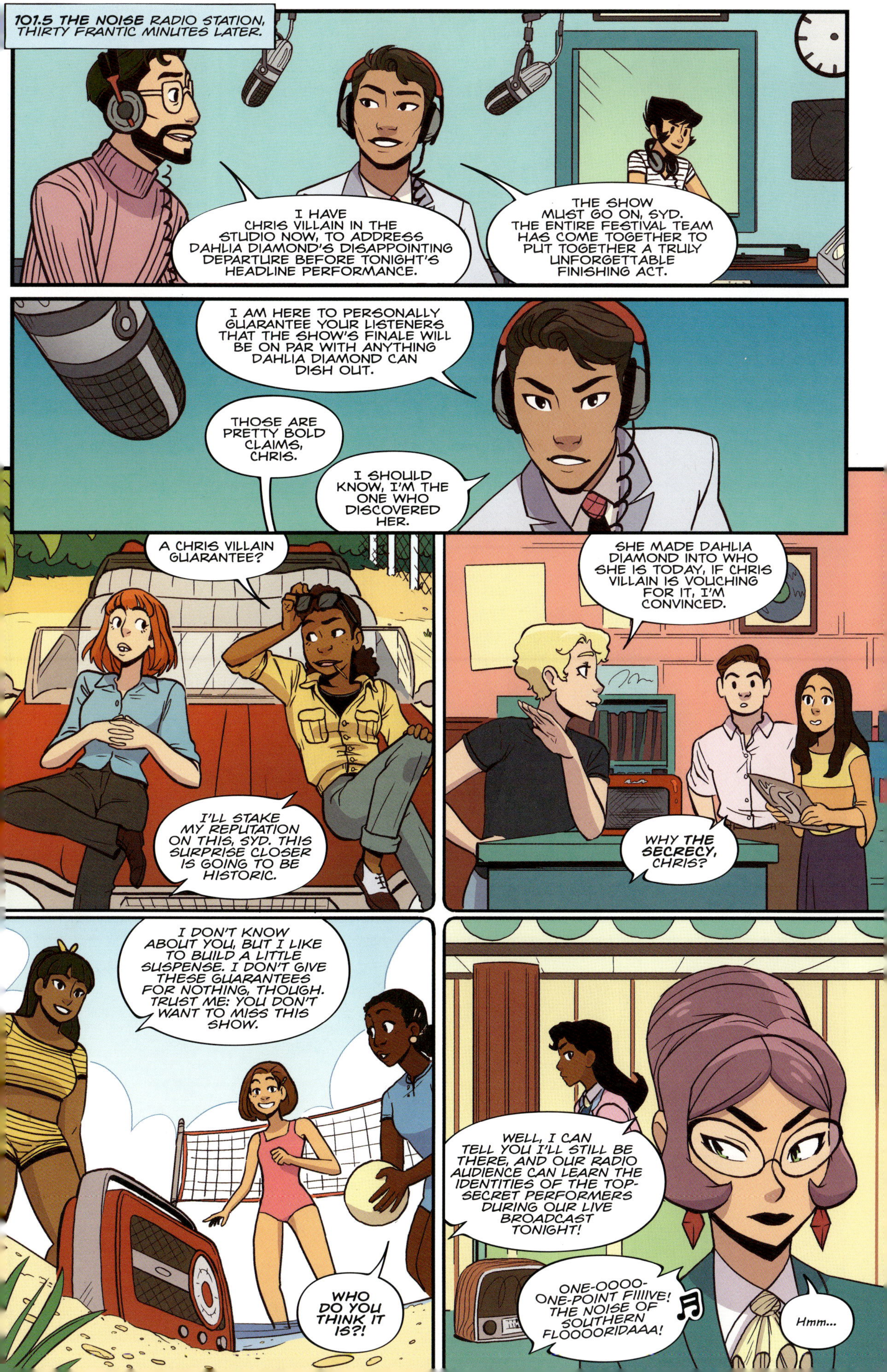

101.5 THE NOISE RADIO STATION, THIRTY FRANTIC MINUTES LATER.
I HAVE CHRIS VILLAIN IN THE STUDIO NOW, TO ADDRESS DAHLIA DIAMOND'S DISAPPOINTING DEPARTURE BEFORE TONIGHT'S HEADLINE PERFORMANCE.
THE SHOW MUST GO ON, SYD. THE ENTIRE FESTIVAL TEAM HAS COME TOGETHER TO PUT TOGETHER A TRULY UNFORGETTABLE FINISHING ACT.
I AM HERE TO PERSONALLY GUARANTEE YOUR LISTENERS THAT THE SHOW'S FINALE WILL BE ON PAR WITH ANYTHING DAHLIA DIAMOND CAN DISH OUT.
THOSE ARE PRETTY BOLD CLAIMS, CHRIS.
I SHOULD KNOW, I'M THE ONE WHO DISCOVERED HER.
A CHRIS VILLAIN GUARANTEE?
I'LL STAKE MY REPUTATION ON THIS, SYD. THIS SURPRISE CLOSER IS GOING TO BE HISTORIC.
SHE MADE DAHLIA DIAMOND INTO WHO SHE IS TODAY. IF CHRIS VILLAIN IS VOUCHING FOR IT, I'M CONVINCED.
WHY THE SECRECY, CHRIS?
I DON'T KNOW ABOUT YOU, BUT I LIKE TO BUILD A LITTLE SUSPENSE. I DON'T GIVE THESE GUARANTEES FOR NOTHING, THOUGH. TRUST ME: YOU DON'T WANT TO MISS THIS SHOW.
WHO DO YOU THINK IT IS?!
WELL, I CAN TELL YOU I'LL STILL BE THERE, AND OUR RADIO AUDIENCE CAN LEARN THE IDENTITIES OF THE TOP-SECRET PERFORMERS DURING OUR LIVE BROADCAST TONIGHT!
ONE-OOOO-ONE-POINT FIIIIVE! THE NOISE OF SOUTHERN FLOOOORIDAAA!
Hmm...

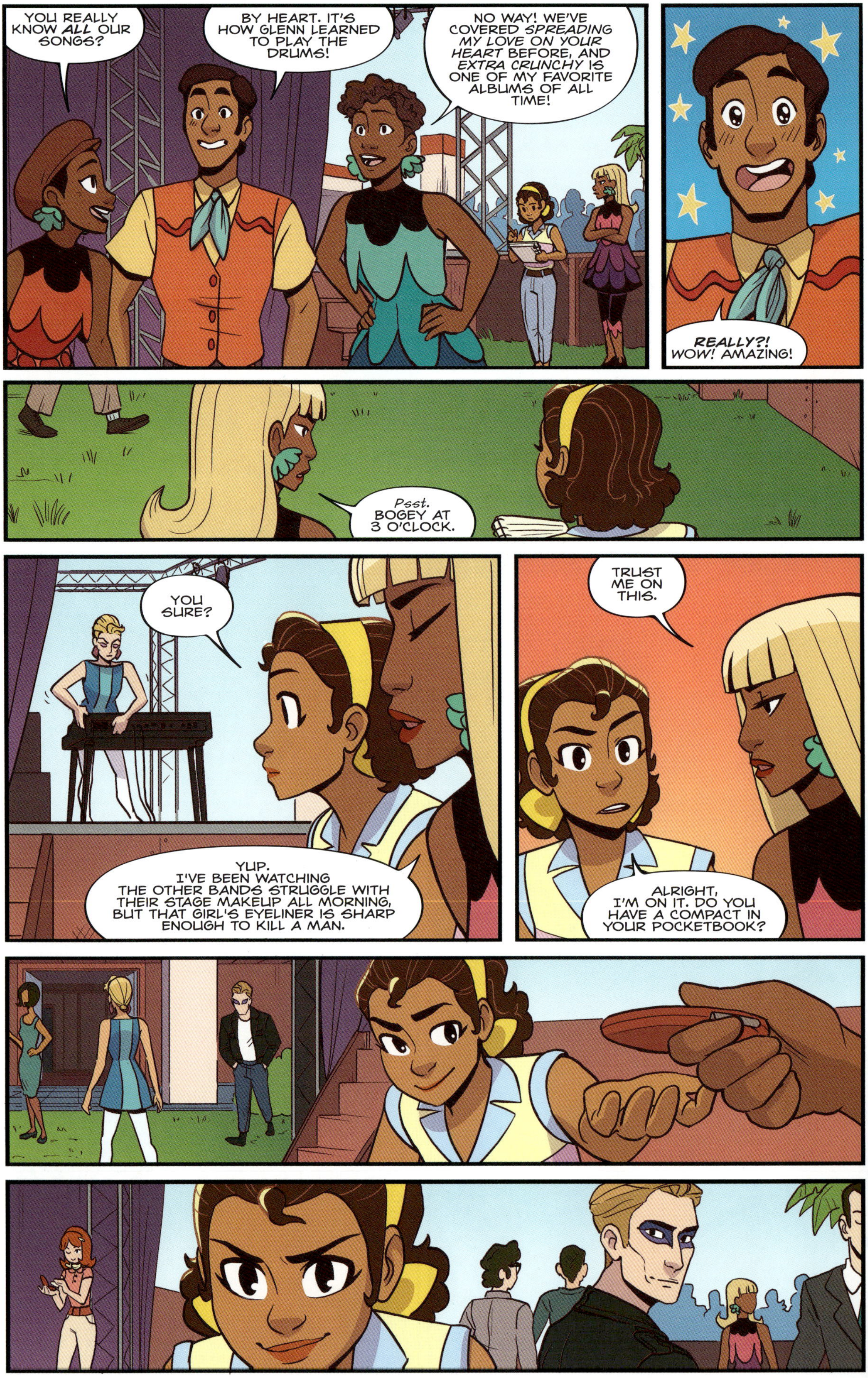
YOU REALLY KNOW *ALL* OUR SONGS?
BY HEART. IT'S HOW GLENN LEARNED TO PLAY THE DRUMS!
NO WAY! WE'VE COVERED *SPREADING MY LOVE ON YOUR HEART* BEFORE, AND *EXTRA CRUNCHY* IS ONE OF MY FAVORITE ALBUMS OF ALL TIME!
*REALLY?!* WOW! AMAZING!
*Psst.* BOGEY AT 3 O'CLOCK.
YOU SURE?
YUP. I'VE BEEN WATCHING THE OTHER BANDS STRUGGLE WITH THEIR STAGE MAKEUP ALL MORNING, BUT THAT GIRL'S EYELINER IS SHARP ENOUGH TO KILL A MAN.
TRUST ME ON THIS.
ALRIGHT, I'M ON IT. DO YOU HAVE A COMPACT IN YOUR POCKETBOOK?

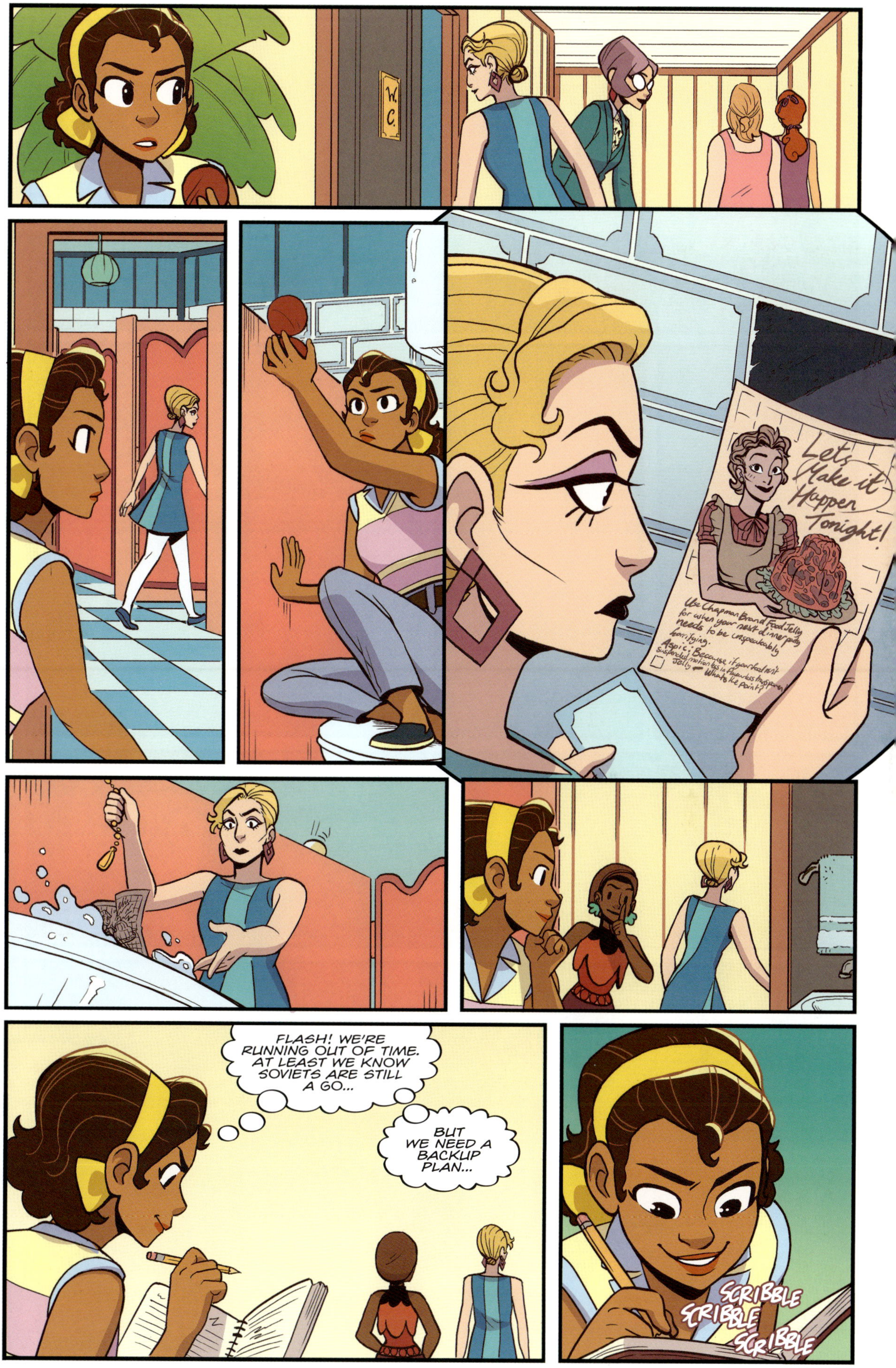
W.C.
Let's Make it Happen Tonight!
Use Chapman Brand Food Jelly for when your next dinner party needs to be unspeakably horrifying.
Aspic: Because if your food isn't suspended motionless in flawless transparent jelly — What's the point?
FLASH! WE'RE RUNNING OUT OF TIME. AT LEAST WE KNOW SOVIETS ARE STILL A GO...
BUT WE NEED A BACKUP PLAN...
SCRIBBLE
SCRIBBLE
SCRIBBLE

101.5
SPR

SNAP

WE'VE GOTTA TELL GOLDIE!

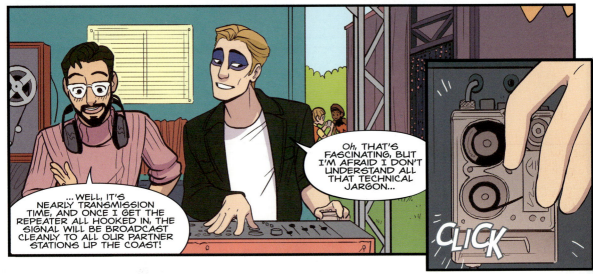

...WELL, IT'S NEARLY TRANSMISSION TIME, AND ONCE I GET THE REPEATER ALL HOOKED IN, THE SIGNAL WILL BE BROADCAST CLEANLY TO ALL OUR PARTNER STATIONS UP THE COAST!

Oh, THAT'S FASCINATING, BUT I'M AFRAID I DON'T UNDERSTAND ALL THAT TECHNICAL JARGON...

CLICK

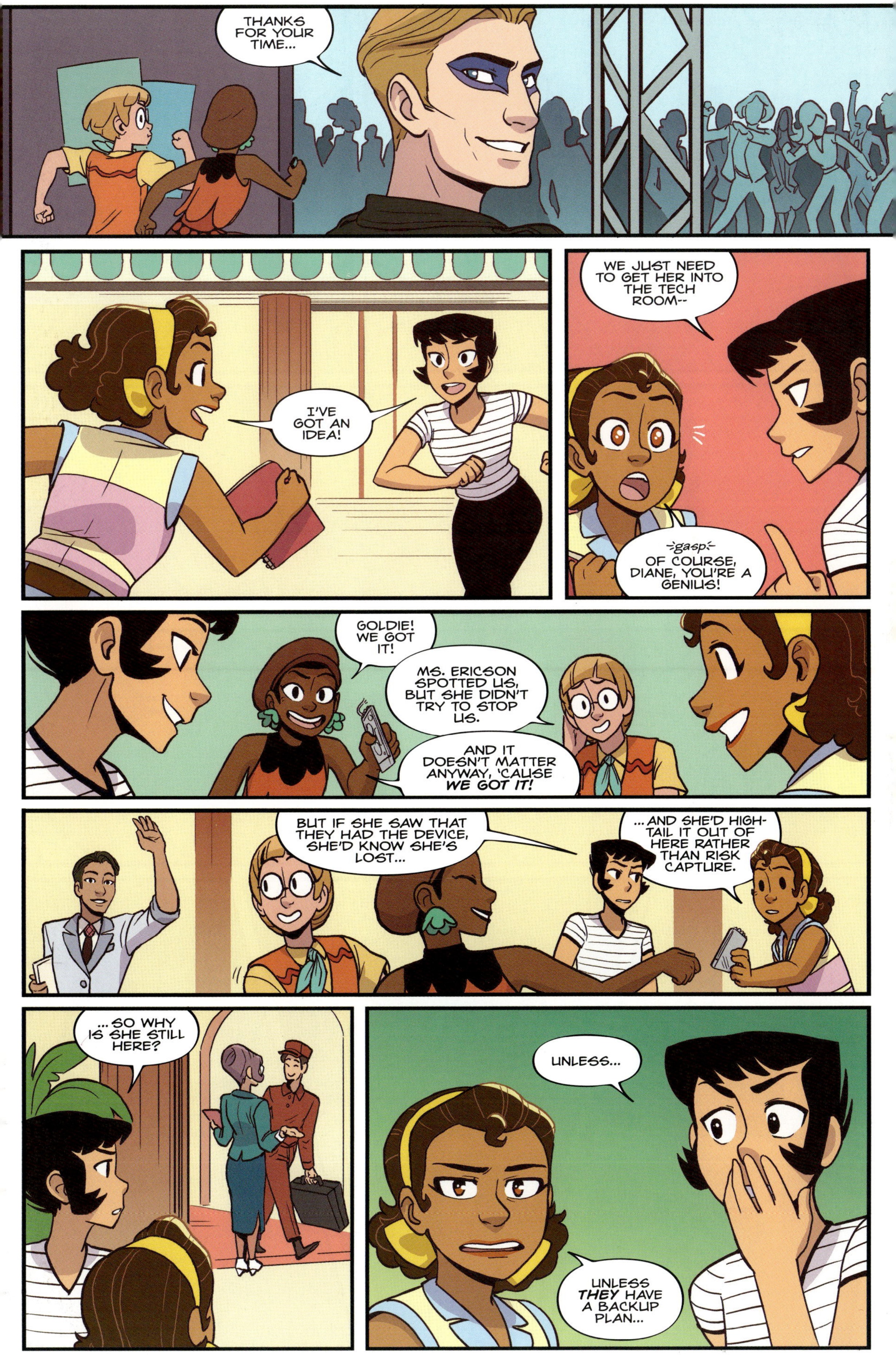
THANKS FOR YOUR TIME...
I'VE GOT AN IDEA!
WE JUST NEED TO GET HER INTO THE TECH ROOM--
-gasp-
OF COURSE, DIANE, YOU'RE A GENIUS!
GOLDIE! WE GOT IT!
MS. ERICSON SPOTTED US, BUT SHE DIDN'T TRY TO STOP US.
AND IT DOESN'T MATTER ANYWAY, 'CAUSE *WE GOT IT!*
BUT IF SHE SAW THAT THEY HAD THE DEVICE, SHE'D KNOW SHE'S LOST...
...AND SHE'D HIGH-TAIL IT OUT OF HERE RATHER THAN RISK CAPTURE.
...SO WHY IS SHE STILL HERE?
UNLESS...
UNLESS *THEY* HAVE A BACKUP PLAN...

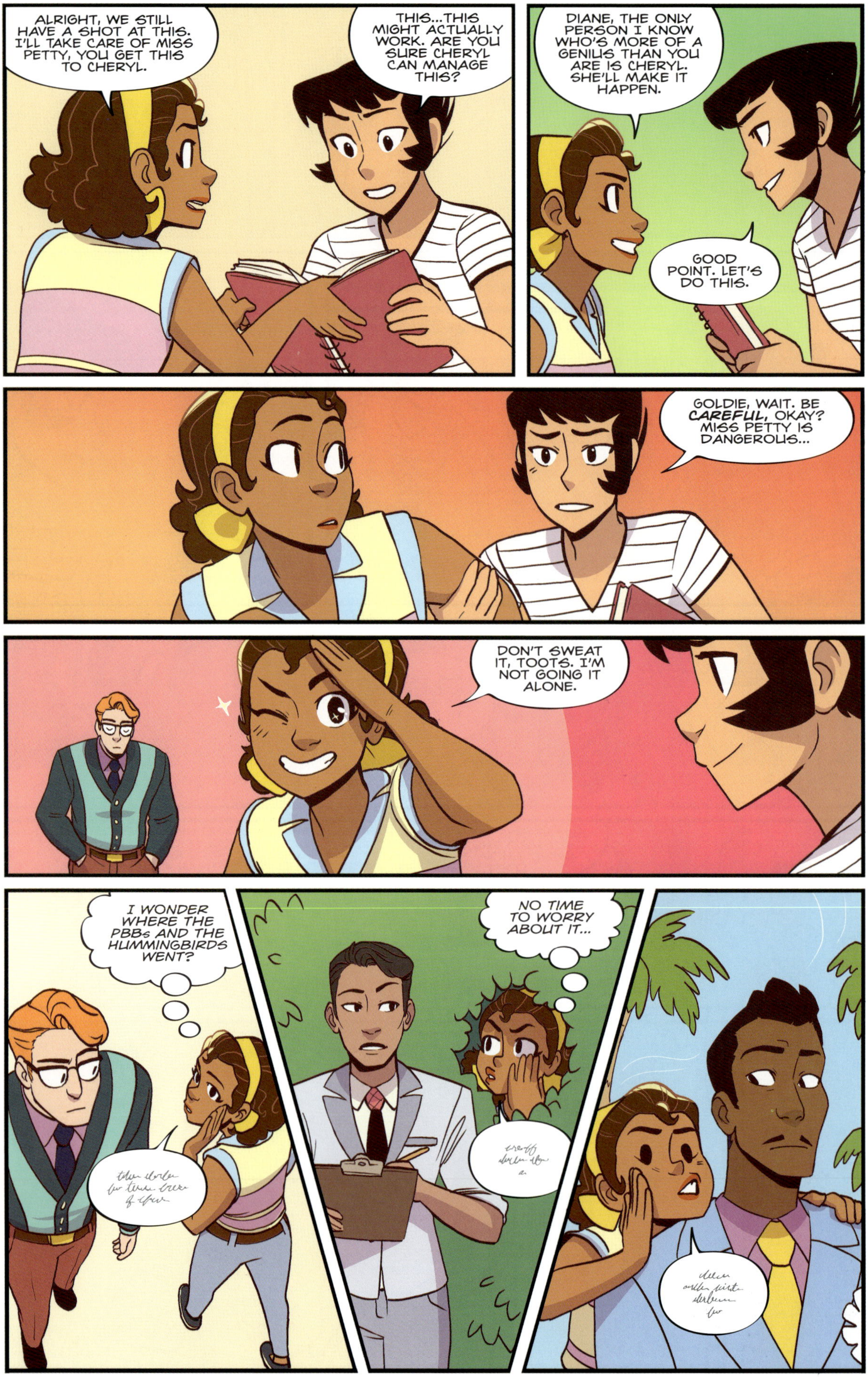
ALRIGHT, WE STILL HAVE A SHOT AT THIS. I'LL TAKE CARE OF MISS PETTY, YOU GET THIS TO CHERYL.
THIS...THIS MIGHT ACTUALLY WORK. ARE YOU SURE CHERYL CAN MANAGE THIS?
DIANE, THE ONLY PERSON I KNOW WHO'S MORE OF A GENIUS THAN YOU ARE IS CHERYL. SHE'LL MAKE IT HAPPEN.
GOOD POINT. LET'S DO THIS.
GOLDIE, WAIT. BE CAREFUL, OKAY? MISS PETTY IS DANGEROUS...
DON'T SWEAT IT, TOOTS. I'M NOT GOING IT ALONE.
I WONDER WHERE THE PBBs AND THE HUMMINGBIRDS WENT?
NO TIME TO WORRY ABOUT IT...

THANK YOU ST. PASCAL!

WOOOoolllloooloo!

LADIES AND GENTLEMEN. ARE YOU READY FOR THE BIGGEST EVENT IN SOUTHERN FLORIDA MUSIC HISTORY?

WOOOolllloooloo!

LADIES AND GENTLEMAN, THIS IS SYDNEY REESE WITH 101.5 THE NOISE OF SOUTHERN FLORIDA, WELCOME TO OUR LIVE BROADCAST OF THE ROCKIN' THE BEACH MUSIC FESTIVAL FINALE!

MISS PETTY!

YOU'RE TOO LATE THIS TIME, CLEVER GIRL! THE BROADCAST HAS ALREADY BEGUN!

GOOD! WHEN THE POWER GOES OUT I'LL HAVE ALL THE EVIDENCE I NEED TO PROVE TO EVERYONE HOW RIGHT I WAS!

I THINK YOU'LL FIND YOUR VINDICATION A COLD COMFORT...

I HOPE YOU'RE ALL AS EXCITED AS I AM, TO BRING OUT OUR MYSTERY CLOSING ACT, BUT BEFORE WE DO THAT...

Heh heh... I GUESS SHE HAD TWO BACKUP PLANS...

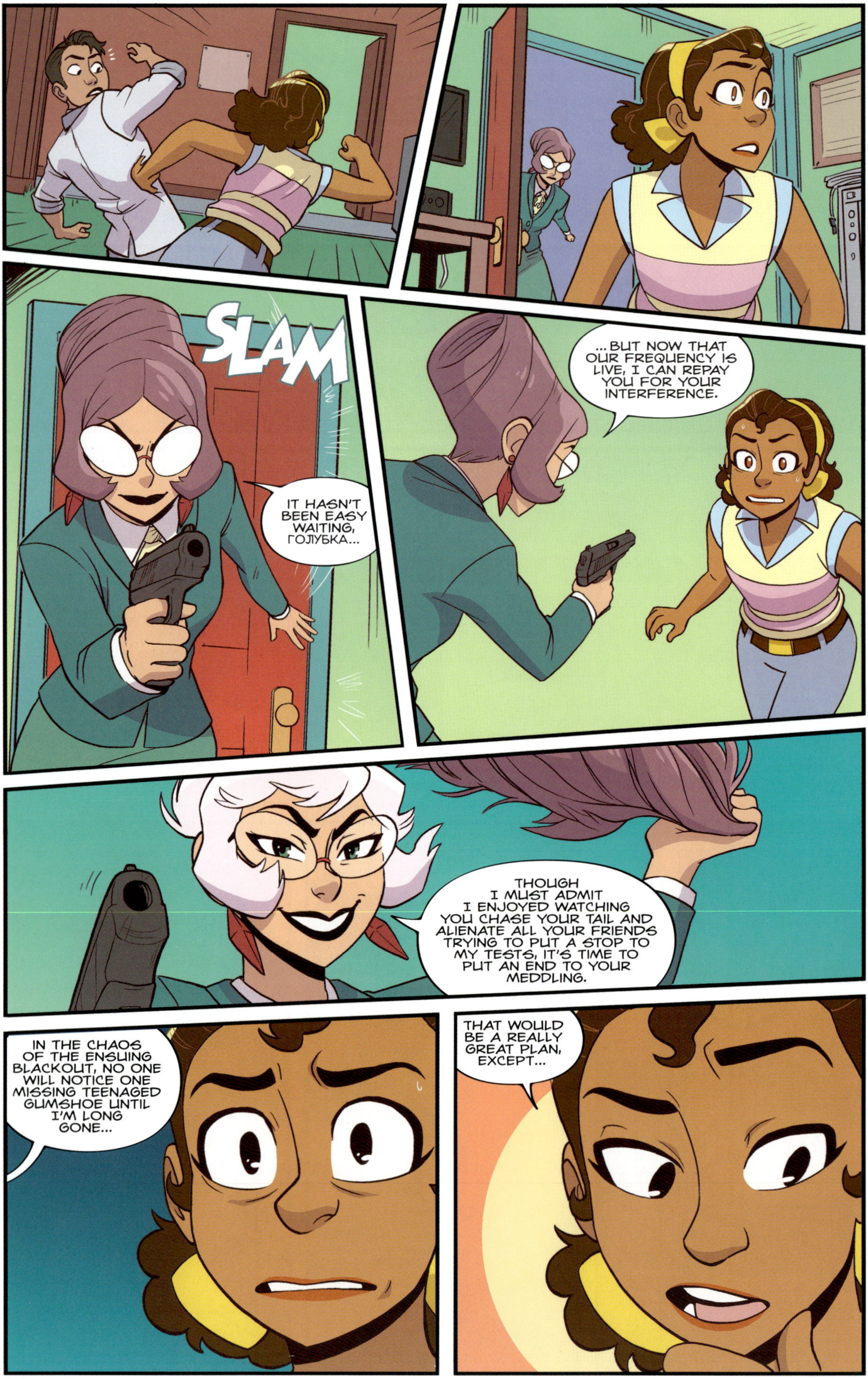
SLAM
IT HASN'T BEEN EASY WAITING, ГОЛУБКА...
...BUT NOW THAT OUR FREQUENCY IS LIVE, I CAN REPAY YOU FOR YOUR INTERFERENCE.
THOUGH I MUST ADMIT I ENJOYED WATCHING YOU CHASE YOUR TAIL AND ALIENATE ALL YOUR FRIENDS TRYING TO PUT A STOP TO MY TESTS, IT'S TIME TO PUT AN END TO YOUR MEDDLING.
IN THE CHAOS OF THE ENSUING BLACKOUT, NO ONE WILL NOTICE ONE MISSING TEENAGED GUMSHOE UNTIL I'M LONG GONE...
THAT WOULD BE A REALLY GREAT PLAN, EXCEPT...

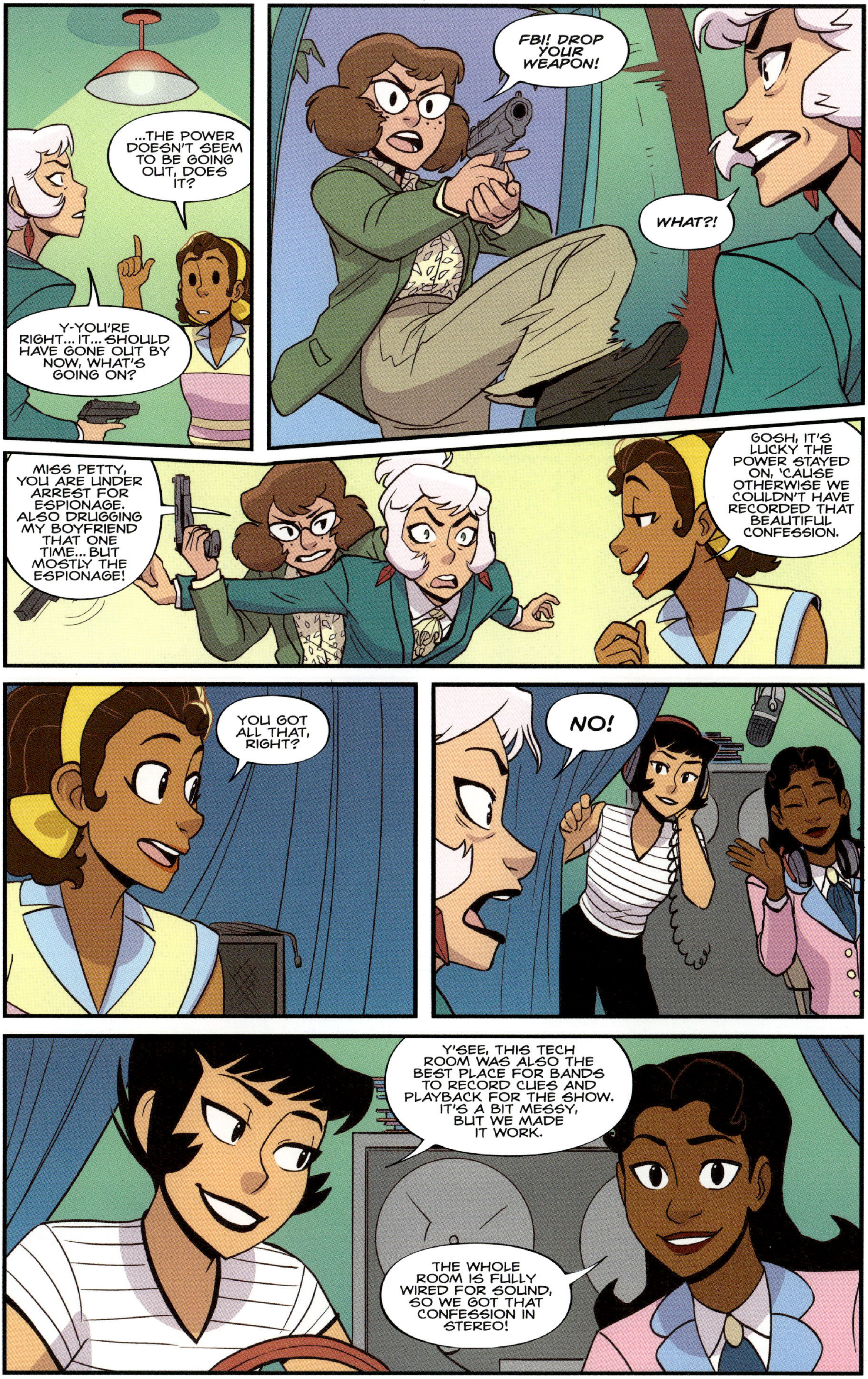
...THE POWER DOESN'T SEEM TO BE GOING OUT, DOES IT?
Y-YOU'RE RIGHT... IT... SHOULD HAVE GONE OUT BY NOW, WHAT'S GOING ON?
FBI! DROP YOUR WEAPON!
WHAT?!
MISS PETTY, YOU ARE UNDER ARREST FOR ESPIONAGE. ALSO DRUGGING MY BOYFRIEND THAT ONE TIME... BUT MOSTLY THE ESPIONAGE!
GOSH, IT'S LUCKY THE POWER STAYED ON, 'CAUSE OTHERWISE WE COULDN'T HAVE RECORDED THAT BEAUTIFUL CONFESSION.
YOU GOT ALL THAT, RIGHT?
NO!
Y'SEE, THIS TECH ROOM WAS ALSO THE BEST PLACE FOR BANDS TO RECORD CUES AND PLAYBACK FOR THE SHOW. IT'S A BIT MESSY, BUT WE MADE IT WORK.
THE WHOLE ROOM IS FULLY WIRED FOR SOUND, SO WE GOT THAT CONFESSION IN STEREO!

BUT--BUT, THE SIGNAL! OUR MODULE WAS IN PLACE--HOW DID YOU?!

YOU MEAN THIS MODULE?

A FAKE! YOU NEVER FOUND THE REAL DEVICE. I CHECKED IT MYSELF! HOW DID YOU STOP THE SIGNAL?!

WE DIDN'T.

WE COULDN'T BE SURE YOU DIDN'T HAVE A BACKUP DEVICE. THE ONLY REAL OPTION WAS TO NEUTRALIZE THE SIGNAL.

WE COULDN'T HAVE YOU SHUTTING DOWN HALF OF THE EASTERN SEABOARD.

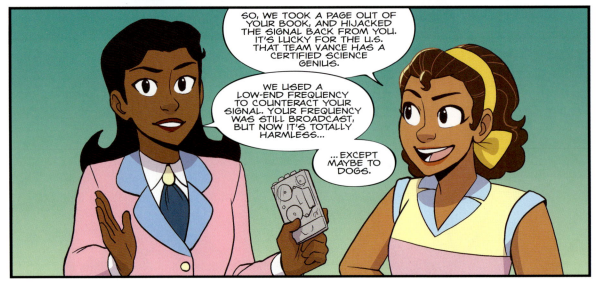

SO, WE TOOK A PAGE OUT OF YOUR BOOK, AND HIJACKED THE SIGNAL BACK FROM YOU. IT'S LUCKY FOR THE U.S. THAT TEAM VANCE HAS A CERTIFIED SCIENCE GENIUS.

WE USED A LOW-END FREQUENCY TO COUNTERACT YOUR SIGNAL. YOUR FREQUENCY WAS STILL BROADCAST, BUT NOW IT'S TOTALLY HARMLESS...

...EXCEPT MAYBE TO DOGS.

IF YOU THINK THIS IS OVER, MY PEOPLE WILL PICK UP WHERE I LEFT OFF!

THEY'RE NOT GONNA GET TOO FAR WITHOUT THEIR KEYS. I THINK MAYBE THAT BLONDE FELLA IS TRYING TOO HARD TO BLEND.

И ВОТ Я СНОВА НЕЦЕНЗУРНО ВЫРАЖАЮСЬ!

CAR TROUBLE, COMRADES?

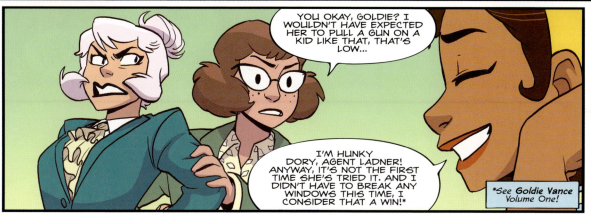

YOU OKAY, GOLDIE? I WOULDN'T HAVE EXPECTED HER TO PULL A GUN ON A KID LIKE THAT, THAT'S LOW...

I'M HUNKY DORY, AGENT LADNER! ANYWAY, IT'S NOT THE FIRST TIME SHE'S TRIED IT. AND I DIDN'T HAVE TO BREAK ANY WINDOWS THIS TIME, I CONSIDER THAT A WIN!*

*See *Goldie Vance* Volume One!

LAILA! *LAILA!* WE GOT 'EM! IS GOLDIE WITH YOU?!

Uh... ⸝ahem⸝ I MEAN: AGENT LADNER, THE SUSPECTS HAVE BEEN DETAINED. WHAT'S YOUR STATUS? OVER.

ROGER THAT, TOOEY. WE'RE ALL CLEAR INSIDE. OVER AND OUT.

GOLDIE!

I'M VERY PROUD OF HOW YOU HANDLED ALL THIS. YOU SHOWED A LOT OF MATURITY...

...BUT I'M GOING TO NEED YOU TO PROMISE ME NOT TO KNOWINGLY WALK INTO A ROOM WITH A KGB AGENT AGAIN IN THE FUTURE...

NO PROMISES, DAD. I'M A DETECTIVE, I HAVE TO FOLLOW THE TRUTH, EVEN IF THINGS GET HAIRY.

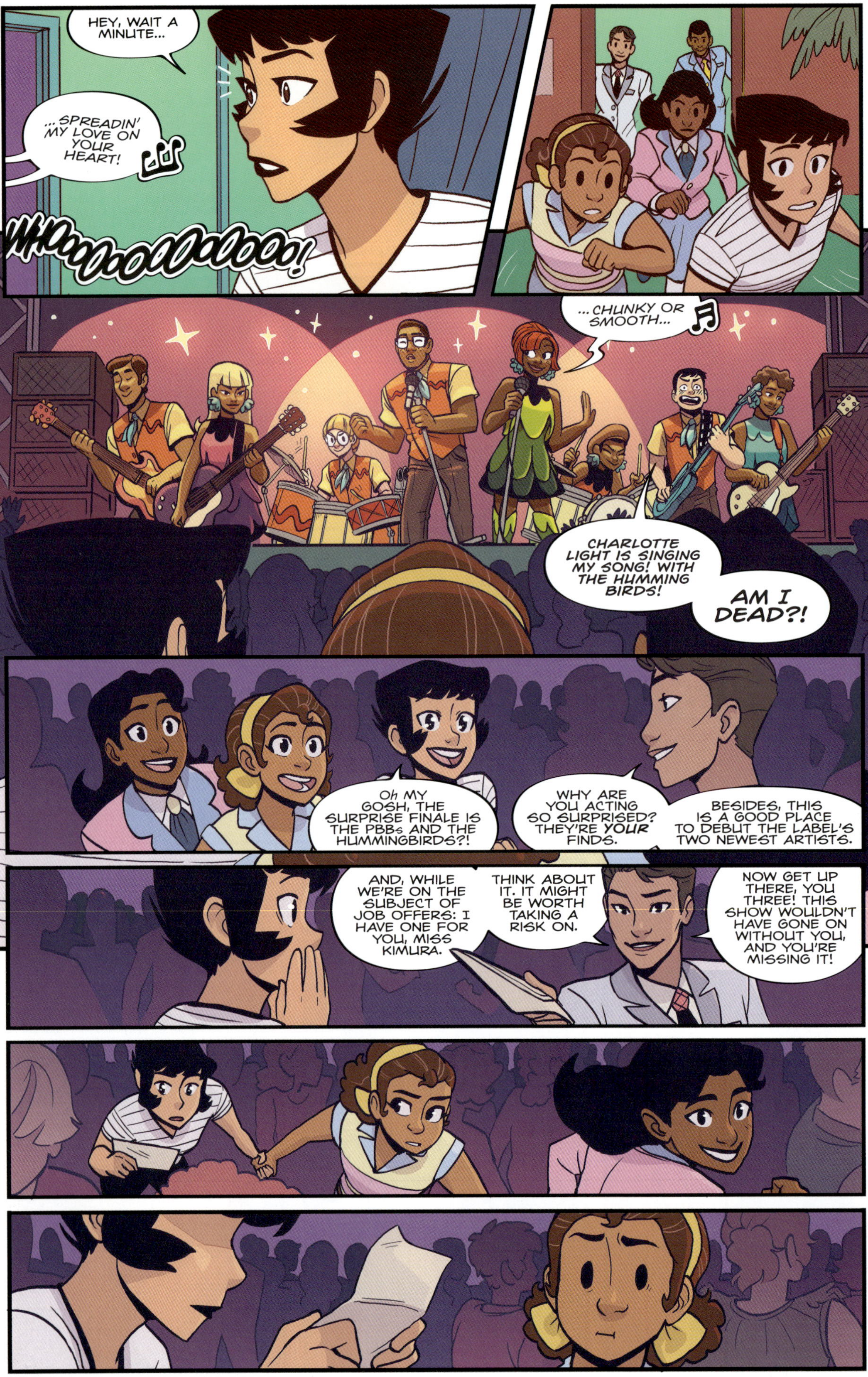
HEY, WAIT A MINUTE...
...SPREADIN' MY LOVE ON YOUR HEART!
WHOOoOoOoOoOoOoOoO!
...CHUNKY OR SMOOTH...
CHARLOTTE LIGHT IS SINGING MY SONG! WITH THE HUMMING BIRDS!
AM I DEAD?!
Oh MY GOSH, THE SURPRISE FINALE IS THE PBBs AND THE HUMMINGBIRDS?!
WHY ARE YOU ACTING SO SURPRISED? THEY'RE YOUR FINDS.
BESIDES, THIS IS A GOOD PLACE TO DEBUT THE LABEL'S TWO NEWEST ARTISTS.
AND, WHILE WE'RE ON THE SUBJECT OF JOB OFFERS: I HAVE ONE FOR YOU, MISS KIMURA.
THINK ABOUT IT. IT MIGHT BE WORTH TAKING A RISK ON.
NOW GET UP THERE, YOU THREE! THIS SHOW WOULDN'T HAVE GONE ON WITHOUT YOU, AND YOU'RE MISSING IT!

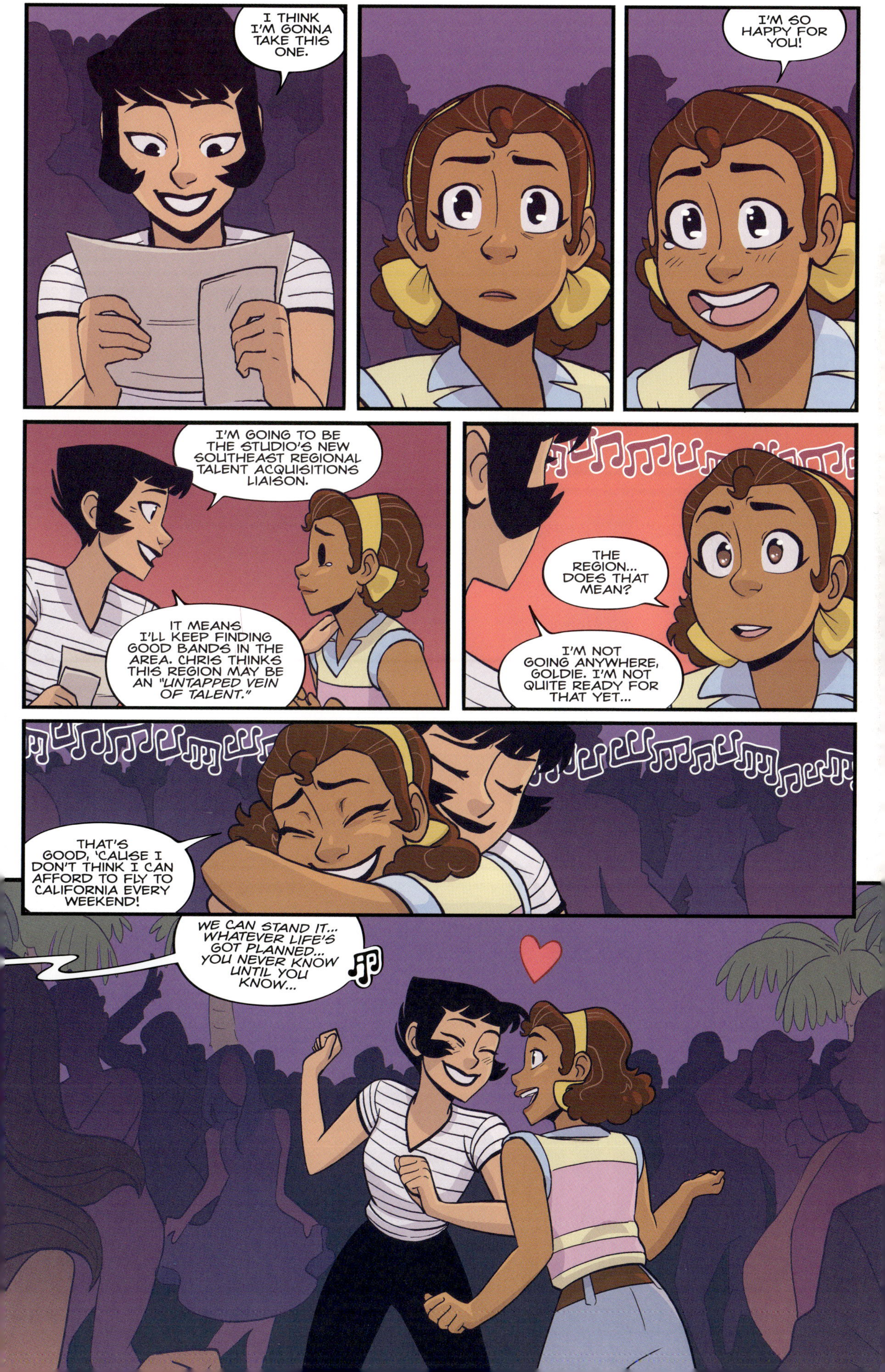
I THINK I'M GONNA TAKE THIS ONE.
I'M SO HAPPY FOR YOU!
I'M GOING TO BE THE STUDIO'S NEW SOUTHEAST REGIONAL TALENT ACQUISITIONS LIAISON.
IT MEANS I'LL KEEP FINDING GOOD BANDS IN THE AREA. CHRIS THINKS THIS REGION MAY BE AN "UNTAPPED VEIN OF TALENT."
THE REGION... DOES THAT MEAN?
I'M NOT GOING ANYWHERE, GOLDIE. I'M NOT QUITE READY FOR THAT YET...
THAT'S GOOD, 'CAUSE I DON'T THINK I CAN AFFORD TO FLY TO CALIFORNIA EVERY WEEKEND!
WE CAN STAND IT... WHATEVER LIFE'S GOT PLANNED... YOU NEVER KNOW UNTIL YOU KNOW...

101.5 THE NOISE, SOME TIME LATER...

♪ YOU SOLVED THE MYSTERY OF ME...

THAT WAS CHARLOTTE LIGHT AND THE HUMMINGBIRDS' LATEST HIT OFF OF THEIR BRAND-NEW ALBUM: MYSTERY OF ME.

NOW, I DON'T GET A LOT OF DEDICATIONS THIS LATE AT NIGHT, SO I'VE GOT ONE OF MY OWN.

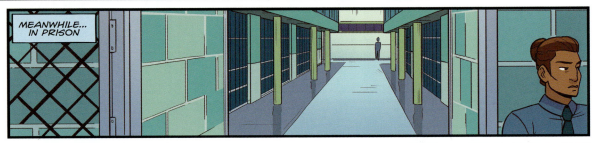

MEANWHILE... IN PRISON

SHUT OFF THAT RADIO, SOME OF US ARE TRYING TO GET AN HONEST NIGHT'S SLEEP!

ONLY HONEST THING YOU'VE EVER DONE, TRISH!

CAN IT, GRETA!

THIS ONE GOES OUT TO MY GIRL, GOLDIE. GO TO SLEEP, DETECTIVE.

‹TEEN DETECTIVE... peh.›

SO, BLONDIE...

I HEAR YOU HATE GOLDIE VANCE AS MUCH AS I DO...

THE END

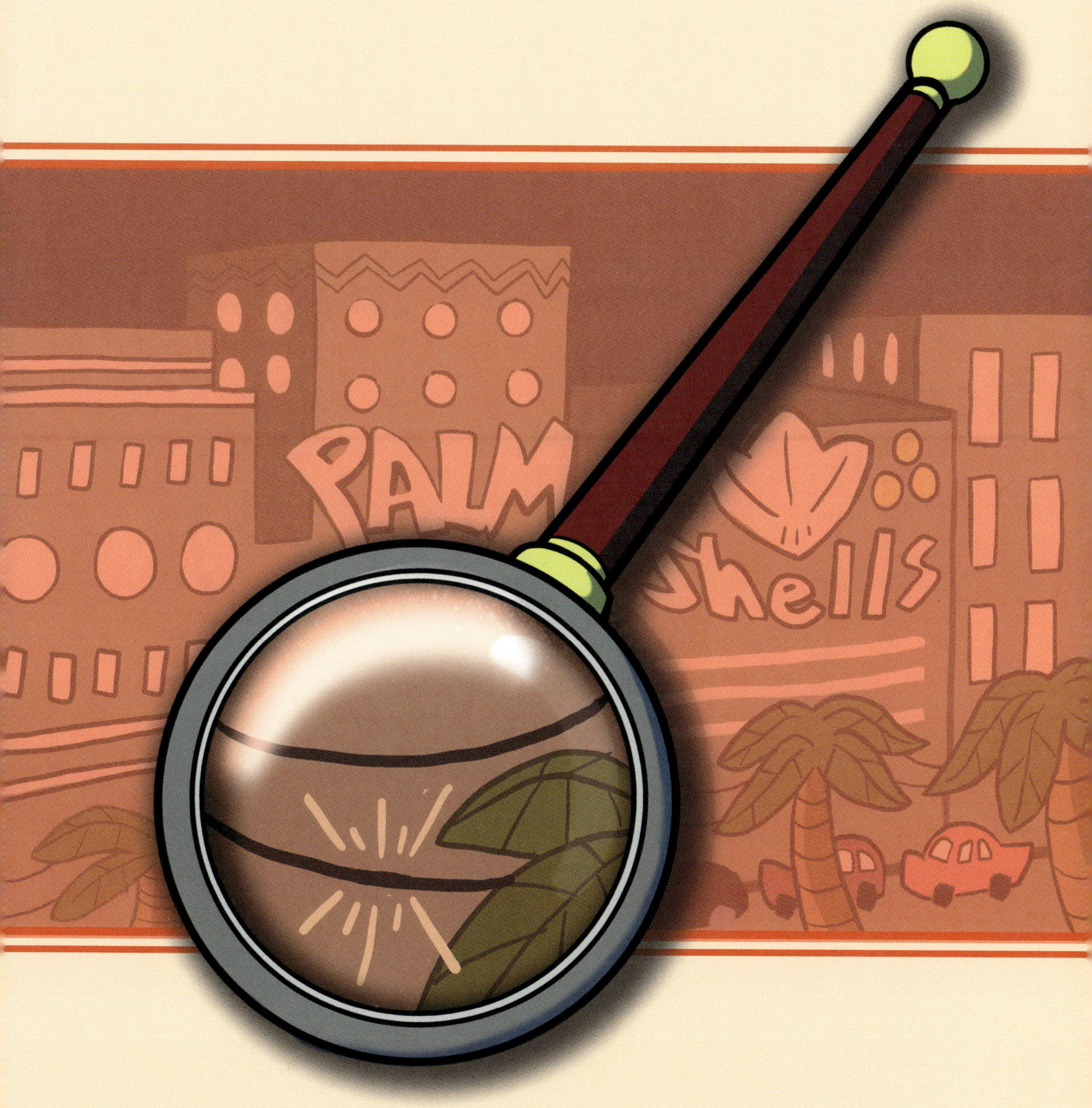
PALM

*Goldie Vance* concept art by **Elle Power**

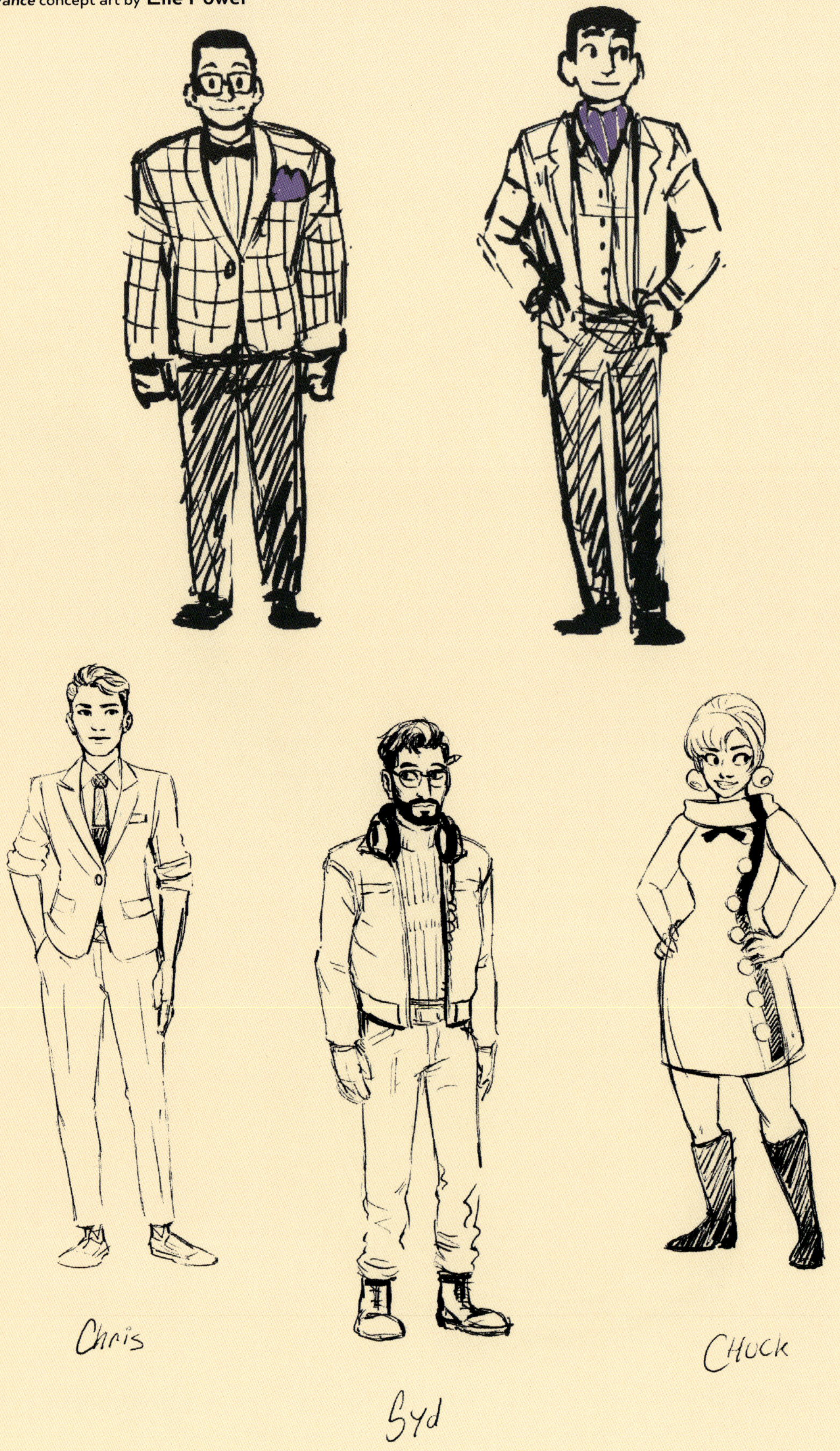
Chris
Syd
Chuck

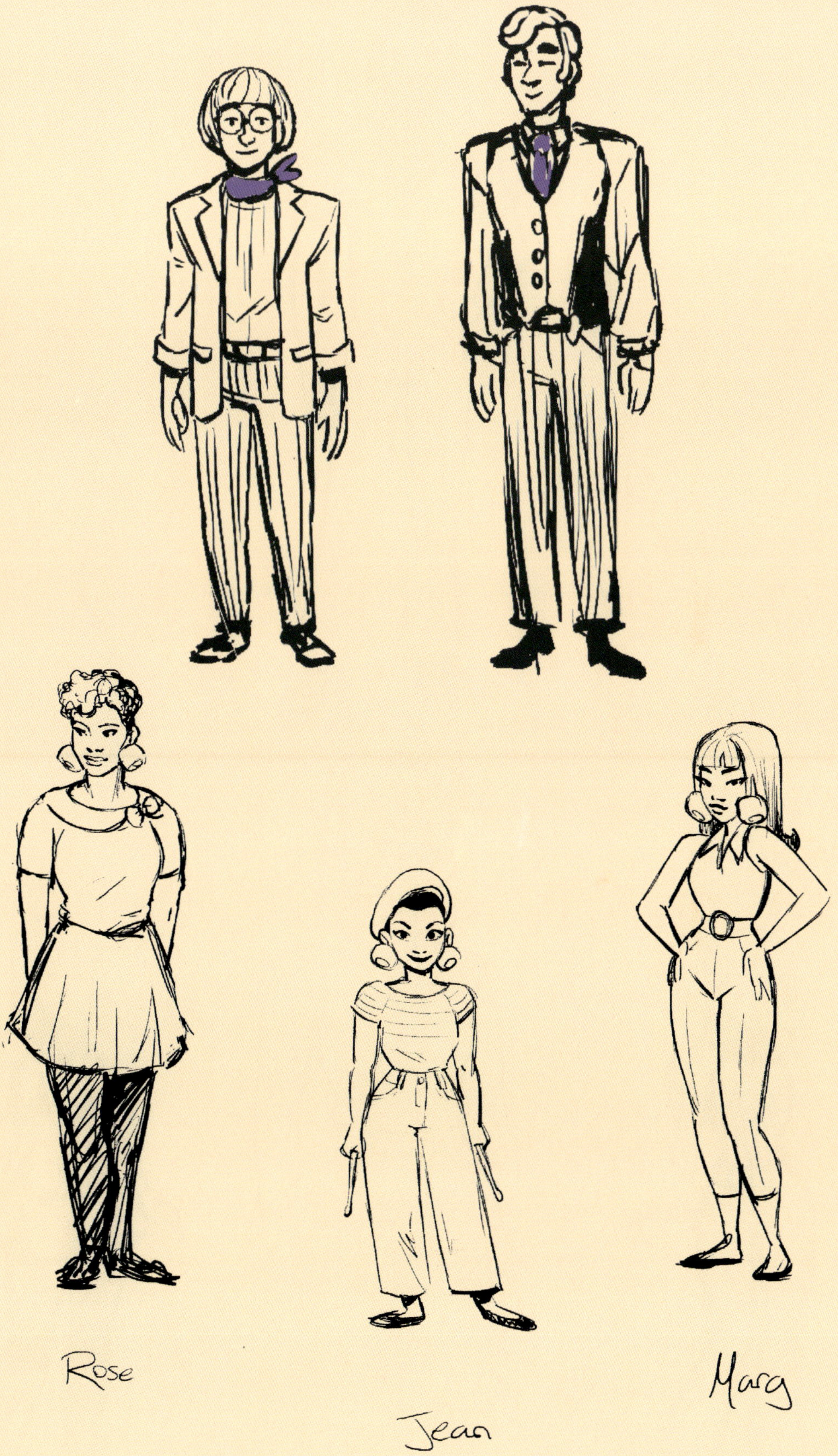
Rose
Jean
Marg

*Goldie Vance* concept art by **Elle Power**

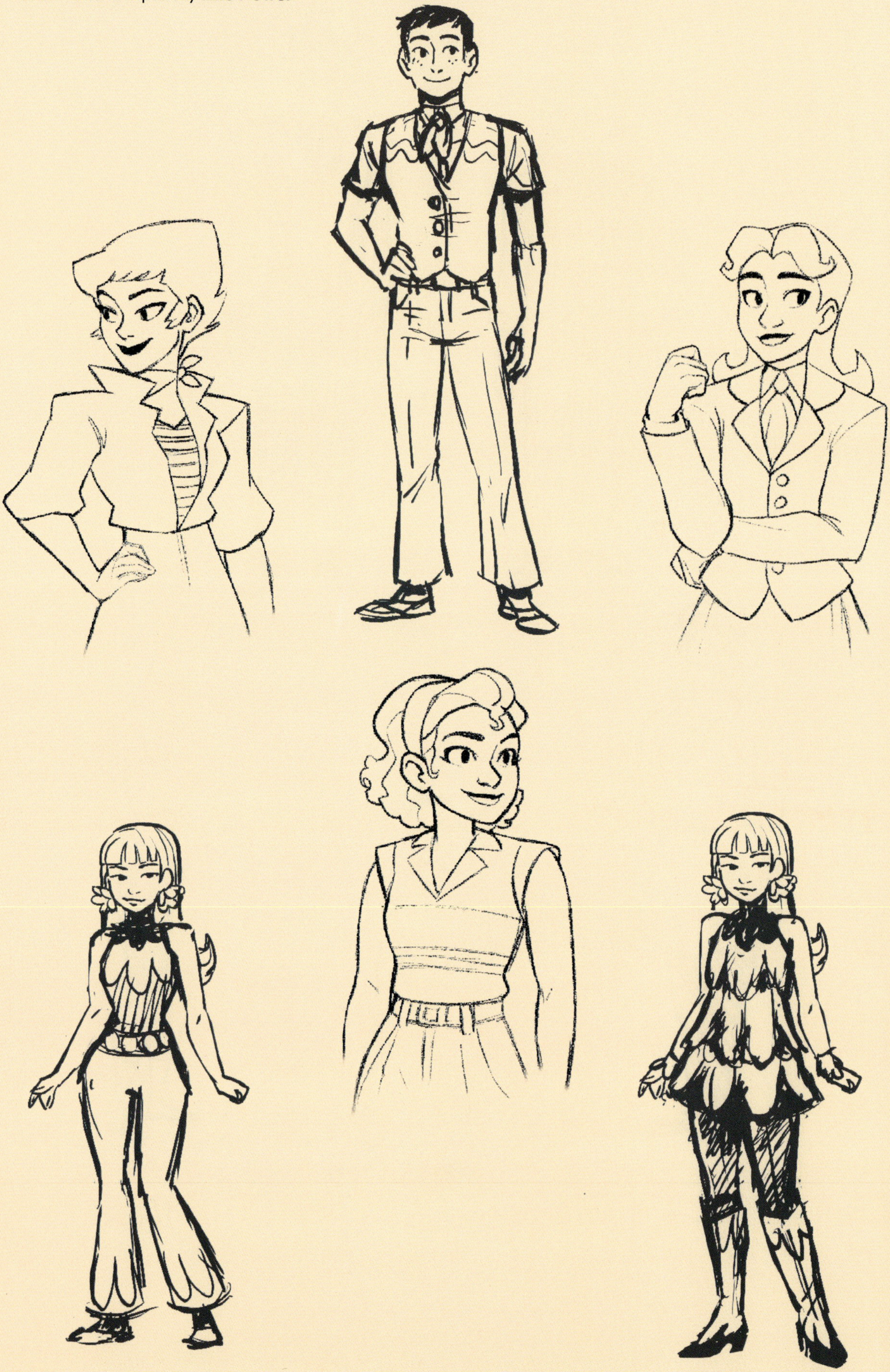

# CASE STUDY

*from script to page*

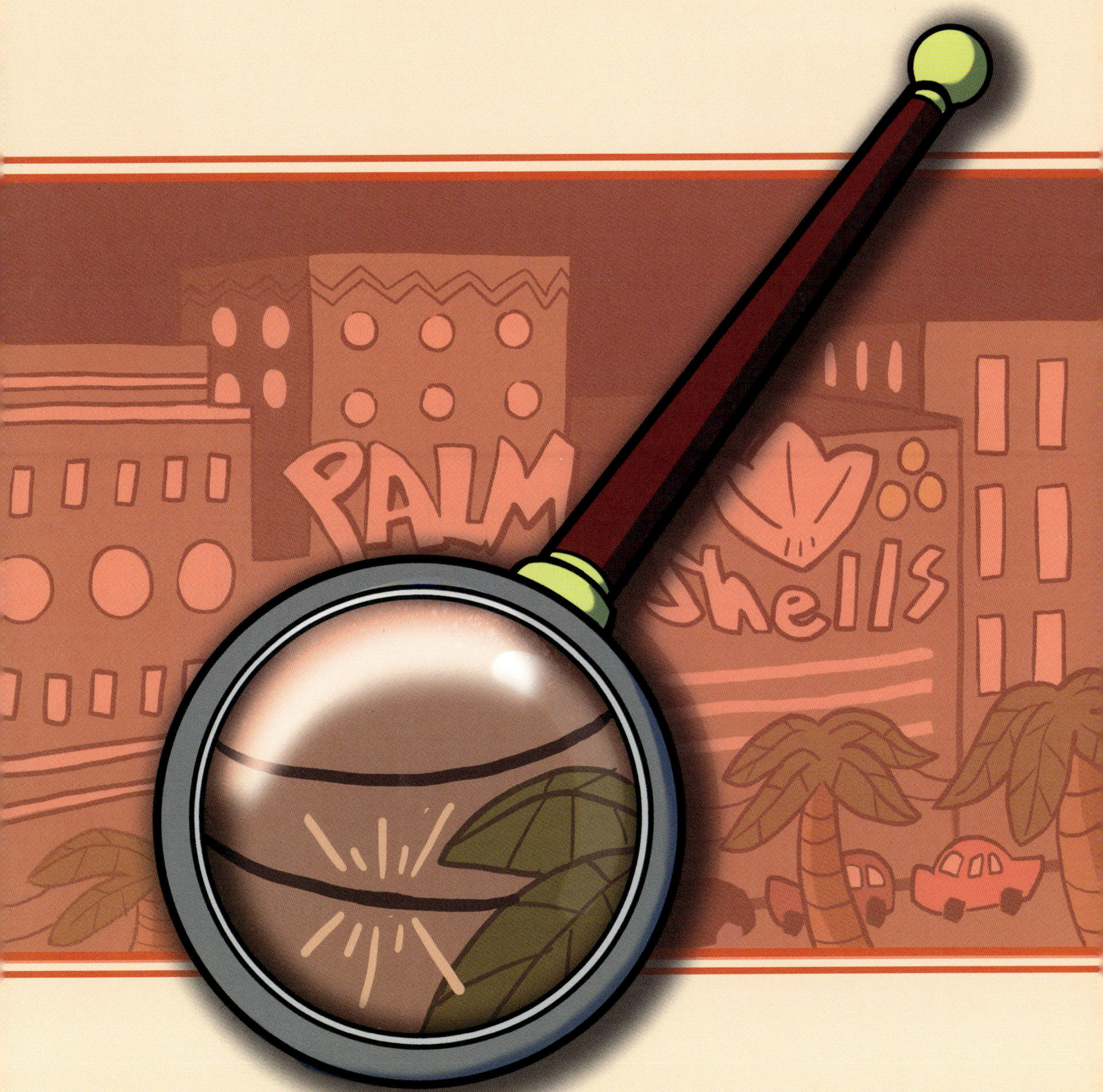
PALM
Shells

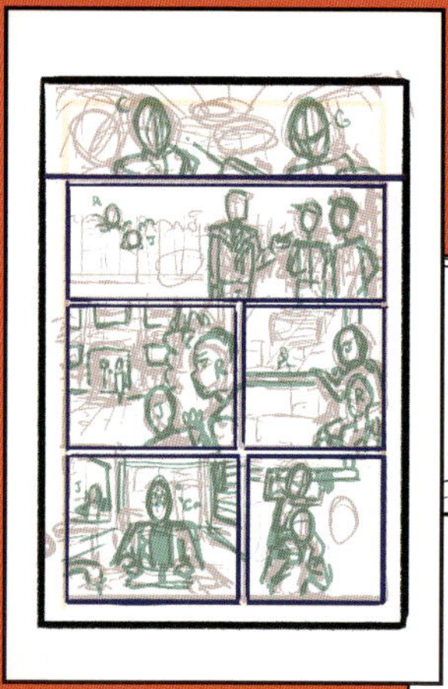

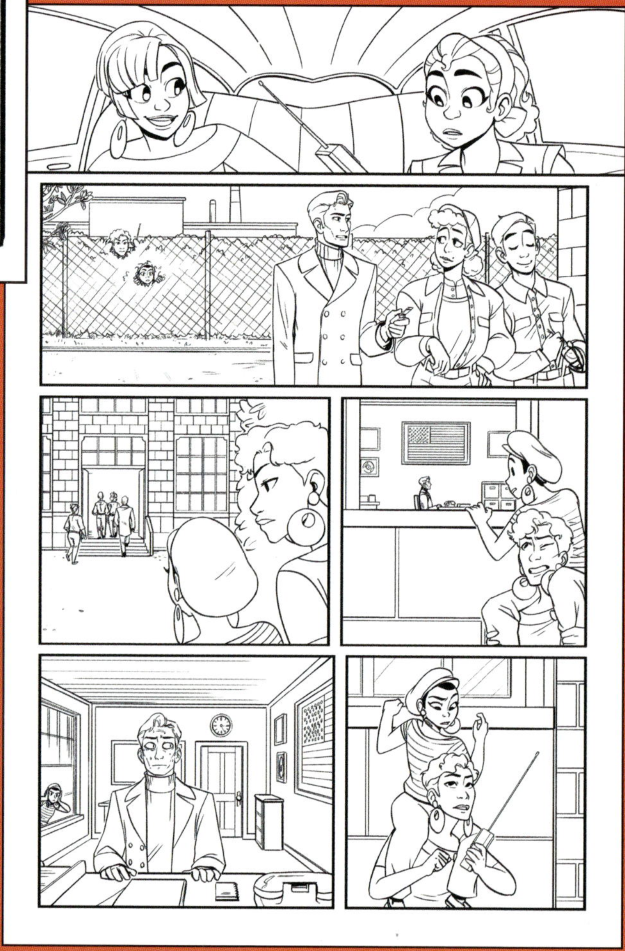

## ISSUE FIFTEEN: PAGE TWELVE

**PANEL ONE:** Goldie and Chuck are still in the car trying to determine their next plan of action.

*CHUCK:* Where to now, Teen Detective?

*SFX (WALKIE):* hiss crackle

*ROSE:* Hey gals, I think we might be on to something on our end. Over.

**PANEL TWO:** Rose and Jean peer over a fence behind a factory, at a tall, blond man with angular cheek bones and piercing eyes (basically Channing Tatum in the submarine scene in *Hail, Caesar!*). He is standing ramrod straight, and wearing a black turtle neck and trench coat and offering some gum to a factory worker outside.

*CHANNING:* Would you like some American gum, fellow worker?

**PANEL THREE:** The workers go back into the building, and Jean and Rose sneak out of hiding.

**PANEL FOUR:** Jean hops up on Rose's shoulders to peer in a window.

**PANEL FIVE::** She sees the man inside an office, sitting bolt upright, eyes wide, sweating and side-eying the American flag.

**PANEL SIX:** Jean looks down at Rose as Rose speaks through the walkie again.

   *JEAN:* I don't think this guy's a very good spy…

   *ROSE:* Yeah, I'm pretty sure this is the place…get over here! Over and out!

## ISSUE FIFTEEN: PAGE THIRTEEN

**PANEL ONE:** Exterior printers, slightly later. Goldie and Diane's cars are parked behind the van on a back road near the printers.

**PANEL TWO:** The girls have set up camp on a ridge where they can see inside the factory with binoculars.

**PANEL THREE:** They are taking notes. Jean sits cross legged, drumming on her own shoes, sighing expressively

    *JEAN:* UUuuggghhhhh…

**PANEL FOUR:** Jean flops over and starts casually drumming on the grass. Goldie patiently continues watching the building and scribbling notes.

    *JEAN:* I'm boooooored…when's the fun stuff? I thought this would all be chasing crooks.

    *GOLDIE:* A lot of investigation work is actually waiting and gathering info.

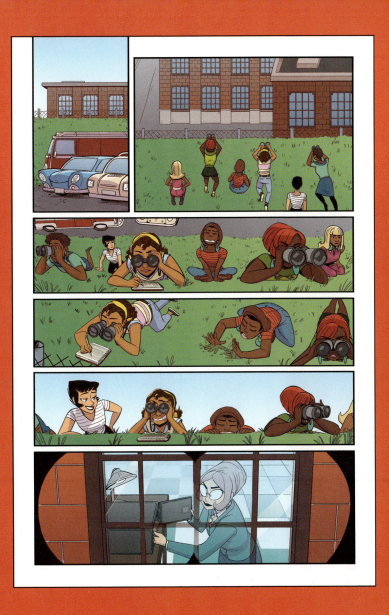

**PANEL FIVE:** Diane smiles down at her, and Goldie smirks, still looking through the binoculars. Chuck points toward the building.

*DIANE:* You're starting to sound like your boss there, Detective.

*GOLDIE:* *snort* Don't tell Walt, he'll die of shock.

*CHUCK:* I've got a new car that just parked. Lady in a uniform, just went in the back door.

**PANEL SIX:** Below, through the binoculars, Miss Petty is entering an office and leaving something in a lock-box.

*GOLDIE:* That's her, Miss Petty! She's…she's leaving something behind!

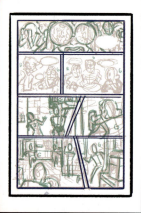

## ISSUE FIFTEEN: PAGE FOURTEEN

**PANEL ONE:** The girls all watch, sharing three pairs of binoculars between them. They see Miss Petty and some of the workers leave for the night in the reflection of the binoculars' lenses. Goldie decides she has to take a risk to get what Miss Petty locked up.

*GOLDIE:* She's heading out. I need to get down there and get whatever it is she just locked up. Dollars to donuts it's the evidence we need. They're closed up for the night, so it shouldn't be too risky...

**PANEL TWO:** Diane nods with determination, and Goldie stares at her, horrified.

*DIANE:* Okay, while you do that, the Hummingbirds can help me look for the Mother and the Master.

*GOLDIE:* The *what??*

**PANEL THREE:** Diane and the Hummingbirds laugh.

*ROSE:* The Mother and the Master are just part of the album printing process.

*DIANE:* That's just what they use to press the records.

*DIANE:* If that frequency was added here, it'll be on those pressings, and we can at least keep the PBB's names clear.

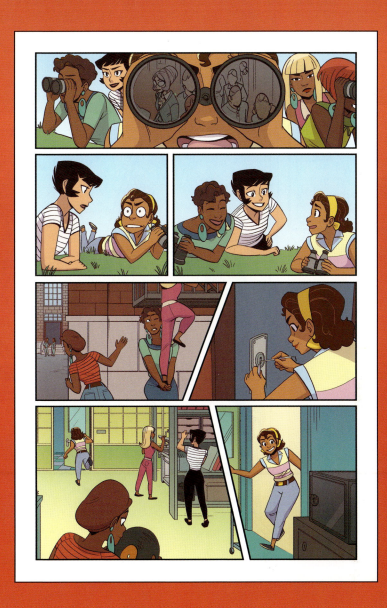

*GOLDIE:* Good thinking! I wouldn't want them to go down for something they had nothing to do with…

**PANEL FOUR:** They find a fire escape – Jean stands look-out on the ground near some pipes while Rose uses her height to help boost the other girls up.

*JEAN:* I'll give you a signal if I see anything.

*ROSE:* Uf!

**PANEL 5:** Goldie picks the lock on the emergency door.

*SFX (LOCK):* Click!

**PANEL 6:** Goldie heads for the main office, and Diane and the others search the factory for the mother and the master and other creepy equipment with nightmare names.

**PANEL 7:** Goldie finds the lockbox under the desk and gets to work on the lock.

*GOLDIE (THOUGHT BUBBLE):* Jackpot!

# ISSUE FIFTEEN: PAGE FIFTEEN

**PANEL ONE:** Goldie is picking into the lock-box when they hear some tapping coming from some pipes nearby.

    *SFX (GOLDIE'S LOCKPICK):* Click click click

**PANEL TWO:** Goldie fiddles with the lock more urgently.

    *SFX (PIPES):* RATTA-TATT-TATT-TATT-TATT!!

    *GOLDIE (THOUGHT BUBBLE): Flash!* That's Jean's warning, someone must be coming!

**PANEL THREE:** She has to get out! Goldie almost has the lock.

    *GOLDIE (THOUGHT BUBBLE):* I have to get out of here, but I almost have this lock!

**PANEL FOUR:** Goldie keeps wrestling with the lock, sweating at the sound of approaching footsteps.

    *SFX (HALLWAY):* step…step…step…

    *GOLDIE (THOUGHT BUBBLE): Almost there!*

**PANEL FIVE:** The lock gives.

    *SFX (LOCKBOX):* Click!

**PANEL SIX:** Goldie pulls a notebook out of the safe (one that looks nearly identical to the one she was taking notes in earlier) just as a voice yells at her to stop in Russian (СТОП!).

    *CHANNING (OUT OF FRAME):* STOP!

DISCOVER
# ALL THE HITS

STEVENSON • ELLIS • WATTERS • ALLEN
LUMBERJANES
BEWARE THE KITTEN HOLY
NEW YORK TIMES BESTSELLING SERIES

Allison + Treiman + Cogar
GIANT DAYS
VOLUME ONE

RIBON • FISH • PEER
SLAM!
VOLUME ONE

Hope Larson • Brittney Williams • Sarah Stern
GOLDIE VANCE
Volume One

THE BACKSTAGERS

TYSON HESSE'S
DIESEL
IGNITION

BOOM! BOX

**AVAILABLE AT YOUR LOCAL COMICS SHOP AND BOOKSTORE**

To find a comics shop in your area, call 1-888-266-4226

WWW.**BOOM-STUDIOS**.COM



**Lumberjanes**
*Noelle Stevenson, Shannon Watters, Grace Ellis, Brooklyn Allen, and Others*
**Volume 1: Beware the Kitten Holy**
ISBN: 978-1-60886-687-8 | $14.99 US
**Volume 2: Friendship to the Max**
ISBN: 978-1-60886-737-0 | $14.99 US
**Volume 3: A Terrible Plan**
ISBN: 978-1-60886-803-2 | $14.99 US
**Volume 4: Out of Time**
ISBN: 978-1-60886-860-5 | $14.99 US
**Volume 5: Band Together**
ISBN: 978-1-60886-919-0 | $14.99 US

**Giant Days**
*John Allison, Lissa Treiman, Max Sarin*
**Volume 1**
ISBN: 978-1-60886-789-9 | $9.99 US
**Volume 2**
ISBN: 978-1-60886-804-9 | $14.99 US
**Volume 3**
ISBN: 978-1-60886-851-3 | $14.99 US

**Jonesy**
*Sam Humphries, Caitlin Rose Boyle*
**Volume 1**
ISBN: 978-1-60886-883-4 | $9.99 US
**Volume 2**
ISBN: 978-1-60886-999-2 | $14.99 US

**Slam!**
*Pamela Ribon, Veronica Fish, Brittany Peer*
**Volume 1**
ISBN: 978-1-68415-004-5 | $14.99 US

**Goldie Vance**
*Hope Larson, Brittney Williams*
**Volume 1**
ISBN: 978-1-60886-898-8 | $9.99 US
**Volume 2**
ISBN: 978-1-60886-974-9 | $14.99 US

**The Backstagers**
*James Tynion IV, Rian Sygh*
**Volume 1**
ISBN: 978-1-60886-993-0 | $14.99 US

**Tyson Hesse's Diesel: Ignition**
*Tyson Hesse*
ISBN: 978-1-60886-907-7 | $14.99 US

**Coady & The Creepies**
*Liz Prince, Amanda Kirk, Hannah Fisher*
ISBN: 978-1-68415-029-8 | $14.99 US

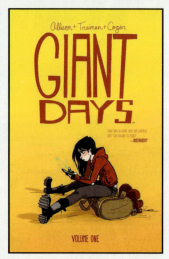

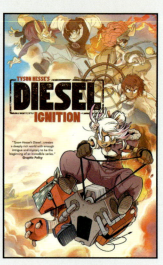

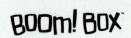